COMING H

To Louise

with best wishes &

happy memories of the

Canal Cruise in Holland

John M Walling

APRIL
2011

By the same author

From Oaks to Avocets
Memoirs

A Parcel of Diamonds
Murder mystery and five short stories

**The Internment and Treatment of German
Nationals During the 1st World War**

COMING HOME

John Walling

Published by Riparian Publishing
5 Tonnant Way
Great Grimsby
North East Lincolnshire
Telephone 01472 587344

ISBN 978 0952 3848-3-0

British Library Cataloguing in Publication Data.
A catalogue record for this book is available from the British Library.

The story is one of fiction based on fact
Most of the main characters are real persons

Printed and bound in the UK by CPI Antony Rowe
Bumper's Farm, Chippenham, Wiltshire
Cover design by Jeff Jacks. Illustrator.
Typesetting by Riparian Publishing, Great Grimsby,
North East Lincolnshire.

In

memory

of my

grandfather

'COMING HOME' FAMILY TREE

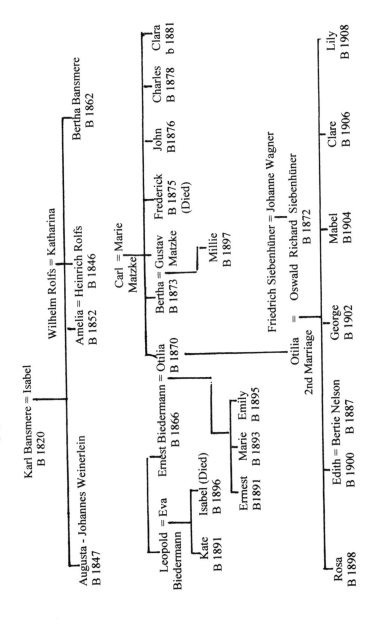

CONTENTS

COMING HOME

INTRODUCTION

There were about twenty-nine thousand Germans living in Britain in the middle of the 1800s, rising to over fifty thousand in the years prior to the 1st World War.

Of the number of Germans who left their country during the 19th century, figures vary considerably, but the consensus of opinion puts this figure at around five million, by far the majority of whom went to the United States of America. The relatively small number who stayed here probably did so for a number of reasons. Some may have discovered when they arrived that their limited means prevented them from going on any further. Others found opportunities which presented themselves at the ports where they disembarked, while some certainly came to join others who had arrived earlier and were making a success of the skills they brought with them, such as tailors, pork butchers and hairdressers. There were certainly opportunities for some tradesmen to set up shops and employ their fellow countrymen, while others found employment as waiters.

This story is based on real people and most of the facts and situations are true, including historical incidents in which people in the story could well have been involved or have witnessed. All the characters have been given their correct names and although they came from different parts of Germany, for the purposes of simplicity and convenience, all have been stated to have come from the same village of Riestedt, near Sangerhausen, in Saxony Anhalt, which was from where the Siebenhüner family originated.

Little or no check was made in the United Kingdom of the immigrants who came over the sea in ships from Hamburg and Bremen throughout the 1800s, and very few of the Germans or Austrians became naturalised. This caused considerable trouble at the outbreak of war in 1914, especially for those men of military age, and, by the end of 1915, some thirty-two thousand had been interned in camps throughout the country. Many were there for the duration of the war and beyond, while thousands of those over military age were repatriated.

There were a number of camps throughout the country where civilian

Germans, Austrians, and a few Turks were interned, but the main camp was at Knockaloe Farm, Patrick, in the Isle of Man. Originally planned to hold five thousand men, the camp was eventually extended to accommodate twenty-three thousand civilian prisoners guarded by some five thousand British soldiers.

They were put into the camps simply because of their birthplace, although some thought, especially in government circles, that all enemy aliens were a serious threat to national security, while others regarded them all to be spies. It was to be in the October of the following year before Knockaloe - one of the last camps to hold German and Austrian aliens - was closed. Only a few thousand from the large numbers that lived in this country before the war were allowed to stay in Britain. Many of those did survive to live comparatively normal lives by setting up businesses and being self-employed, and together with their families were eventually accepted as equal citizens in their local communities.

This novel tells the story of one of those families, how they came to be here in England, and what happened to them throughout their lives.

The strain and trauma of what these people endured during their lifetime was not apparent to future generations as very few, if any, spoke about what they had been through, with the result that little or no knowledge about their past was known until after they had died.

CHAPTER ONE

6th October 1921

Amelia took her husband's soft, limp hand into hers and gently held his long slender fingers which had worked so deftly all his working life as a tailor, sewing together the cloth for the suits he had made for almost sixty years. Now they were at rest, their work finished, the white bones almost showing through the pale and wrinkled loose skin covering them. Henry took off his spectacles, sighed deeply and closed his eyes. Amelia feared that he would not be with her for very much longer as she sat by his bedside in the small sparsely furnished bedroom. The previous evening he had collapsed with violent pains in his chest. After the doctor had called, he just lay in his bed occasionally slipping in and out of consciousness. Amelia leaned across his frail body to kiss him gently, first on the forehead and then on his thin pale cheeks almost devoid of flesh. He now appeared to be sleeping peacefully.

She stared into the open fire at the last glowing embers in the tiny bedroom grate, and recalled the early, uncertain days after they had left their lovely village in Saxony Anhalt to come to England. Her mind went back to the time they had sat side by side at their wedding feast. Was it really over fifty-one years since that day when they were married, and when her young handsome Heinrich had given her hand a squeeze telling her not to worry about the future?

*

January 1870.

"There's nothing to worry about, Amelia." Heinrich gave his bride's hand a gentle, confident, squeeze. "We've an exciting future ahead of us." He put his face close to hers and smiled reassuringly.

Heinrich Rolfs was a tall man, slim, extremely handsome and six years older than Amelia. His neat blonde moustache and bushy side-whiskers gave him the appearance of looking slightly older than his twenty-four years. He had promised to marry Amelia as soon as she had reached her 18th birthday, although at times had wondered whether he should have waited for her to become a little more mature. She was young, shy and innocent, but these were some of the things which endeared her to him.

Amelia had been so excited about the wedding and the ambitious plans they had made beforehand for their future life together, but was now feeling sad about leaving behind everything and everyone she knew and loved. She smiled back at Heinrich as Friedrich Siebenhüner called out loudly to them from further down the hall.

"The village isn't going to seem the same without you two."

Heinrich had to answer in an equally loud voice in order for his friend to hear over the noise. "We'll still think about you all while we're away, Friedrich. Do you not envy us?"

"I don't know whether I'd risk what you're doing," Friedrich shouted back, pointing his finger in their direction as if to emphasise his point, "but I wish you both luck." He didn't want it to sound as though he fully approved of their decision, but he envied Heinrich in another way: Heinrich had married the girl that all the young men in the village desired, himself included.

Amelia Bansmer looked radiant in her white satin wedding dress as she sat next to the husband she had married less than an hour before. Her light brown hair, neatly arranged in plaits, caressed the sides of her young face, her cheeks a deep pink coloured from spending most of her life outdoors. Her bright blue eyes glistened as she looked lovingly at the new gold ring on her small wedding finger. Yet she was feeling somewhat apprehensive about leaving for ever her lovely village of Riestedt in the German Province of Saxony-Anhalt. It was a big step to take, and, even at this late stage, she wondered whether they were doing the right thing. But she knew that it was too late now to have doubts. Everything had been arranged for their departure and they would be leaving for England first thing next morning.

Amelia knew that she was going to miss the lovely peaceful countryside around her home, with its kaleidoscope of contrasting colours throughout the seasons, the early morning chorus of the songbirds, and the cosy warmth of the farmhouse where she had been born some eighteen years earlier.

She would also miss the strong pungent warm smell of cattle in the sheds, their rough leathery hides pressing against her face as her hands squeezed and pulled expertly at the animal's thick warm teats in turn during milking time. As she sat daydreaming about what she would miss the most and what she was about to leave behind, she recalled the sounds which had always been part of her life and had previously taken for granted. She would never hear again the familiar heavy plodding of the shire horses on the cobbles as they pulled their squeaking carts laden with hay, corn or sugar-beet, nor the crisp rustling of the dry straw as she stacked the stooks of corn in the fields at harvest time.

Sitting in silence, she remembered the joyous picnics in the meadows, and the fresh dry sweet smell of the hay after turning. For the last time she had visited the beautiful wooded mountainous region to the northwest, where she had enjoyed the outings on those lovely scenic journeys into the foothills around Harzgerode with her father in their horse and trap. But most of all she would miss her family: her mama and papa, and her sisters Augusta and Bertha. Now, with Heinrich, she had decided to exchange all this for what they expected would be the bare, busy streets of London's East End.

She leaned forward to glance at her older sister close by as if to seek her approval for the decision they had made. She too was looking at her and Amelia wondered whether she might have been reading her thoughts. Augusta gave her a reassuring smile, as if giving her blessing to the venture her sister was about to undertake. Amelia smiled weakly back and then breathed a deep sigh. She knew that she was going to miss everything and everyone terribly.

Aware that someone else might be watching her, she glanced around to see if there might have been anyone else who could tell what she had been thinking, but all the wedding guests were either eating or talking, completely unaware of the turmoil whirling around inside her head. They were mostly people from the village of Riestedt with whom she had grown up and knew well, but they also included many of Heinrich's friends from the nearby town of Sangerhausen where he had worked as a tailor in his father's shop from an early age. Some of the young men worked in the copper mines close to the town, and Heinrich, in contrast to them, always looked a little more distinguished by his smart appearance and clean complexion.

Heinrich had known Amelia Bansmer ever since she used to come into the shop as a little girl with her father. Karl Bansmer would place her on a chair while he talked politics with Heinrich's father, Wilhelm. It was even at that young age that Heinrich fell in love with her, promising himself that when she was old enough he would ask her to marry him. Being some six years older than Amelia, he had waited patiently for her to begin to take notice of him. When that happened, and because they were often seen together, everyone took it for granted that they would eventually marry, not least Heinrich's mother, Katharina.

Heinrich had learned tailoring from his father, and became quite expert in every aspect of the trade by his early teens, but now, at twenty-four years of age he was about to leave the country of his birth and, together with his bride, start a new life in England. Many young people had already left and were still leaving for a variety of reasons. The country had not fully recovered from the crop shortages and high prices of the 1850's, which left memories of hunger and bankruptcies. In addition, there was now a lot of unrest due to the French government threatening Germany over territorial claims. All this, so soon after the Austrian-Prussian war, would mean that compulsory mobilisation was inevitable and many young men were anxious to leave the country to escape being called up to serve in the army.

Still uncertain as to whether they had made the right decision about leaving, Amelia turned towards her father to ask again the question she had asked herself a thousand times. "Papa....," she began, but then stopped abruptly as she heard Heinrich whispering in her ear.

"Are you happy?" he asked her, in a most endearing way.

She turned her face towards him. "Of course," she said, answering his question with sincerity, and she was - wonderfully happy, married to the only real love of her young life. However, she had wanted the additional reassurance from her father that they were doing the right thing, but intuitively Heinrich had known what she was about to ask her papa and had deliberately interrupted the question she was about to ask him.

Her father had recognised the uncertainty in Amelia's voice and, reaching out to touch her hand, startled her by speaking in quite an abrupt manner, "This is the most important day of your life, Amelia, and you have a wonderful future ahead. I have every confidence in Heinrich, and I know he will be a good husband to you." He paused and then continued thoughtfully, "I envy you both leaving our wretched Fatherland, although you know that we will miss you both terribly." Then, squeezing her hand as if to give her the assurance she was seeking, he added, "Now stop worrying, enjoy this moment and eat your food."

Instantly she experienced that same feeling as when she was a little girl sitting in her place at the table in the farmhouse at mealtimes. It was something in the tone of her father's voice that caused her to believe for a moment that she was not really married, but as he continued to gently squeeze her hand, she suddenly felt a pang of excitement. A new country would give them a fresh start in life, and, instead of fear and the threat of more wars, hopefully a more peaceful existence.

She had been only fourteen years old when some of her friends' older brothers had been either killed or wounded fighting for Austria against

14

the Prussians. The conflict had been too complex for her to understand, but she clearly remembered the Prussian soldiers marching through her village in Saxony-Anhalt during the summer some four years previously. All this had happened when Saxony, together with other lesser German States, had given unqualified support to Franz Joseph of Austria against the armies of William 1, King of Prussia. Now the men were talking of the inevitability of another war, this time against France, and as Saxony was now part of the German Confederation, Heinrich too would no doubt be required to serve in the army. In common with others of his generation he was reluctant to do so. This had been one of the main factors which had decided them to leave and go to live in London as soon as they were married.

Heinrich leaned towards his bride and put his arm around her shoulders, hugging her to him. "Now, my girl, stop looking so serious. This is your wedding day. Are you beginning to feel sorry already that you married me?"

"Of course not, Heinrich. I was just thinking about our new life in England."

"I've told you before, there is nothing to worry about," Heinrich said quietly. He looked past Amelia towards where her father was sitting, and put his finger to his lips.

"Shhh, I believe your father is about to propose our toast."

Karl Bansmer was a big man in every sense of the word. He was heavily built, forty-six years of age, handsome, with a very large moustache and long side-whiskers covering most of his weather-beaten face. His deep cleft chin was round and smooth and his hair was beginning to turn grey. He had spent some considerable time dressing earlier that morning, and looked very smart in his new suit which his friend, Heinrich's father, had made specially for him. Herr Bansmer was a person of considerable influence in the community and as a local farmer was well known in the village and beyond.

That morning he had felt extremely proud as he witnessed his daughter's marriage in the lovely 15th century St.James Church which dominated the market place in the nearby town of Sangerhausen. Although disappointed that he had not had a son to carry on with the farm, he was very proud of his three daughters, Augusta, Amelia and young Bertha, but he also felt very sad that his favourite daughter was going away, and that he would probably never see her again. However, he wanted the day to be a happy one for Amelia and was determined not to let his own feelings spoil it for her. He stood up and banged the table with his spoon to attract the attention of the guests.

"My dear friends," he began, "as you can imagine, I have mixed feelings in proposing the toast to the bride and groom...." As Karl Bansmer began to speak, he found himself shaking with both emotion and nervousness. He was not used to making this kind of speech and wished that he could have spoken about farming or politics, the subjects he knew more about. But he wanted to sound sincere, even though next day his son-in-law was going to take his lovely daughter away from him for good. He reached down to clasp her hand as he talked. With a lump in his throat he told the guests of the days when she and her older sister, Augusta, played so happily on the farm together, and when their family was made more complete when young Bertha had been born.

"...and then," he continued, "our peace was shattered and our State humiliated." His body stiffened and his manner changed noticeably. He was now on to one of his favourite topics as he related what had happened to his beloved country during the past few years. "We rightly ignored the Prussian ultimatum ordering Saxony to demobilise and to accept their reform proposals, and as you know, four years ago, when hostilities began against Austria to whom we had an allegiance, we were occupied by the Prussian soldiers within the first three days of the conflict."

Now he was in full flow. Puffing out his cheeks in anger, his audience listened attentively as he continued with bitterness in his voice, "the millions of taler imposed on all of Saxony by the Prussians - in spite of the huge sum it cost for the dubious privilege of paying for the Prussian occupation - could have crippled the State's finances for a very long time, but thankfully the money arrangements made by our government saved the day but for how long? All this could be for nothing. Bismarck's ambitions to obtain a unified Germany will inevitably lead to a war against France in order for him to achieve his political objectives. As we now all belong to a German Confederation, Saxony will be part of this conflict which can be only weeks away, and then, God help all our young men."

Karl had not planned to say all of this, and some of it may not have been an accurate assessment of the political situation, but it helped him come to terms with his daughter's leaving. He paused, in an attempt to calm himself down, before concluding, "So, in proposing this toast to my loving daughter, Amelia, and Heinrich, who I am confident will take great care of her, I wish them well. They go to their new country with my blessing, and I am certain that they will have a better future there than they would have if they had remained here in our so called new Germany."

Everyone rose to toast the young bride and the bridegroom, not least the best man, Johannes Weinerlein, who had nodded in approval of everything that Herr Bansmer had said, indeed, he had often heard his own father express those very same views. He clicked his heels as he stood to attention glass in hand.

Johannes had served his three years army service, but he had seen little of the fighting. The overwhelming supremacy of the Prussian army had been successful everywhere and the main Austrian forces were quickly defeated with the loss of thousands of men. His regiment had hardly had time to reach the borders when Saxony had been invaded, and now, as with most of his fellow countrymen, he feared the consequences of another war with France, not of defeat, but of the repeat of the bloody carnage that would be inevitable during the fighting.

Johannes had returned to farming after leaving the army. As well as working on his father's farm, he had always helped their neighbour, Herr Bansmer, with his harvest each year. It was hard and backbreaking work, especially cutting the sugar beet and loading it on to the horse-drawn carts. Although it was only a small farm, Karl Bansmer always found it necessary to employ extra labour from the village. Karl Bansmer's two eldest daughters had also helped with some of the lighter jobs, and Johannes always enjoyed their company when they were all working together, even more so when he was close to Augusta. He had grown up with Karl Bansmer's eldest daughter, who was now twenty-three, and only six months younger than himself. Now it was his turn to do his duty as Best Man by proposing a toast to her and the other bridesmaids.

As he rose to speak, he looked towards little four-year-old Ernst Biedermann and his six year old brother, Leopold, both dressed smartly in their new outfits sitting next to Amelia's eight-year-old sister, Bertha, who was one of the bridesmaids. The children would not have understood what Heinrich's father had just said, but as he looked towards them, Johannes wondered what sort of future they would have in this troubled country. In spite of having indulged in a considerable amount of wine, Johannes made a good job of his speech, purposely dwelling a long time in his complimentary remarks to Augusta, causing her to blush unashamedly.

Very soon after all the formal proceedings had concluded, a small orchestra at the end of the hall played Viennese waltzes.

"Thank you, Johannes, for your kind words," Augusta said gratefully, smiling up at him as they joined the bride and groom on the small dance floor in the only large building of the village.

He looked for the first time into her blue eyes and saw the small dimples in her cheeks as she smiled. He had never noticed before that she was so beautiful. Was it her lovely dress that made her look different from how he usually saw her? Before he had joined the army he had listened to some of his friends talking about wanting to marry her. Johannes looked closely into her face as they danced around the floor and wondered why she had never married one of them. Upon his return home from the army, he had fully expected to find that Friedrich Siebenhüner or Carl Matzke had managed to persuade her to marry one of them. They were both a year older than Augusta, but had not been called to serve in the army because they had worked in the coalmines near to the town of Halle. Friedrich was still single, but Carl had since married one of the village girls. They too were guests at the wedding, together with Carl's wife, Marie, and their baby son, Gustav.

"You dance very well, Augusta," Johannes told her, and then clumsily spoilt the compliment by adding, "for a farmer's daughter." She looked at him disapprovingly, and although feeling a little hurt, said nothing. She was happy just to be his partner on the dance floor and to feel his hand holding her own, for she had loved him for as long as she could remember. Although he often teased her, he had never shown her any real affection. Would he only ever think of her as just a farmer's daughter she wondered? She could feel the warmth of his hand as it rested on her waist. He held her gently yet firmly, and she wanted the waltz to go on forever.

"I think I prefer you like this to milking the cows, laying sheaves or pitch forking the wheat," Johannes suddenly announced, and Augusta felt his hand squeeze her own more tightly than before. As he let go of her waist, she gave a full twirl at the end of the dance and, spinning round, fell into his arms, her face close to his. They stayed like that for a moment and Johannes suddenly wanted to tell her how beautiful she looked, having regretted the unkind things he had said to her. "I think you are..." he began, and then stopped short of what he was about to say suddenly aware that all eyes in the room were watching him. Instead, he gave her a brief but tender kiss on the cheek. "Thank you, Augusta," he said politely, and went away hurriedly to join his friends feeling that perhaps he had made a fool of himself.

"We saw that," Friedrich ribbed as he approached them. Carl Matzke laughingly added, "We'll get you married off yet."

Johannes felt his face burning as his cheeks took on a bright red colour. "Oh no you won't, I think I got carried away for the moment. It meant nothing," Johannes said, not wanting them to know exactly how he really felt. "Let's open another bottle of wine." It was a happy evening and the dancing continued for some hours until Amelia and Heinrich left their guests as their long journey to England commenced the very next day.

The next morning, Karl Bansmer took Amelia and Heinrich in his horse and trap the 25 kilometres to Halle, where they were to stay the night before catching the early morning train to Berlin. It was a bitterly cold journey and Heinrich and Karl spent most of the time on that long journey in deep conversation discussing the implications of the political unrest in Germany. Amelia sat in silence for most of the way her eyes taking in for the last time every blade of grass and flight of bird and listening to the clicking of the horses' hooves on the hard ground. The frosty cobwebs on the bushes appeared more beautiful than ever she had seen them and she felt sad as the early morning sunshine melted the white silken threads until she could see them no more. In spite of them all being well wrapped up against the raw January air they were all feeling very cold when they arrived in Halle. As her father handed Heinrich the small amount of luggage they were taking with them, Amelia couldn't hold back her tears.

"I'll write to you, papa, as soon as we reach London," she said between sobs.

"Now, now my girl. No more tears. I want to see you smiling as I leave. That is the way I wish to remember you." Karl Bansmer gave his daughter his large handkerchief to wipe her eyes, and kissed her forehead. "London is not the other end of the earth!"

As he set off on the long journey back to Riestedt, she continued to wave to her father until he was out of sight, then sat down by the side of Heinrich with a heavy heart. She could not bring herself to believe that she had left her home for good. The ride in the trap in the cold air of that January day had chilled her through to the bone, and Heinrich put his arm around her as she shivered. "You feel frozen, my love; come, snuggle up close to me."

Amelia looked down and saw that she was still clasping her father's handkerchief, and began to cry even more. Heinrich thought it best to say nothing until she had dried her eyes, and then tried to comfort her by talking enthusiastically about their future life together. Heinrich's words gave her reassurance that all would turn out well once they had arrived in London, and then perhaps, in a year or two, he told her, they would be able to return to see their parents.

Next morning they caught the train to Berlin, a journey that took over four hours. Heinrich had been to Berlin previously, but for Amelia it was the first time she had travelled on a train. Soon after leaving Halle, she could hardly control her excitement as they passed through the lovely countryside. As the train rumbled along the track north of Dessau on the way to Belzig, she thought that the scenery was even more breathtaking.

"Look! Heinrich, how those snow-covered mountains glisten in the winter sunshine? They look so beautiful." Now she had begun the journey she felt the excitement of the occasion which was beginning to overwhelm her, "I think we're going to have a wonderful time in London," she added.

Heinrich was surprised at her sudden outburst but pleased that she had overcome her disappointment at leaving. He put her tiny hands into his. "I know we are," he said.

Amelia pulled her long black shawl tightly over her head when they arrived at Berlin's Wannsee Railway Station and kept close to Heinrich as they made their way to the place from where the train for Hamburg would depart.

The platform was crowded, but they noticed that most of the other passengers waiting to board the train appeared to be of Russian origin, carrying large bundles of clothes and looking very impoverished. Small children clung tightly to their mother's long dresses, and babies wrapped up against the cold were cradled snugly in their mother's arms. Most of the men were unkempt in their open-necked shirts and shabby overcoats. Amelia looked proudly at her husband knowing that underneath his smart long coat he wore a well-tailored dark woollen suit, white shirt with a stiff collar, and a silk tie.

She suddenly felt sorry for all the poor individuals around her, who possibly possessed nothing more than what she could see, some, no doubt, fleeing their country for roughly the same reasons that they themselves were leaving.

Heinrich had already explained to Amelia that his father had told him that people who had left some twenty years ago for the United States, had written home telling of jobs, and better opportunities over there, which had been the inspiration for more people to go to find out for themselves. He now told her that these Russian people waiting for the

Hamburg train had probably heard similar stories from their friends or relations who had left earlier in their search of freedom from religious oppression, heavy taxation and social constraints, in the hope of finding a better life in the New World.

Amelia was saddened at the thought that the future of these people was so uncertain, but in a funny sort of way, they gave her a feeling of contentment that her own life was so securely mapped out.

As they walked past the people towards the other end of the platform, Amelia whispered, "I think we are lucky having somewhere to stay when we arrive in London, Heinrich. I expect that most of those Russians were forced to leave their homes and have nowhere to go."

"I believe that most of them will be hoping to get to America," he explained. "When they get to England, they will be going on to Liverpool, and from there to the United States. They may look impoverished, Amelia, but don't be deceived by their appearance. No doubt they will all have their steerage-class fare enabling them to get there, but they also know that it is not certain that they will all be accepted. They are prepared to take their chances."

Heinrich saw from Amelia's expression that he had not really answered her question. He smiled. "Certainly our fellow travellers would think us very fortunate if they knew our plans, but none of us are going off to a future which is certain, Amelia."

It was the first time that she had heard Heinrich express any doubts about their destiny and it made her feel a little uncomfortable. There were other German passengers on the platform, and Heinrich raised his hat politely to the ladies with a brief exchange of "Guten Tag," as they passed by. Further on at the far end of the platform, was a group of people each carrying a 'perineh' (a sort of bed-roll). Heinrich recognised the men in their loose fitting black clothes to be Jews. Their bodies were thin and their faces looked drawn and emaciated. The small children looked frightened, their eyes wide open and staring.

"I have heard that Russia is beginning to expel these people from their border regions," said Heinrich quietly as he saw Amelia's puzzled expression, "and I understand that they are also being persecuted and hounded in Rumania. In many cases their lives have been threatened and who can blame them for trying to seek sanctuary in another country."

Amelia looked lovingly at her husband, admiring him for the way that he had shown such compassion in his voice whilst explaining the plight of these poor souls. She thought that he must have gained a great deal of knowledge about worldly events from the people who had visited his father's shop in Sangerhausen. Suddenly, her thoughts were interrupted by the noise of the huge steam engine coming alongside, pulling the long line of coaches, which would take them to their final destination of that day.

The young couple had already had a long day travelling and spent most of the time sleeping during this uneventful and tiresome 240-kilometre journey to Hamburg, arriving in the late evening cold, hungry and tired.

Their ship was not due to sail until early next morning, so they found a small hotel close to the docks where they enjoyed a supper, but slept fitfully. It was a cold morning when they awoke. Icicles hung down outside their window, and the frost had created beautiful intricate patterns on the inside of the panes of glass. After enjoying a breakfast of bratwurst and thick crusty bread, they made their way to the harbour to meet the captain of the ship that was to take them to London. Here too, they had been told that Amelia's cousin, Bernhard Bansmer, the ship's carpenter, would meet them and tell them of the arrangements he had made when they arrived in London.

Captain Kuiper had been Master of his ship - the "Henrietta" - for many years, and was an experienced sailor. In his younger days, he had taken trading ships under sail to and from Magdeburg on the Elbe river, where he had first joined as a deck hand when he was only thirteen years of age. Later, he had been one of the first to learn how to steer the new steam ships in the 1840s. Now in his middle fifties and overweight, his large greying beard, moustache, and thick side-whiskers hid most of his face. Beneath his bushy eyebrows, his blue eyes were small but kindly and he smiled broadly as he met the young couple.

"You must be Amelia and Heinrich Rolfs," he said, extending his right hand towards them. "I think you are very brave to travel at this time of the year - not many do. We finished unloading last night and will be moving out at high tide in about three hours time. Unfortunately, there's much drift ice in the estuary which we'll only be able to pass through with the assistance of the Hamburg tugs." Noticing the young couple's concern he gave them a reassuring smile. "But there's nothing to worry about, we'll get through."

Heinrich paid the nine taler, which he had been told to pay being the cost of their journey to London. The captain put it into his pocket without a word.

"Now if you would like to follow me, I'll take you to meet Bernhard who will show you to your cabin where you will eat and sleep."

They pulled their coats tightly around them as they walked briskly across the harbour to where the ship was berthed. It was freezing cold and the sea gulls screeched loudly as they flew lazily over the ships, not caring about the ice-cold air.

Amelia had never met her cousin Bernhard previously. She had only been two years old when he had left the village to join his father to work as an apprentice carpenter on board the ships. Bernhard's mother had died soon after her son was born, and Amelia could not even remember ever meeting her Uncle Klaus. Like Bernard, he too had been a carpenter on board the trading ships, but had drowned in the Elbe following a collision. Amelia's mother had told her that following his father's death, Bernhard had joined the "Henrietta". He came towards them smiling broadly, his small stature giving him a child-like appearance. Amelia smiled as she noticed that his long straw coloured hair almost covered his ears.

"You've certainly grown into a fine young lady, and 'Einrich's a lucky man," Bernhard remarked as he held both of her hands at arms length, then pulled her towards him to kiss her on both cheeks. Amelia averted her eyes as she felt herself blushing at his remarks.

"'Ow's Uncle Karl and Aunt Isabel? - 'aven't seen them since father got killed."

Amelia felt a lump in her throat when Bernhard enquired about her parents. She immediately recalled how she kissed her mother goodbye and, later, waving to her father in Halle.

"They're both fine and send their regards," she answered bravely.

Bernhard explained the arrangements he had made for them when they eventually arrived in London, as they walked around the ship.

"There's some rooms I've found for you close to Broad Street Railway Station. It's a large three storey 'ouse in a terrace, and you'll 'ave two rooms on the second floor. The ground floor's occupied by 'Erman and Willemine Wilke - the tailors I wrote t'you about, and e's agreed for you t'work with 'im. 'E 'as some rooms above a pawnbroker's shop in Middlesex Street nearby - reckons that e's got enough work for both of you. 'E told me that e's looking forward t'having another experienced tailor working with 'im. E's already got three assistant tailors all living in the same 'ouse".

"How old are these people?" Amelia asked. She was hoping that he would be able to tell her that some were of her own age.

"Oh Willemine's only twenty-three and 'as a little baby born in August last year and 'Erman's a few years older but 'is assistants Luke Brandas and 'Enri Ewes are in their early twenties then there's Friderieke Luhm a

23

tailoress she's only about seventeen and young Lize Willemine's sister she's sixteen year old and does all the jobs in the 'ouse."

Amelia smiled again as Bernhard had said all that without taking a breath. She was astonished that there would be so many people in the same house, but pleased that she would not be the youngest there.

"Oh, I nearly forgot," Bernhard added, "there's also John McGill. E's a Scotsman on the top floor with 'is daughter and little George 'is stepson."

"What do they do?" Heinrich asked. He wondered whether they too were tailors.

"Well, John's a boot closer and e's about fifty - something. Janet oo's twenty-one does the same job as her father as well as looking after little George oo's only four years old."

Amelia looked puzzled. "A boot closer? What's that?"

Bernhard laughed, "I thought y'might ask me that. Boot closers do what it says they do! They sew the tops on the boots so they'll fasten together see? In the East End many people do lots of things in their 'ouses and a number of folk make leather shoes for the theatre people."

"It sounds an interesting 'ouse - I mean house," Heinrich remarked, "and also very crowded, but at least we will have a roof over our heads. I'm pleased for Amelia, too, that nearly all the people are about our own age."

Bernhard showed them their cabin, which was only small but contained two single bunk beds.

"Not really designed for an 'oneymoon couple I'm afraid," Bernhard quipped, "but you should be comfortable 'ere."

Just before the ship was due to sail, the young couple went back on deck with Bernhard to watch the ship leave the harbour, but they were distracted by the sight of people boarding a ship alongside. Amelia thought that she recognised some of the children she had seen on the platform in Berlin and again on the train travelling to Hamburg.

"They aren't as lucky as you two," announced Bernhard nodding his head in their direction, "You probably saw some of 'em on the train from Berlin."

"But they've got such a long journey ahead of them. They will be frozen by the time they get there." Amelia's heart went out to those children huddled close to their parents in the icy cold morning air.

"Most of 'em will be off to America to start a new life there."

"But they look so cold. How will they get to America - how much does it cost to get there?" she asked. She was still concerned, especially for the children, and recalled some of the frail and sad faces she had seen in Berlin.

"I've 'eard that the Great Central Railway Company in England offers cheap package deals to Germans, Russians and Poles leaving their 'omes for a new life in the West. I believe it's about ten shillings in English money which'll be enough to take 'em to the ports of 'ull or Grimsby in England," Bernhard explained.

Amelia was still not satisfied. "But what will happen to them when they get there, and how will they get to the ships to sail to America?" She knew enough to realise that the immigrants would be on the wrong side of the country when their ship docked.

"They'll be fed and looked after and then travel by train to Liverpool where they'll be able to get cheap packages on the grain ships returning empty to New York. It'll cost 'em about two pounds. They'll probably live on tea, salted 'erring and black bread during the journey. Sadly for a number of reasons the American authorities may not accept all of them. Let's 'ope they 'ave a fairly quiet voyage across the North Sea...and us too for that matter," Bernhard added out of consideration for his new travellers.

Amelia noticed that a number of the other passengers standing on the forecastle of the other ship were well dressed: some old men, some happy girls in groups, babies in arms, and men with decorative pipes in their mouths puffing out clouds of white smoke into the cold air. She hoped in her heart that they would have a safe journey and gave them a little wave as their ship began to move. At first, the 'Henrietta' was pulled by the tugs through the drift ice to the mouth of the Elbe estuary. The ship then made good headway across Heligoland Bay and into the North Sea to begin the long four hundred miles or more voyage to the Port of London.

Two days later, and at early light, the ship berthed in the Royal Victoria Dock in London's East End. The Captain had already made a list of his few passengers in case it was required by the official from the Board of Trade, but as often happened, no one met the ship. Bernhard hailed one of the larger cabs and gave the driver the small amount of luggage Heinrich and Amelia had brought with them. Then climbing into the cab, they set off to go to their new home in Bishopsgate.

The journey from the docks was a harrowing experience and not at all how they had imagined it would be. As they travelled along Middlesex Street to their destination, a variety of odours and smoke from roadside fires drifted into their cab. Mixed smells of meat cooking, hot chestnuts, potatoes, and other things they could not identify, mingled with the strong, nauseating smell of horse dung, churned by the wheels of the vehicles. They noticed that some of these carriages with heavy loads were pulled by teams of lean, sweating animals, with snorting nostrils and white froth dripping from their mouths. A barrel of wine, that had obviously just fallen from a passing wagon, lay on the road spilling its contents. Amelia sat in shocked silence as she watched men, women, and even children, scooping up the strong smelling liquid into containers with their dirty hands as the wine poured out on to the cobbles. Amelia's own hands were to her face, not knowing whether to cover her mouth and nose in order to stifle the obnoxious smells, or to put her fingers in her ears to quell some of the noise.

The street was crowded with men, women, and children, some dashing about, as if they had no time to get where they were going. A variety of different sized vehicles and hansom cabs dodged each other as they seemingly made their way in all directions, their wheels resounding over the cobbles in unison with the clicking of horse's hooves. Everyone appeared to be either shouting, laughing, crying, or calling out their wares. Some men in dirty aprons, had large trays balanced on their heads containing bread, cakes or vegetables, while others carried sides of freshly butchered, blood red meat over their shoulders.

It all appeared chaotic to the young couple who had just arrived from the country and in complete contrast to the sort of life-style they had left behind.

Heinrich noticed a look of despair in Amelia's eyes as they met his and Bernhard saw it too and laughed. "You'll soon get used to this, cousin Amelia," he told her. "In fact you'll probable enjoy it," he added, in an effort to make light of what had appeared to have disgusted her.

"I don't think that I ever will," Amelia said quietly, more to herself than for anyone to hear.

When they arrived in Artillery Lane, she also found the old four-storied terraced property very disappointing, and the rooms Bernhard had found for them, dirty, dingy and dilapidated. Amelia thought that she had better make the best of it for Heinrich's sake, after all, there was no where else to go.

Later that evening they met Hermann Wilke and his wife, Willemine, who Amelia took to straight away. From the first day that they worked together, Hermann recognised that he and Heinrich would make an excellent partnership being immediately impressed by the newcomer's tailoring expertise. Amelia worked hard to make the two rooms they had on the second floor look as homely as she could, but in the first few months following their arrival, she often sat by the fire, alone with her thoughts, wondering whether they had done the right thing by coming to London, especially as she now knew she was pregnant. But perhaps a baby would make all the difference to their life in England.

CHAPTER TWO

July 1870.

Augusta Bansmer lay in the long grass of the meadow of her father's farm with her eyes closed. She was almost asleep in the warmth of the summer sun. Johannes Weinerlein sat by her side, his arms wrapped around his knees, deep in thought as he contemplated his future.

The last few years had not been good for the farms. Crops had been poor and now the prices of grain had dropped steeply. Cheap imports from Russia and the United States had undercut Germany's agricultural prosperity, plunging farmers into prolonged depression. In addition, the harvest failures of recent years accentuated their despair and many farmers and agricultural workers had left to go to America. Neither his father's farm nor that of his neighbour, Karl Bansmer, was doing very well and Johannes was worried what might happen if there was another war.

In Riestedt, some of the young men had already been conscripted into the armies of the Southern German States, and soldiers who had returned told of large concentrations on the borders with Alsace around Landau. A conflict between Germany and France seemed inevitable and everyone believed that the aggressive intentions of both countries would soon lead to war. Johannes had had enough of the army and war, but also believed that the future held no hope or prosperity for farmers. Why couldn't his father have persuaded him to be a tailor like Heinrich?

He turned his head and looked down at the girl who he had known all his life. She looked different from how he used to see her helping on the farm. The last time he remembered her looking so serene was at Amelia's wedding. She had never asked him what he was about to say to her after their dance and he now recalled how she appeared to enjoy it when he had kissed her on the cheek. He suddenly had an urge to kiss her again but this time on her mouth. He leaned over to do so, kissing her only briefly and tenderly on her lips. He was surprised how warm and soft they were.

Without moving, she opened her eyes slowly. "Why did you do that, Johannes?" She asked him the question almost whispering it.

"It was a sudden impulse and I thought you were asleep."

"Is that all? And I thought..."

He finished her sentence for her....."you'd like me to do it again."

He kissed her again but longer this time pressing his lips firmly against hers. Augusta felt her heart pounding with the excitement and could hardly believe that this was happening. She had wanted him to do this for as long as she could remember.

Gently he brushed her hair from her face with his hand and then saw that her eyes were full of tears.

"Have I made you cry?" he asked, sounding concerned.

"No! no! I'm not crying. I'm happy, happy because..." and she'd rehearsed the next bit so many times waiting for this moment, that she found it so easy to say..... "I love you, Johannes."

He smiled down at her, and then threw himself on to his back looking up at the swallows weaving their way across the bright blue summer sky in search for food. "I must be the blindest person in Riestedt," he announced laughing. "Here I am," he called out to the birds, "with the girl who I have known all my life and could not imagine what life would be without her, and yet have not realised until now how much I love her." He tore at the grass with his hands at the same time, angry with himself for not telling her all that before now. "I don't know why I haven't kissed you before," he said, without turning towards her.

She lay on the grass listening to him rant while she herself was in a state of euphoria and hardly daring to breathe.

"But you did, at Amelia's wedding - on my cheek." Augusta reminded him, laughing. "Don't you remember? "

They both lay motionless for a while until he suddenly turned in her direction, playfully throwing the handfuls of grass all over her. He now held her tightly in his arms. "I'm never going to let you go, Augusta." He held her face in his hands as he kissed her tenderly at first. She threw her arms around him and they kissed passionately, their bodies pressed tightly together.

After a while he sat up and held her tiny hand, his thoughts returning to what he had been thinking about previously. "But what future do we have here? Let's get away, as your sister and Heinrich did. I don't want to do any more farming. Look how miserable our fathers are! What do you think?"

His sudden burst of enthusiasm frightened her. She was stunned and remained silent for a while looking at the man who had always loved farming. Augusta had told him about the letter she recently received from her sister in London telling her that she was to have a baby in

October and that they were very happy. Amelia had also told her that Heinrich was working hard and had already formed a partnership with Herman Wilke and that they were doing extremely well. Augusta had given the letter for Johannes to read, so perhaps it was this which had influenced him in wanting to join them.

Augusta had been taken by surprise at Johannes' outburst. "I don't understand. Where do you want to go and what would you do? Our life is farming. Can't we be as happy here in the countryside as in a foreign city? And what is the attraction of travelling abroad apart from the adventure? Johannes, are you being serious?"

"I haven't just come up with this idea, Augusta. Please think about it."

Augusta sat up and put her head down on to her bent knees and closed her eyes. She could not believe what Johannes was proposing. At this moment to leave Germany was unthinkable. Being the eldest daughter, she was aware of her responsibilities to others as well as her own feelings. There was her father to consider, who had always been so kind and loving to them all. Had he not already lost one daughter? Would this be the way to repay him for all his kindness by going away as Amelia had done, probably never to see each other again? She sat up, looked closely at the man she had always wanted and loved for years, and in her moment of happiness suddenly felt frightened that if she answered in the wrong way, she could lose him.

"Can't we talk about this another time, Johannes, because I don't want to think about anything else at this moment other than just being together for ever and ever?" She snuggled close to him as he promised not to mention it again until she did. He held her warm and responsive body firmly but gently in his arms as he kissed her again.

*

Karl Bansmer was walking his shire horse back to the farmhouse after a long day in the fields, slowly enough to enable the big stallion to cool off after pulling the loaded hay-cart from the meadow to the farmyard from first thing that morning until early evening. He unhitched the horse from the cart and, now released from the constraints of the shafts of the huge wooden carrier, the huge animal made its way slowly across the yard to the water trough.

It would still be another forty minutes or so before Karl himself could relax after his day's work. First he led the horse to the stable and took off the bridle, collar, harness and lines, and after wiping and hanging up the tack, sponged the body sweat from the animal, then wiped the dirt which had accumulated during the day off the animal's fetlocks. He then checked for stones that might have been buried deep in the hooves which could cause the animal to be lame. After a final and careful look for cuts and abrasions, the farmer filled up the rack with fresh hay adding a few chopped cracked oats that his horse enjoyed. Although the stallion slept standing up, Karl always put down some clean wheat straw before leaving.

"Did you see Augusta while you've been in the fields, Karl?" his wife asked as he entered the house.

"Hasn't she been in for her meal then yet?" Karl sounded concerned.

"Well no, she has not been back to the house since early afternoon. I thought that you might have seen her across in the far meadow. That is where she usually goes when you don't need her to help you."

Karl had remembered seeing her go in that direction about the same time his wife had mentioned.

"Yes I did see her, and she was walking over there with Johannes Weinerlein," then added as an afterthought, "I don't understand why Augusta hasn't married that fellow. Johannes is a nice enough chap and single, but she doesn't seem to be interested in young men."

"Then you don't know your daughter," his wife said with disdain as they sat down to eat their evening meal. "What you haven't noticed in all these years, Karl, is that there has only ever been one man in Augusta's eyes and that has been Johannes, but he doesn't seem to have ever shown any real affection for her even though they have always been good friends."

Karl didn't answer, he knew that he was out of his depth trying to understand the complexities of the minds of the women in his life, and when it came to love, well, it was really none of his business. However, what he did know was what his neighbour, Martin, had told him about his son, Johannes. "What I do know," Karl said with a superior air, "is that according to his father, Johannes doesn't seem to be as interested in farm work as he used to be since he came out of the army, so perhaps he is not the best person to have for a son-in-law, even if she might want to choose him for a husband."

Isabel smiled to herself as she allowed Karl to have the last word on the subject. She knew that her daughter would make up her own mind whatever anyone else thought about it and, in spite of what her husband had just said about Johannes, she knew that Karl thought highly of him, almost as much as he would a son of his own.

The sun had almost gone down behind the tall conifers beyond the boundaries of his neighbour's farm, throwing shadows across the land as if drawn by giant's fingers when Johannes and Augusta returned to the farmhouse. Karl was asleep in his favourite chair when Augusta burst into the room. She was clinging on to Johannes's arm. At the sudden noise, her father awoke with a start.

"Mama! Papa!" was all that Augusta could manage to say at first and she went to her mother who embraced her. Isabel had never seen her daughter look so happy. Karl gave his daughter a hug and kissed her on both cheeks, then took the hand of Johannes into his own and shook it warmly.

"I do hope you know what you're doing son. She's a strong girl that daughter of mine," he joked.

During supper they all talked about when they would marry, but Johannes never mentioned anything about what he had suggested to Augusta in regard to leaving. However, at that time they were not to know that their joy was to be short lived and their arrangements to marry postponed. Later that month, news spread that France had declared war on Germany, and only a few days later, Johannes received notice to immediately rejoin his old regiment, the Royal Saxon X11 Army Corps.

*

In a dimly candle-lit bedroom on the second floor of the old terraced house where Heinrich and Amelia Rolfs had their two rooms, Otilia Rolfs came into the world. It was not the best place in the world for a baby to be born. Willemine Wilke rolled down her sleeves and handed the baby to Amelia, while young Lize, who had been at hand keeping her sister supplied with all that was required throughout the birth, sat on the bed touching the tiny soft fingers of the new life that had just been born in that dilapidated room.

"She's the prettiest thing in all the world, Mrs Rolfs," Lize said quietly, not wishing to disturb the now sleeping child.

Amelia felt tired, weak and exhausted, and moving the shawl away from the tiny face whispered, "She is my beautiful little girl," and pressed her lips gently in a kiss on the baby's forehead.

As soon as the two women had left, Heinrich came into the room and knelt down by the side of the bed. "So this is my lovely daughter Otilia, and you are the cleverest wife any man could wish for." He kissed them both very gently and touched his wife's pale cheeks as if trying to bring them back to their usual rosy colour.

Amelia smiled at her husband, and then at the baby, "And you now have a family to look after."

Heinrich felt jubilant as she reminded him of his extra responsibility but after a while thought that she looked tired. " I'll leave you to sleep now and come to see you later when you've rested."

Mrs. Wilke had a cup of strong coffee waiting when he came down the stairs.

"Come and drink this before you go to work, Mr. Rolfs," she called.

"That's very kind of you," replied Heinrich politely, and then added, "Maybe I should be drinking schnapps, not coffee," but then his smile left his face as he looked about him.

"That is not the way a happy man should look, Heinrich, especially after the birth of his first-born. What's wrong? Is something the matter?"

Heinrich's shoulders sagged a little and his usual reserved manner disappeared. Willemine had never seen him like this: he was normally so upright, proud, and always appeared to be in full control of every eventuality, but now his head was bent forward and he had lost his normal composure.

Mrs. Wilke could see that he was finding it difficult to find the right words, but thought it best that she did not interrupt lest he stopped himself from telling her what was on his mind.

Heinrich thought about how different the birth of their baby would have been in the countryside they had left. The fresh clean air coming through the window of the farmhouse and the sounds of birds singing in the trees outside as if to herald the birth: their two families coming to visit them and the joy their parents would have had in seeing their first grandchild. Heinrich was having mixed feelings about his newly born baby upstairs in their dismal and tiny bedroom. "It's not at all how I thought it would be here in England before we came. I don't want you to take this personally, Willemine, but I think you will agree that this house, which is damp and alive with vermin, is not the ideal place to bring up a baby."

Too obsessed by his own thoughts for his family's welfare, he had forgotten for the moment that his kindly neighbour had given birth to her own baby barely five months earlier in the same building, and was making the best of it. After all, the conditions in which they lived were far better than many others in the East End of London. Mrs. Wilke remained silent for a moment or two, and then put her arm around Heinrich's shoulders.

"I know exactly how you feel, and when you see Herman, tell him what you have just said, and he will tell you that he said almost the same words when Allo was born. Now drink your coffee and perhaps we will all find somewhere better to live as time goes by, and stop worrying - Amelia will cope and the baby will be fine."

Heinrich was more aware of his surroundings as he walked to his place of work in Middlesex Street. He noticed more than previously the strong smell of horse dung churned by the wheels of passing horse-drawn drays in the narrow lane, the dirty bare-footed children playing at the end of the street and, as he walked by, the black sewer-rats that quickly disappeared down a grill in the road close to the new Synagogue. He turned the corner where Bert in his rags always sat, selling his lucifers and clay pipes, and looked with disdain at the mangy looking cats which roamed wild everywhere. Heinrich quickened his pace as he approached the building where they rented their workrooms above the pawnbroker's shop.

Now anxious to break the news of his new arrival to his friends, his mood changed suddenly as he reached the door that led to the stairs to the upper floors of the building. He bounded up them two at a time and burst into the room, grinning. Herman was trimming the edges of the material of a partly made suit, tape measure draped round his neck and pins jabbed haphazardly into his waistcoat.

He turned his head as Heinrich entered. One look at his colleague told him what he was about to hear. "Well! Boy or girl?"

"It's a girl, - and I'm a papa!" Heinrich answered in a voice somewhat louder than he normally used.

"This calls for a celebration," Herman announced as he reached underneath the cutting table and produced the bottle of champagne that he had bought for them to mark the occasion. "Everyone, stop what you are doing; Heinrich's a papa!"

The two assistants, Henri Ewes and Fridericke Luhm, both came from the other room, followed by Luke Brandas wearing his usual broad grin, and still carrying the hot iron he had been using to press the finished clothes.

"What are you going to call her, Mr. Rolfs?" Fridericke asked as she shook his hand, her face turning a bright pink as she did so.

"Oh, Amelia's already decided that," Heinrich replied proudly, "It's 'Otilia'."

Friderieke started to say that it was a pretty name but stopped suddenly with a shriek as the cork shot out noisily from the bottle. She had never even seen a bottle of champagne before. Her eyes were transfixed on the glasses as she watched them fill with frothy bubbles and then settle to a reveal clear sparkling liquid. She wondered whether she would like it.

"So now my little Allo will have a playmate," Herman said cheerfully as the glasses were raised in a toast to the new baby.

"From now on," Heinrich announced with authority, "now that I have a baby born in England, I wish to be known as Henry - not Heinrich!"

"To HENRY Rolfs and his new baby," they all shouted, and everyone laughed and raised their glasses again - all except Fridericke who drank hers too quickly, the bubbles coming down her nose and causing her to splutter.

It was not quite the normal routine they were all used to that day: people came to congratulate Mr. Rolfs, and some of the women brought items of baby clothes. Rachael Levi, from the second-hand furniture shop across the road, gave him a lovely white shawl she had crocheted for her own babies.

"So give Amelia this for the baby," she said as she handed it to him, "she will find it useful now that the weather is getting colder already."

Henry went home earlier than usual that evening carrying the presents he had been given, including two bottles of wine he had bought to celebrate the birth of his daughter. Amelia was sitting up in bed and the baby was sleeping when he arrived.

"I am so happy, Heinrich, I could burst!" Henry put the gifts on to the bed.

"People have been so kind: Herman produced a bottle of champagne, and we all toasted our baby." Henry paused and then asked, "Has Mrs Wilke been to see you?" He wanted to find out whether she had told Amelia about the conversation he had had with her earlier in the day.

"She has been wonderful and so helpful to me all day: bringing food and advising me how to feed and look after baby, and making sure that my visitors did not stay too long to tire me out. Why don't you take her one of those bottles of wine in appreciation for what she has done?"

"She didn't say anything else to you?" Henry asked anxiously.

What else should she have said apart from giving me advice?"

Henry just shrugged his shoulders and was relieved that Mrs. Wilke had kept silent about what they had discussed that morning. He then told Amelia how he had decided to change his name to Henry, and that they should now try and be like an English family for the sake of little Otilia who was, after all, English.

"So now, not only do I have a new baby, but I have a new man called Henry Rolfs," she teased, "so Henry Rolfs, please would you make me a nice cup of tea while I finish this letter to my dear mama and papa telling them of our wonderful news."

Henry went into the other room and used the water to make the tea, which had been boiling continuously in the kettle on the hob for most of the day, cut a few slices of rich fruit cake that Mrs. Wilke had made for them previously, and returned to the bedroom where Amelia was sucking the end of her pencil looking thoughtful.

"Have you found any accommodation for Augusta and Johannes yet, as I want to include a message to them in my letter to mama whether or not we have managed to find any rooms for them?" She could tell immediately from Henry's expression that not only had he already found somewhere, but that he had forgotten to tell her about it.

"I meant to tell you the other day, but with all that has been going on, I forgot.

Sam Long told me that he'll have a couple of rooms free in the house at number 16. I told him about your sister wanting to come from Germany, and that it might be some time before she could arrive because of the war, but he very kindly said that he would keep them for her as long as he could. I'm sorry, my dear, it had completely slipped my memory."

At that moment, the baby stirred in her crib and started to cry.

"Pass her to me, Henry - see I have not forgotten to call you Henry! - she is probably hungry."

"If you can finish your letter tonight," he told her as he left the room, "I'll take it with me to post on my way to work in the morning."

Henry poured himself a cup of tea and sat down in his favourite chair by the fire. This had been quite some day he thought: the months of waiting over, and now they were a real family. Tomorrow, he would begin looking for another house, but then he wondered whether perhaps he should wait until after Amelia's sister arrived from Saxony. Christmas would then be over, so maybe it would be best to leave the search even until the Spring. As he contemplated the alternatives, his eyes closed and he fell into a deep sleep.

He awoke with a start and looked up at the clock on the mantelpiece: it was almost nine o'clock and he had been asleep for about half-an-hour! He wondered whether he had heard gentle knocking which had caused him to waken. He thought that Amelia would probably be asleep by now, and not wishing to disturb her, went quickly to the door and opened it quietly. John McGill and his daughter, Janet, from the top floor stood outside on the landing.

"Och man, congratulations on da birth ov ya wee bairn. We apologise fa da late ca', but we just got in an' he'rd da nooze, an' hoped ye'd join me in a wee dram t'wet da bairn's heed. We knocked a couple of times and thought ya'd maybe gan ta bed," and he held up a half full bottle of Scotch whisky as he entered the room.

Henry considered that he was doing quite well in learning the English language during the time he had lived in London, but as usual with Mr McGill, he had understood little of what he had said. However, his action with the bottle of Scotch in one hand, and the fact that he was carrying two glasses in the other, clearly told him the reason for his visit, and the words he had spoken in his broad Scots' accent were of minor importance.

His daughter, Janet, was a Londoner, and although she too could copy her father's way of speaking, she was always careful when talking to the Rolfs to try to speak in a way that they would understand. Indeed, Henry often looked to her to interpret what the old man said. Only the other day as Henry passed them both on the stairs, he was greeted with, "Och guid mornin' ta ye, Mr. Rolfs," but although he had been able to guess what the greeting meant, Janet had caught Henry's puzzled look, and with a smile had explained the words to him.

Henry noticed that Janet was also carrying something hidden under a cloth when she came into the room with her father.

"I expect that your wife has been unable to do much cooking, so I've brought you an apple strudel that I've made."

Henry was moved by her kindness. "I will eat it with my supper, - alright?"

"Alright," Janet replied, aware that he was asking her whether he had said the right words. "That was very good," she added. "Your English is getting better and better every time I talk to you."

They drank the 'wee drams' quickly, John McGill continually raising his glass in a toast to the 'new bairn', as he put it. Immediately after they had left, Henry looked in the bedroom and saw that Amelia and the baby were both sleeping soundly. Earlier, his wife had eaten a meal that kind Mrs. Wilke had brought her, but Henry was hungry having had little to eat all day. He made himself a supper consisting of smoked German sausage, pickles, cheese and currant bread, accompanied by a bottle of light ale, and then concluded his meal with a generous helping of Janet McGill's strudel.

Soon afterwards, he turned off the gas mantles and, creeping silently into the bedroom, peeped into the tiny cot to take a last look at his daughter. He then undressed and got into bed, being very careful not to disturb his wife. It had been a long eventful day, and one of the happiest he had spent in his life.

CHAPTER THREE

1870-1871.

Isabel Bansmer was thrilled to receive a letter from England, and let out a shriek of joy when she read the news of the birth of her daughter's baby, but then as she read on, her expression changed, as she could not believe it to be true that Augusta was planning to leave Saxony and join her sister in London. She re-read the letter, but there was no mistaking the fact that Heinrich had found somewhere for her eldest daughter and Johannes to live. Augusta must have written to Amelia to ask her to do this for her, but had said nothing about it to either herself or her father. Why had she not discussed it with them? Had she something to hide? And what of Johannes? She was aware that Augusta was missing him dreadfully, but did he know about this? Her daughter had not heard from him, as far as she was aware, since he had gone to the war in July. It was unthinkable that she had planned this without his knowledge. Isabel was so upset that she began to cry and was still weeping when Karl came home for his lunch.

"What on earth are you crying for?" Karl asked, and then saw the letter his wife was holding with the Queen Victoria stamp on the envelope. "Oh no! Something has happened to Amelia!" and he snatched the letter from out of his wife's hand to read.

"No, no, Karl, nothing's happened except that she has had a daughter and both are well."

"And you are crying because of that?"

Karl expressed surprise and began to read the letter eagerly, but as he read on his mood changed to bewilderment, then anger. Still holding the letter in his hand he looked at his wife, her cheeks wet with tears and her eyes red with crying.

"She has no right," he bawled, throwing the letter down on to the table. "She has no right to make these decisions without consulting us first." The more he thought about it, the angrier he became. "I do believe that she and Johannes planned all of this before he went into the army. They have not considered you, or me for that matter, and then there is poor Bertha who will have lost both her sisters if she goes. No, Isabel, I'll put my foot down. She'll not go and that's final." Karl put his arm around his

38

wife's shoulders and gave her his handkerchief to dry her eyes.

"Now come, Isabel," he said tenderly, "wipe away your tears and forget all about it. I'll deal with it when Augusta comes home. Meanwhile let us think how happy Amelia must be with our first grandchild."

"I wish they were nearer so we could visit them, Karl. I fear we shall never see her again or the baby."

"Nonsense, Isabel. In her letter she says how well Heinrich is doing. When he has saved enough money they will come to see us, and we'll see our grandchild then." In his heart, Karl did not really believe what he had just said, but he could not allow his wife to think in any other way than that she would see her daughter again sometime in the future.

"But what about Augusta, Karl? Why has she deceived us so? Have we not been good to her? Is she so unhappy here that she has to go away to London? Oh! Karl, I do not understand what is happening in our country that is causing so many people to go away to live in the United States and England."

Karl ate his supper in silence wondering what had caused Augusta and Johannes to make plans to leave their homeland: the trouble was that he could think of too many reasons why they should not stay! It had seemed right for Amelia, so why not Augusta? His first reaction had been to condemn the decision they had made, but was he right to do so? Perhaps he had been too hasty in saying that he would stand in his daughter's way. She had her whole future ahead to live her own life with the man she loved. Was it right that he should spoil it all by opposing what his daughter wished to do?

Augusta had always had a strong resolve to do what she wanted. They were a happy family, but would his lack of support put her in the impossible and unfair position of deciding between her parents' wishes and those of her future husband? The only uncertainty, however, was if Johannes did not return from the war! He had heard of so many soldiers being killed or badly wounded. He looked towards his wife who was also deep in thought, and wanted to tell her what he had been thinking, but how?

"Isabel, we live in hard times, and our country seems obsessed with war." He was talking very quietly, hoping that she would understand what he was about to explain to her. "You won't know as we men do, that heavy fighting has been taking place since August in the areas around our borders with France in the Districts of Alsace and Lorraine, and our local boys are being killed and wounded in the process. I know you don't fully understand all of this, but I'm trying to explain how the

39

young must feel in this country. Most of them were reluctant to go to war, in spite of them being loyal to Saxony and commanded by our own Crown Prince, Frederick Charles, but they had no choice, and no one knows what sort of hell they are going through. The latest news is that the German armies, including the Royal Saxon Corps, have got Paris under siege, but it is believed that there's still much more fighting to take place before this war is over. We hope and pray that Johannes will soon be returned to us safely. In addition," he continued, "you also know what a lean period we farmers are going through, with bad harvests and low prices. Is this what Johannes has to look forward to when he returns?" There was no point in talking as if he might not return, he thought.

He waited a while before continuing, hoping that she was taking it all in. "I tell you Isabel, if we were still young, I would take you away from all this, and now I've given it careful thought as to what Augusta is apparently planning to do, I can understand why they want to get away to start a new life as Amelia has done - and by all accounts with some success."

"So we have brought our children up for them to go far away and never see them again, is that what you are saying?"

Karl had never argued or had a serious disagreement with his wife in all the years they had been married, but he was aware that his wife would take some convincing to come round to his view of the situation. He hoped that she would try and think about it as he had done, and that she too would see how futile it would be to try to stop Augusta and Johannes from doing what they wanted. "I think we should give her a fair hearing when she comes in, Isabel: we cannot hang on to our children forever."

Isabel looked long and hard at her husband, her eyes sad, and although she would not admit it, in her heart she too was beginning to doubt whether they should be standing in their daughter's way.

"But they are not married, Karl, and Amelia said in her letter that Heinrich had already found somewhere for Augusta to live, presumably to wait there until Johannes could join her when he came out of the army. Why couldn't she have waited? What's her hurry?"

"I think we had better leave the questions until Augusta comes home, don't you? Meanwhile, let's think about our first grandchild instead, what's her name again?" They said the name "Otilia," in unison, and held hands as if it was their own child that had been born.

*

Paul Biedermann farmed a medium-sized holding similar to those of his friends Martin Weinelein and Karl Bansmer, growing sugar beet and lucerne in rotation on his land. The lucerne he used as fodder for the few cattle he kept for milk and meat but, as with his neighbours, he was barely making a living. He and his wife were walking back from Sangerhausen where they had been to visit relatives. They had left their five-year-old son, Ernst, and his two-year-older brother, Leopold, with Augusta Bansmer while they had been away. It was late when they arrived home, and Augusta was beginning to get concerned in case her parents might be worrying where she was. "Won't you stop and have a meal with us?" Heidi asked.

Augusta refused. "I really ought to get back to the farm. I think Mama will be worrying about me," she said laughing, and then added thoughtfully, "even at my age."

"Any news from Johannes?" Paul asked the question really more out of concern than expecting her to reply in the affirmative. Apart from news received from a few badly wounded men who had returned, very few letters had come back from the 'front' as far as he knew.

"No, I haven't heard. It's now been almost four months since he left, but I expect they are not able to write letters, and no news is good news," Augusta said bravely.

"What do you plan to do when this war is over and he comes out of the army?"

Paul wanted to make it appear that it was only a matter of time before Johannes would return.

"I'm waiting to hear from my sister in London to see if we can start a new life over there. She seems to be very happy, and Johannes and I discussed this before he left, as his heart is not in farming. It gives us something to think about and look forward to. I have not even told my mother and father about it yet, but I will do as soon as I hear from Amelia, so it's a secret until I do. You won't tell them will you?"

"You seem very excited about it, Augusta," Heidi said, giving her a kiss on the cheek. "I hope that everything turns out all right and we wish you both every happiness."

Augusta had been there all day, and was unaware that her parents had already received the letter from her sister that very morning. So she set off home, well wrapped-up against the bitter November wind, and made her way towards the farm track which led to her parents' farm, thinking all the time of how to break the news to them. "Perhaps I ought to tell them about our plans tonight as soon as I get in," she told herself. "Paul and Heidi seemed to take it well about our leaving, so perhaps Mama and Papa will too. I think I may have been worrying over nothing."

She quickened her steps, anxious to get home and explain everything to her parents.

*

In the middle of January, after over five months of war, Johannes was camped with a Brigade of the X11 Corps in the region of Aulnay, North of the river Marne, some eight miles from the centre of Paris. Although there was still fighting in many other parts of France, the mood of the soldiers was such that they could see the end of the conflict was near. Bombardment of the French capital by German heavy artillery had been going on daily for over two weeks, and as the city had been under siege since early September, one more decisive battle would, they believed, end this bloody war.

Johannes was war-weary, cold and hungry, and his thoughts were of home and Augusta, whom he had not heard from, or seen, since that wonderful July day when they had declared their love for each other. Was it really only six months ago? The Royal Saxons had successfully fought their way from the Moselle valley to the position they now held, but Johannes had lost many of his friends on the way. In August, for instance, in the villages near Metz, the French army had held their positions in spite of heavy artillery fire and repeated attacks by the German army. After two days the Royal Saxon Corps, under the command of their own Prince Frederick Charles, had come into the attack, and with the use of plenty of artillery, took only half an hour to drive the French from their positions. They had then pushed northwards and attacked the unprotected French flank.

However, not all the battles had gone well for the Prussians. At the village of St Privat, a decision by Prince Augustus Wurttemberg to press home the attack by the Guard Corps was made before the troops had time to prepare, and without any covering fire, they made their way up the slopes of the bare open fields in the face of the French guns. The result was a massacre. The mounted officers and the foot-soldiers fell in large numbers, and in twenty minutes over a quarter of the men had been killed or wounded. It was only by the Saxon army's outflanking movement that the French were beaten.

This bloody battle had been the beginning of many such scenes that Johannes had witnessed during the last few months: the horrific spectacle of mutilated bodies, of friends dying in agony, and the large number of burnt corpses and hideously mangled horses of the cavalry lying on the battlefield, haunted his dreams in what little sleep he had had.

Now, Johannes was lying shivering in the cold January night on the outskirts of Paris and, with a German victory almost certain, he thought that at last all this horror was behind him. However, next morning his Brigade was called to reinforce the troops around St Quentin to the north, and help to scatter the defeated French army there. It proved to be more difficult than at first thought, and a fierce battle took place. Johannes, with his Brigade, struggled through the muddy fields in the fog and rain as they advanced towards St Quentin. The French fired on them as they approached, and Johannes fell wounded, a bullet shattering the shinbone of his left leg. He lay there for some time, listening to the shouting of the men as they went into battle, the crying out of the wounded, the roar of the artillery, and the constant firing of rifles becoming fainter as the fighting moved further away. His thoughts were with Augusta and he wondered whether he would ever see her again, but after drifting in and out of consciousness, he woke up to find himself in a field hospital.

Just over a week later he learned that, at last, an armistice had been signed, which meant that he would soon be returning home

CHAPTER FOUR

1871-1872.

Four months had passed since Johannes had lain on that battlefield near Paris, in the belief that he would probably lose his leg, or at least never be able to walk again. Neither had happened, but he had a pronounced limp due to his left leg being now slightly shorter than his right. Augusta had visited him every day since he returned home, but he had refused to discuss the subject of their future, and on more than one occasion, even suggested that they did not have one. "Who wants to marry a cripple?" was his usual reply when Augusta brought up the subject of marriage, and he preferred not to discuss it any further.

Deep in thought, he leaned against the farm gate looking across his father's fields. Although not yet confident enough to leave his walking stick behind, he had managed to hobble the fifty yards or so unaided for the first time. The early morning sun reflected against the new fresh greens of the leaves in the trees and hedges and the spring flowers in the meadows glistened with their bright colours. The birds at that early hour heralded a new day with joyful song and cheerfulness, all in complete contrast to the way Johannes himself was feeling. He was suddenly aware of the sound of quiet footsteps behind him getting nearer, and guessed correctly that it was Augusta who was approaching.

"You've done very well to get this far, Johannes, I told you that you would be alright again, but you wouldn't believe me." She slipped her arm through his and snuggled up to his shoulder. "I do love you," she said confidently.

As usual she received no response from him, and he just stared across the fields. He knew that he had been very lucky not to lose his leg, but he found his incapacity difficult to live with.

"There is no way that I can be of any use again to my father on the farm, and you say that I'm alright?" He gave an unpleasant grunt, which indicated a rejection of what she had said.

Augusta felt a lump come into her throat. "Johannes, you must not give in." She had become used to his rebukes, especially if she was being optimistic about his future or recovery, and tried to ignore them, but at the same time, she understood his despair.

Do you remember, Johannes, almost a year ago, as we lay in that field over there in the summer sunshine, I told you that I loved you, and that I'd never leave you. Do you remember?" Augusta did not wait for an answer. "Well, I meant it, and still do. I love you and always will. But now that you are beginning to make almost a full recovery, and will be able to live a normal life - although perhaps not in farming, I want you to tell me truthfully, do you still want to marry me?" She started to shake a little, and regretting that she had given him no other alternative other to answer either yes or no to the question. Still clinging tightly to his arm, she bit her bottom lip and tried to hold her breath until he answered: she would die if he said no.

He turned his head, and for the first time since he came home his face was devoid of tension and uncertainty. It was not the question she had asked but what she had said about doing something else other than farming which had aroused his interest. He had thought of nothing else since his return other than not being able to do what he had always done. Now she was suggesting what he had thought impossible - to leave farming. He wondered what she had in mind. He looked into her face and suddenly he felt his confidence return that had been lacking previously.

"Do you really think I could do something else to earn a living, Augusta?" he said quietly.

Instead of the rejection she had feared, it had sounded more like a cry for help. "But of course, and we can do it together if you will let me help you."

He put his arm round her shoulders pulling her towards him. "I've been so unfair to you, Augusta, and you've been so kind and loving throughout my recovery. Of course I've always loved you, but I couldn't bear to think of you tied to a cripple."

Augusta tried to interject but Johannes put his hand up to stop her. "No, let me finish what I want to say: heaven knows you deserve an explanation from me. I know that you would like us to go over to your sister in England, and if you believe that we could make a go of it over there, then I'm willing to try."

He had not mentioned marriage, but Augusta felt an enormous sense of relief that he was at last sounding more optimistic in his future. However, he had not answered her question of whether he wanted to marry her, and what he had said had sounded more like a temporary partnership arrangement than anything more permanent, but she would be content with that, so long as they were together.

"Oh, Johannes, of course we could make a go of it, and I could teach you to sew," she said excitedly. "There is nothing wrong with your hands. Perhaps there would be places for us in the tailoring trade when we get to London: my sister and Heinrich seem to be doing all right."

"Maybe Heinrich's father would take me on as an apprentice for a while to learn tailoring," Prompted by Augusta's suggestion, it was an idea that suddenly occurred to Johannes. "I would not ask for pay: I wonder if he would do it? Meanwhile, you had better write to your sister, Amelia, to ask Heinrich to find out if those rooms are still available."

Augusta had not seen him so enthusiastic about anything since he had come home. As she helped him walk back to the farm, she felt happier than she had been for a very long time.

*

Almost two years had passed since the first time that Sam had offered Henry the rooms for his sister-in-law and Johannes. In reply to Amelia's letter to her sister at that time, Augusta had told her that life was so uncertain for them with Johannes still being in the army, that any future plans to leave Germany would have to be delayed until the war with France was over. Augusta had then written again to tell her about Johannes being wounded, and Amelia had almost dismissed the idea that they would still be coming to join them in London.

She had been disappointed that they had not arrived, especially as she wanted to show off her baby to her sister. Then, about a year ago, she had heard again from Augusta that she and Johannes would still like to come, but now she knew that it would be more difficult to find somewhere for them to live. A large new railway station was being built in Liverpool Street, next to the existing Broad Street Station, and men working on the site had taken up every room in the surrounding area. Some of the houses were so overcrowded, that beds were occupied continuously in relays for the full 24 hours each day. There was a saying that 'Beds were never cold in Bishopsgate'.

Sam Long had remembered that Amelia had asked him to let them know if he had some sort of accommodation where her sister could stay if they came to England.

"Is yer sister-in-law and 'er 'husband still interested in coming 'ere, Mr.Rolfs?" Sam Long asked Henry, as he called to him down the street when he saw him coming home late one evening, "'cos I've got them rooms empty again if they was."

When Henry told Amelia about this latest offer that Sam Long had made, she was overjoyed.

"I must write to Augusta in the morning to tell her the good news. They must be thinking that after all this time we don't want them to come! You didn't tell Mr. Long that they were not married, did you, Henry?" There was a touch of anxiety in her voice as she put the question.

"No, I did not, but I don't know why not," Henry answered firmly.

Henry was concerned that Sam would think badly of them for withholding that information. "It does not seem fair on Sam not to tell him that he's letting his rooms to an unmarried couple!" he added.

"She has never mentioned marriage in her letters to me," Amelia said thoughtfully. "Perhaps when she receives my letter, they will marry before they leave." She felt satisfied with her conclusions, and then, to put Henry's mind at rest, added, "So there is no need to mention it to Mr. Long until we know one way or the other."

"Well, I am still not very happy about it," Henry snorted. He looked towards his wife for an assurance that she would be able somehow to put matters right with Sam Long before they arrived.

Amelia decided to say no more about it and to let the matter rest there. Augusta, after all, was the oldest of the three sisters, and the way that she chose to run her life was her own affair. Secretly, however, Amelia was more worried about how her parents would feel about her sister not being married, if that was the case. Augusta had said in her letters how much she was in love, and that Johannes had made a good recovery from the severe leg wound he had received in the war. In addition, she had told her how he had been making good use of his time learning tailoring with Henry's father while they were waiting to come to London.

Amelia also thought of young Bertha who was about to lose another of her sisters, but being so much younger than herself and Augusta, she would not have been affected by the traumatic events in Germany which had been one of the main reasons for their leaving. Suddenly, she realised that Bertha would be at least ten years old now, and must have changed considerably in the two and a half years since she last saw her. Lost in these perceptions, she was vaguely aware that Henry had spoken to her.

"What are you thinking about, Amelia?" Henry asked for the second time.

Amelia was aware that Henry obviously wanted to carry on the argument about her sister, but she was anxious now to change the subject.

"Oh nothing really, I was just wondering why we had not heard any more from cousin Bernhard since he married at the beginning of last year," she lied.

Their attention was drawn towards baby Otilia crawling across the floor of the room towards the fireplace.

"Watch her, Henry, don't let her get too near that fire."

Henry picked her up and held her on his knee. He loved to be with his daughter and made every excuse to hold her in his arms. Due to working long hours with Hermann Wilke, he saw very little of her when she was awake.

"I do believe she is going to be a beauty like you, Amelia," he teased.

"Oh get away with you, Henry. I don't feel very glamorous in this drab place and I do wish that we could get away. I saw two more mice again today running across the bedroom floor: I do worry about Otilia."

Amelia took every opportunity to complain about their rooms, as she felt that Henry was too pre-occupied with his work to really bother to look for somewhere better to live. However, this was not exactly true. He had made some enquiries about rented accommodation in much better property in streets behind Broad Street Station, but had been told that there was nothing available at the present time. Herman Wilke had introduced him to a landlord he knew, who owned some of these houses in Shoreditch, and Henry had been to see the property which was much more desirable than where they now lived. He knew that Amelia would like the area if only they were able to move, but had not mentioned it for fear of disappointing her should it not happen. For this reason, he too was now anxious to change the subject.

"Do you know where your cousin Bernhard went to live? Didn't he put his address on his letter when he wrote to say he had married? Is he still on the 'Henrietta'?"

"Why all these questions, Henry? You have never appeared interested in Bernhard before!" Amelia said, showing surprise.

"Well, it was you who mentioned him when you said that we hadn't heard from him. He must have been on your mind."

Henry gave Otilia a big kiss on the top of her head and put her back down on the floor. She had been wriggling to get away all the time they had been talking. He sat her down next to the musical box for which he had paid ten shillings from a stallholder in Petticoat Lane. It particularly appealed to him as it had been made in Germany and the tunes it played reminded him of home. He lifted the lid and moved the lever to set it in motion. Otilia was completely fascinated as she watched the tiny hammers moving jerkily back and forth to strike the silver bells, while the metal keys hit the spikes of the slowly revolving roller to create the lovely tinkling tunes.

"I just thought that he might have brought his wife to see us before now, that was all," Amelia continued, still trying to forget about her sister.

Henry thought that he would go along with this conversation. It would stop his wife from asking any more questions about finding a new place to live.

"Who did he marry did you say?"

"Mother told me in one of her letters that Bernhard had left the ship and is now working in Hull. Perhaps I didn't tell you that he married a woman called Elizabeth Jack. I remember mama telling me that she was a widow - and his landlady!"

As Amelia picked up Otilia to get her ready for bed, Henry rose from his chair to get his supper, "I think he is very clever to marry his landlady: won't have to pay rent anymore!" He chuckled at his own joke, and then called after Amelia as he went in the store cupboard, "You won't forget to write to Augusta in the morning, will you?"

"Of course not, Henry, I will do it first thing," Amelia said quietly as she took their daughter to the bedroom.

Henry turned up the gaslight, and then deliberately and carefully crushed two cockroaches with his heel that he saw scurrying across the floor. He really must have another word with one of those landlords next time he saw them, he thought. Amelia was right; this was no place to bring up a child.

*

It was Saturday in the first week of July, and the sun beat down from a cloudless sky. Amelia had just returned from a hot, crowded Petticoat Lane, and was about to make herself a cup of tea when she heard a knock on the door. "I wonder who that can be?" she said out loud, as she began to open it. She stood there for a second staring at the two people outside, then her eyes filled with tears of joy.

"Augusta....Johannes," was all that she could say at first, as she put her arms around her sister, giving her a big hug. "It has been such a long time."

While Amelia was wanting to know all the news from home and asking about her mama and papa, young Lize Wilke, who kept house for older sister Willemine while she helped with the tailoring, ran to the work-rooms in Middlesex Street, to break the news of Augusta's arrival to Henry. She arrived out of breath and it took a while for him to understand that his sister-in-law had arrived. He hurried back home to greet them, hoping to find that Johannes was now his brother-in-law.

"What a crowded journey we have had from the docks! I have never seen so many people in one place...," were Augusta's first words in her native tongue as soon as Henry came through the door.

Henry kissed her on both cheeks and shook Johannes warmly by the hand.

"....we came by The Tower of London," she continued almost without stopping, "and along the road which the cabby told us was Petticoat Lane, and there were crowds of people and horse-drawn cabs, and carriages of all shapes and sizes. We saw men carrying lots of baskets full of fruit and vegetables on their heads, stalls full of clothes, men carrying sides of meat, beggars, street-sellers, and everyone seemed to be shouting at once!"

Augusta was so excited that she wanted to tell them everything that she and Johannes had seen on their journey from the docks. Henry waited patiently for her to stop talking to enable him to find out what he wanted to know. He looked to see if she was wearing a wedding ring, but her hand was hidden in the baby's clothing as she held his daughter in her arms.

"....and there were all the men at the top of the road working on a new building - I expect you know what it is they are doing, building a railway station or something the cabby told us - but the smell of horse dung on the roads did remind me a little of the farm," she said smiling, "but all the children we saw looked so pitiful, most of them in ragged clothes!"

She paused in order to get her breath but Henry had left it too late to ask his question before she started again.

"I expect you know that Johannes is now an expert tailor and do you think he will be able to get a job, Heinrich?" She paused, again, this time waiting for him to answer. However, Johannes laughed out loud at what she had said.

"I don't know about an expert, Augusta. Heinrich's father had said that I had shown promise as he tried to teach me about the trade, but I have a long way to go before I will be considered to be an expert!"

At last Henry saw the opportunity to get a word in. "Well," said Henry firmly, at last being able to speak, "first things first," (he would tell them later about him now being called Henry and not Heinrich) but now he had to know - "Are you married?" he asked bluntly.

Augusta stopped smiling and looked at Henry coldly. She wondered why he should ask that question. What had it to do with him? But then she smiled again as she suddenly realised that she had not told them what she had intended to tell them as soon as she had arrived.

"No, Heinrich, we are not." She looked at him quite fiercely at first and then her face resumed its happy smile as she reached out to put her sister's hand into her's. Her eyes had a sparkle as she explained the situation to Amelia. "On the boat coming over Johannes said that we would get married as soon as possible when we arrived in London. You know what mama is like, Amelia, she wanted us to get married properly like you did, and invite all our friends to the wedding. I tried to explain to her that we really didn't have time, as we wanted to come here as soon as possible after we received your letter. Poor mama: she was so disappointed." Then lifting the baby high in the air between her outstretched arms, she addressed her reply to Henry's question to the child in English, "....so, little Otilia, you vill soon be having a new uncle."

There was nothing more that Henry could say. He now realised that perhaps he had been too impatient in wanting to ask the question that had been worrying him, so he quickly changed the subject and asked about his own parents.

While Augusta was giving him the news that they were both well, Amelia thought that her husband was looking very worried in case Augusta might have been offended so, wishing to put right immediately any harm that might have been done to their relationship, she thought it best to give an explanation to her future brother-in-law, as to why Henry had been so blunt.

"Henry has been understandably worried, Johannes, about whether you were married or not, especially as he had managed to find rooms for you to live together. We were both concerned about what Mr. Long would think if he found out that you were not married, but I am sure he will understand when we explain to him what you have told us. So let us forget it now." Amelia smiled and concluded that that was the end of it and no harm had been done.

"What's all this name of 'HENRY'?" Augusta said with a chuckle.

Henry was relieved that she appeared not to have been offended by his directness, and Amelia explained that Henry had wanted to be called Henry instead of Heinrich, for Otilia's sake.

Later, Henry went with them to their rooms and introduced Augusta and Johannes to Sam Long. His fears had been unfounded, Sam being most understanding about their situation. He even suggested that as he knew the Reverend R.D.Duncan, who was curate at St.Mark's parish church of

Whitechapel, he was sure that he could get him to read the first banns out for them next day at the Sunday Morning Service, to enable them to get married as soon as it was possible.

"I know 'e speaks good German, and I fink bo'f of you ought to go to church tomorra'," he suggested, turning towards Augusta, "cos it'll look bad if y'aint there."

Augusta had learned quite a lot of English before coming to England, but because of Sam's cockney accent she had found it impossible to understand everything that Sam had said. Henry noticed the glazed look of Augusta's face so he translated it for her.

"Tell him that of course we will go, Henry. We would want to anyway! Perhaps you and Amelia would come too, and we can give thanks to our Lord for our safe journey and family re-union."

"I'm sure that Amelia will think it a lovely idea, and when you have settled in, come and join us for some supper, and I'll open a bottle of German wine which I've saved for an occasion such as this. You come too, Sam, we'll be pleased to have your company, and thanks for your help and understanding."

Just over three weeks later, Johannes and Augusta were married by the Reverend R.D.Duncan, with Sam Long and Amelia Rolfs signing the register as witnesses. Little Otilia cried loudly throughout the ceremony while both young Friderieke Luhm, and Mrs Wilke who sat next to her, also cried but for a different reason, each soaking a handkerchief with their tears as Johannes and Augusta recited their vows.

Henry went to bed happy and light-headed that night, not only because he had consumed more than his normal intake of wine, but also because he worried no more about his sister-in-law and Johannes. Normally he was so tired after working long hours that he found no time to express his love for Amelia, but the day had been one of romance, which had rekindled his own emotions.

Amelia too, was in a state of euphoria, not only happy at being united again with her sister, but also because the ceremony had brought back memories of how she had felt on the day when she was married to Henry. Their arms were wrapped around each other as they lay together, remembering the day's events and telling of their love for each other.

"I can feel your heart beating," Henry whispered excitedly as he moved his hand around underneath her nightdress. He undid the bow beneath her chin, and she pulled his head down on to her bare breasts. In the warm summer night they made love, then fell into a deep contented sleep.

CHAPTER FIVE

1872-1888.

Only four months after they had arrived, Augusta and Johannes began to doubt whether they had done the right thing in coming to London. Their living conditions were not all they had hoped for. Their rooms were damp and cold and overrun with vermin, and the degeneracy they could see around them was almost too much for them to bear. Augusta was saddened too by the sight of the poverty-stricken barefoot children in the streets and was heartbroken to see the little chimney sweeps, no more than five or six years old, permanently black with soot and covered in cuts and sores received from their ordeal inside the tall chimneys of the large houses. Prostitutes regularly walked past her house from their lodgings in the squalid streets of Whitechapel making their way to ply their trade with the men who were constructing the new Liverpool Street Station across the road.

"I don't feel safe going out after dark, even to walk the small distance to visit you," Augusta told her sister.

"I would hate to be taken for one of those girls of ill repute."

Amelia laughed, especially at the words she had chosen to describe the whores, but she agreed with her that she would be unwise for her to do that. " 'The King's Arms' gets very busy in the evenings, and I would not like to think of you in danger of being accosted by the men who hang about outside." Amelia squeezed her older sister's hand, and then added reassuringly, "Sam Long will take care that no one comes into the house where you are living, so there's no need to worry about that."

Augusta had been so excited when they had first arrived in London, but now that the cold winter weather had set in conditions outside were not as attractive as they had previously seemed. Obnoxious street smells arising from a mixture of smoke from the chimneys, gas from the street lamps and horse dung, all trapped in a blanket of thick fog, greeted them in the dark winter mornings and often hung around all day. Flea-ridden dogs wandered the streets, thin and scruffy, endlessly searching for scraps of food that people had thrown out for them. Mangy-looking cats prowled in every corner. It had been so different on the farm they had left back home in Saxony where everything was clean and the air fresh even on the coldest of days. Rain was welcomed on the farm and was essential for the growth of the sugar beet and corn, but here in London the rainwater looked dirty turning the pavements and roads into a messy and smelly quagmire, and only a long downpour had the desired effect of washing the place clean.

Johannes was not very happy in his work either. His leg seemed to hurt him much more in the damp atmosphere. His fingers were becoming sore with hours of pinning up the suit material and the endless stitching he was given to do by Mr.Wilke. It would have helped if he could have used the new Singer sewing machine on occasions, but Friderieke Luhm, the young 18-year-old seamstress from Neustettin, was the only person allowed to use it.

"You must concentrate, Johannes, and follow the chalk lines carefully," Herman Wilke explained. "We cannot afford to waste cloth and it only delays the delivery of our orders. We have so much competition in this part of London, especially from the Jewish quarter, and more and more people are coming here all the time from Europe - most of them experienced tailors."

Johannes despaired at Mr. Wilke's attitude towards him and often he would go home late in the evening feeling very unhappy.

"Mr.Wilke still not satisfied with your work?" Augusta would ask him when he looked as if he had had a bad day. She could not really help him any more and he was always too tired to want to accept her advice anyway.

"This damn leg doesn't help," grumbled Johannes. "After sitting still for such a long time I find it's difficult to move it when I eventually stand up. I'll never be able to work like Mr. Wilke and Henry do, with one leg somewhere tucked underneath their bodies as they pin-up and sew. Mr.Wilke has even worn a smooth groove out of the wooden block with his shoe where he sits nearly all day long!"

Augusta did not like to hear him grumbling and was anxious to change the subject as she put out his meal. "I got a nice piece of veal from the butcher this morning and made you a Wiener Schnitzel for your supper." It was one of Johannes' favourite meals and, as he ate, Augusta read out the letter she had received earlier in the day from Germany.

"Two of your friends, Carl and Friedrich, wish to be remembered to you, Johannes, and the Siebenhüners - you remember, they were married last year - have had a baby boy, Richard Oswald."

Johannes was not very interested in babies and his wife knew it, but she was anxious to give her husband something else to think about other than work. As she read the letter through, Johannes wondered whether he had been too inconsiderate in leaving his father to cope with the farm without him, especially as the old man would be finding the work harder to do in the later years of his life. He now realised that he was not really cut out to be a tailor and was missing the farm life dreadfully. Perhaps he had been too hasty in deciding that he would be unable to do farm work because of the injury to his leg. He was not as incapacitated as he had expected to be and exercise appeared to be better for his leg than sitting still for long periods: he kept these thoughts to himself, however.

When Henry came home the following evening, Amelia told him about how unhappy their brother-in-law appeared to be. Her sister had been to see her during the day and wondered whether Henry could do anything to improve the situation.

"I could ask him to come with us to Abraham's," Henry suggested, "and perhaps he would then begin to feel that he was part of the tailoring community, but to be honest, Amelia, he is not making much progress and I don't hold out any hopes that he will ever become a good tailor."

"It's early days," Amelia pointed out hopefully; "you surely must give him a chance to improve."

Henry mumbled something to the effect that they had given him lots of chances, but thankfully his wife did not hear what he had said, or perhaps chose not to. She was thinking more about her sister and how disappointed she would be if Johannes could not carry on in the trade and would be forced to move away, then suddenly remembered the news her sister had told her. "Augusta had a letter from home yesterday giving her all the news and your old friend Friedrich is the father of a little boy."

"Friedrich a papa! Impossible!" Henry quipped. "He's probably had a boy on purpose so that he can follow him in the mines. He will have him down the pits as soon as he can walk if I know Friedrich!" Henry roared with laughter. "What have they called the little fellow?"

"Richard Oswald, I think Augusta said."

As she spoke, Henry lifted his young daughter up into his arms and addressed his next remarks to her. "I miss our old friends, Otilia, and if we were still back home you would probably be marrying that little rascal Richard Oswald Siebenhüner in about twenty years time!" He then returned to thinking about his brother-in-law. "I'll try and have a word with Abraham to see if he will have a word with Johannes. He'll probably take more notice of him rather than any advice I would give."

The following Friday evening Henry and Johannes set off on the walk to

Abraham Solomon's house and met him coming out of the Synagogue nearby.

"So this is your brother-in-law, Henry, is it?" Abraham asked as he shook Johannes's hand. "I'm so pleased to meet you. Henry has told me so much about you already and you are very welcome to come to my house. As you probably know, we do not do any cooking on our Sabbath, so my dear wife, Esther, prepared a meal earlier today for us to eat tonight."

Abraham introduced Johannes to a number of his friends, dressed in dark suits and some wearing large flat black hats or, as in Abraham's case, an ordinary black trilby. Abraham had a kindly face, Johannes observed, or what he could see of it beneath his large black and grey beard. He tried unsuccessfully to guess how old Abraham might be. He looked over fifty years of age, but had the stature and clear skin of a much younger man: he was later to learn that he was only in his late thirties.

As they made their way towards Whitechapel carts passed by along the still busy Middlesex Street with their lanterns flickering in the cold late evening air. Many shops, dimly lit by gaslight, were still busy with customers, while all those owned by the Jews were closed and shuttered. This was due, Abraham explained to Johannes, because the Jewish Sabbath began shortly after sunset on Friday evening and continued until Saturday night.

Amelia and Augusta had arrived at the Solomons' house in the late afternoon, purposely to witness the traditional start of the Jewish Sabbath. They had watched as Abraham's wife, Esther covered the table with a lovely white damask cloth and laid out the best silver, placing two specially baked braided loaves on a board next to a cup of wine. She had then lit the candles on the table and prayed for God's blessing on her work and for her family.

The candles burning in the house gave a warm and friendly glow when the men arrived. Esther, wearing her best dress, welcomed them at the door. "We will rest a while before we eat and you can tell me about your troubles," Abraham said sympathetically, looking towards Johannes. "Henry has told me that you are unhappy here. Perhaps I may be able to help."

Surprisingly, Johannes found it very easy to explain why he did not think things were working out for him as well as he had expected they would. He began first to tell them about his feeling of hopelessness when he returned home from France with his injury, which prevented him from continuing to work on his father's farm. He told of his wish to leave Germany with Augusta and start a new life in England.

"I'm not really cut out to be a tailor, but the opportunity presented itself to learn the trade under Henry's father and then wait for the right moment to come here to England and make a new career for myself, but...." Johannes hesitated; everyone had been so supportive, but no one had ever asked him to tell them what he really thought before. "....but to be truthful," he continued, "my heart is still in farming and I long to be back home."

It was the first time that Augusta had been aware of her husband's hankering to be back on the farm in Saxony, and his revelations took everyone so much by surprise that no one spoke for a while. Augusta felt that she had let her husband down and tried to say something, then thought it best at that time not to interpose. Abraham was the first to speak.

"Because of what you have said," he said quietly, "I cannot advise you what to do, Johannes, but your heart will probably dictate what your final decision will be."

Augusta went over to where Johannes sat and, taking his hands into hers, spoke to him quietly, "Do you want to go home and talk about this?"

"No! no! no!" Abraham interjected, his arms raised and the palms of his hands turned outwards in protest at the suggestion. "Home? No! Let us not talk any more, but enjoy ourselves. Tonight is an evening when we welcome our friends, and Esther has prepared a meal for us to enjoy. Come, sit round the table and join with us in our family festival."

Abraham offered the men a yarmelka, or skull-cap to wear, and then, after everyone had sat down at the table, gave a blessing over the loaves of bread which he referred to as 'challot', chanting in praise of his wife and reciting verses from the bible. After taking a portion of bread and wine for himself, he passed the loaf and bottle to his guests for them to help themselves before Esther brought in the meal. This consisted mainly of fish, which she had prepared in the traditional way by covering it in flour and beaten egg and then lightly frying in oil.

Throughout the evening, no one referred to what Johannes had said earlier, but Augusta wanted desperately to talk to her husband about what they were going to do and where their future lay.

"It's not going to be easy," Johannes explained to his wife when they got home, "but I don't think I want to stay here, and if we move away from this area, what else could I do?"

"After what you said this evening, I don't know what you want me to say. If I try to persuade you to carry on, people would think that I was forcing you to stay here. If we moved they would think that I had not supported you enough or that I hadn't helped you to continue to persevere with learning the tailoring trade."

"Nonsense, Augusta, all that we would be doing is going back to my father's farm in Saxony to do what I'm best at and what I know about."

"But I thought that you didn't have your heart in farming. You always said that your leg would prevent you from going back to it anyway!" Augusta was completely taken by surprise at his change of attitude.

"Well, I suppose it's a question of missing what I had always taken for granted. I could always run the farm and employ some casual help like my father always did. I have been thinking, too, that as he gets older he will need someone and he only has me. After all, I always promised him that I would run the farm when he was too old to do so himself and I feel now that I have let him down. As far as the leg is concerned, I'll just have to put up with it. It's not too bad really," he now admitted.

All the time Johannes was explaining, Augusta realised that it had not been a sudden impulse that had caused her husband to open his heart to Mr.Solomon, but something that he must have been thinking about for some time.

"The only thing that has been worrying me..." Johannes stopped for a second or two, and moved over to where she sat and took her hands into his, "is how you feel about going back and leaving your sister. You had so looked forward to being with her again before we left home and now there's little Otilia...."

Augusta freed one of her hands and placed two fingers on her husband's lips to stop him from talking and then took his face gently between both of her hands. "Of course I'll miss them, but I told you a long time ago," she said lovingly, "that I will never leave you and wherever you go, then I will go too, because I love you. You are all that matters to me. To be truthful, Johannes," it was now Augusta's turn to say what she really thought, "I can't wait to get back to the countryside, so let's go home."

"I feel that we have been here for years," Johannes confessed. They both laughed together and felt happier than they had been since coming to England.

Just three months after Augusta and Johannes had left to return to Germany, Amelia's second baby came into the world with little fuss. She named the baby after her younger sister, Bertha, because she had dark hair like her. She was a healthy baby, but Henry was concerned for both his children as so many in the district did not survive the first year and even many more died when they were still very young.

Time passed uneventfully for the next two years, when Amelia gave birth to their third child, Frederick, who developed breathing problems soon after he was born. It was a bitterly cold February morning and the damp conditions of the house were not good for the baby. The doctor said that he would give him only a week to live, but on the fourth day Frederick died during the night. Henry was heartbroken and blamed everything and everyone, but he knew that the real culprit was more than likely the house in which they lived.

Next morning he visited Harry Haws, an undertaker who had his dark suits made by Herman, to arrange the funeral. Following a very short service conducted by the Reverend Duncan (the same man who had married Augusta and Johannes some two and a half years previously) the tiny coffin was carried to the cemetery in the hearse pulled very slowly along the streets by two fine looking jet black mares. A young boy wearing a well-brushed top hat and a dark suit, which was somewhat too large for him, led the sad procession. It was a very cold day, and the small group of family mourners together with a few friends, stood by the graveside their eyes full of tears as the tiny coffin containing Henry's little baby boy was lowered slowly down into it. That same evening, Henry called on that landlord whom he had visited previously and who owned some better property away from the area.

"I would be very grateful if you could find a house for me and my family in one of your much more desirable properties than those where we now live in Artillery Lane." Henry asked humbly, stumbling over the words and trying to put them in the right order.

Mr.Kearly, the landlord, listened to Henry's request, but interrupted him when he began to be told about the baby's death and what Henry had thought to have been the cause.

"I had heard about your baby Mr Rolfs, and I'm very sorry about that and I do have some good news for you. Some rooms are coming empty in a couple of months' time and you can have those if you'd like. It's rather a large part of the house in Earl Street but you'll need it with all your family and helpers. The rent will be more than you are paying now, but it should suit you very nicely. It is a hard thing to say, but your son's death, causing you to come and see me this evening, may have been a blessing in disguise. I've only learnt today that the first six houses where you live at present are condemned, along with other property in the area; they are due to be pulled down. It will be difficult to house all those

59

people who live there and they'll be a rush for rooms to rent tomorrow when the news is known."

Henry could hardly believe it: new rooms in a newer house in a far better area, and no overcrowding as there was in Artillery Lane! After warmly shaking hand of his benefactor he thanked him most profusely and hurried home to tell his Amelia the good news. She was overjoyed and could hardly believe it. She looked around at the home they had lived in for the past five years. "I don't know what this other house you've found for us is like, Henry, but anything will be better than this horrid place." Although they moved immediately the rooms became vacant, the loss of her baby son gave them much unhappiness for a while afterwards. However, in the Spring of the following year, Amelia gave birth to a healthy son whom they named John, after her brother-in-law Johannes.

Henry no longer worked with Mr Wilke in Middlesex Street and obtained his own orders for the work he was doing. Now that they had more room he could work from home, taking in lodgers who were experienced in tailoring to help him. His business thrived, albeit modestly, and, during the next five years, Amelia had two more children: Charles was born two years after John, and then Clara three years later.

Now that he had a bigger family to support, Henry worked even harder and enjoyed the time that he and Amelia spent with the children. On Sundays they would go to church in the morning and, if the weather was fine, stroll through the park in the afternoon. They remained friends with the Wilke family, but some of the others he had known when he first arrived in London had moved away when the houses were condemned. Henry also had many business acquaintances, mainly in the tailors' shops in and around Middlesex Street and there was, of course, his old friend Abraham Solomon whom he saw regularly.

"I cannot believe how the years are going by so quickly already," Abraham remarked to Henry as they sat together drinking coffee, "and those girls of yours are going to make someone very happy one day. They are so good-looking, my friend."

Henry was proud of his family, especially of his lovely daughter, Otilia, whom he had always thought of as his favourite, although he would never let the others know how he regarded her.

CHAPTER SIX

1888.

On a fine April morning, Henry and Amelia Rolfs, and their five children walked back home after attending the morning service in St.Leonard's Parish Church.

The years had passed by uneventfully and now their children were growing up far too quickly. The two boys, John and Charles, together with the youngest girl, Clara, were still at school. Otilia, who was now in her seventeenth year, and Bertha, who was fourteen, both helped their father and had done so from the day they had completed what little education they had had. John too would be leaving the church school in July and would soon be joining them, while their mother also found time to help her husband, stitching in the linings and sewing on buttons.

The rooms were a hive of activity most days, the work often continuing late into the evening. In addition to his family, Henry had found it necessary to find extra help. John Ziesemir was one who had been with him for a number of years. He had learnt his trade whilst serving his apprenticeship in a tailor's shop in Whitechapel Road. Another who had been with him for some time was Charles Bender who specialised in making long morning coats, while Mr. Bender's young daughter, Dora, who had been taught well by her father, put an expert finish to the work with her fine stitching. In addition, Matilda Huller from Berne, also lived in the same house, and was employed by Henry mainly to iron and press the clothes and arrange collection by the retailers.

Henry was very proud of what they did and took great pains to ensure that their work was of a very high standard. He often boasted that he would be able to recognise any suit of clothes that left their establishment, anywhere. To try and prove his point, he would sometimes accept his own challenge by standing outside the busy Liverpool Street Station from seven o'clock in the morning and, for an hour or so, watch the businessmen and junior clerks coming in on the early trains. He said that he could usually tell who was wearing his suits and who was not.

Late one evening when Henry returned from one of his calls, he entered the room where most of the work was carried out and was surprised to see Amelia still working. He quickly noticed that there were more unfinished garments around her than he had ever seen before.

"Are you working on all these at the same time?"

"We've been working hard all day to try and get all these done," she explained without looking up at him, "and I've hardly had time to cook meals or do any house work. I really could do with some domestic help, Henry," and then added almost without a pause, "perhaps you would have a cold supper tonight, so get yourself some food from the larder while I finish this jacket."

Henry was a very tolerant man who was not easily upset or aroused, but the only thing that could disturb his equanimity would be to find that his meals were taking second place to everything else. He knew his wife better than she thought he did, and guessed that she was making the excuse that she had been too busy to get him a meal because she had an ulterior motive. She had mentioned a few days ago, something about getting someone in to help with the domestic work, but he had dismissed the idea of another person looking after him, especially as he enjoyed his wife's cooking and the meals she prepared.

"Do you mean you want a cook?" he asked, not believing for a minute that she would do such a thing as employing someone to cook his meals.

"No, Henry, don't be silly, I mean someone to do all the household chores that take time: dusting, bed-making, cleaning, preparing the vegetables, that sort of thing. If we had someone to do all that I could still do all the cooking, and have more time to help you."

Henry breathed a sigh of relief, but Amelia had not quite finished telling him the plans she had made. "The extra turnover would enable us to cover the tiny cost of feeding a servant girl, and relieve me of the housework. There's a lot to do, Henry, and I do enjoy helping you."

He thought that there must be logic somewhere in her argument, but he was too tired to work it out, and in any case he was caught in a trap. It looked to him like - no servant - no dinner!

"Alright, you win, Amelia, but where are you going to find a girl you can trust?"

His wife stopped what she was doing "It so happens that I was talking to Mrs Cannon at number 26, and she has a granddaughter in Twickenham who she thinks will be suitable. She said that she was not very bright, but a good little worker."

"And how old is this, 'not very bright good little worker', who you have suddenly found to be suitable and who lives the other side of the City?"

"She's nearly fifteen, her name is Mary Cannon, and she's willing to work for just her keep. Her food will cost very little and we can easily put another bed in with Dora and Matilda. They have already said that they wouldn't mind."

Henry looked at his wife and smiled. This was not something that she had suddenly thought of as being a good idea: she had had it all worked out before she even asked him for his approval. Amelia saw him looking and knew what was going through his mind. She gave a little chuckle and immediately put down the garment she had been working on. "I think I'll finish that tomorrow," she announced. "You sit where you are and rest, Henry, and I'll get you a nice meal."

Henry now realised that when he found her still working, it was all a ploy to get him to approve what she already arranged. She had manipulated him to agree by using blackmail, but at least he knew now that he would not have to get his own supper.

He sat back in his chair to relax but looked towards his two eldest daughters and thought how pale they looked. "I hope you girls have been out today." Henry was concerned that they were not getting enough exercise or fresh air, and remained far too long in the house. He was feeling a little disgruntled and his daughters just happened to be in the firing line.

"Yes we did, Papa," Otilia answered, "and we walked along City Road, past the barracks, then back across the field."

Henry picked up the 'East London Observer' that he had bought from a newsboy earlier in the early evening. "And how many young Grenadier Guards did you see on your walk? You know I don't trust them, not since they attacked the people demonstrating in Trafalgar Square last November."

"Papa, we don't know what you have against the soldiers. Some of them look quite respectable young men and very handsome in their uniforms."

Henry thought about pursuing the matter further, but wondered whether he was being a little unreasonable. He had had a lot of sympathy for some of the crowd who were Socialists, and they had been demonstrating over the exploitation of their labour by some employers, even though the Police Commissioner had banned the rally. Henry knew that the soldiers had been asked to assist the police, and that they had had no choice but to do what they had been ordered to do, but it seemed to him to be wrong that the working man had been suppressed when trying to express his dissatisfaction with some of the things that he himself believed to be wrong.

"Well as long as you don't talk to them and ignore them if they try to talk to you," he said from behind his newspaper, "I know what some of them get up to."

The girls giggled at that, and their father gave a grunt of disapproval of their flippancy as he turned the pages of his paper.

After his meal, Henry walked down into Bishopsgate to arrange the collection of the finished articles of clothing from his house, and collect payment for the work that had been done. His weekly visit also included meeting with the many friends that he had made, mainly his own countrymen.

"Did you know that a couple of young men from your part of Germany are in London and living somewhere in Whitechapel?" someone asked him. "I heard they are both cooks working in the hotels."

Henry did not know any cooks, and in any case, if they were young men, they would have been very young when he left eighteen years ago, possibly not even born! "Do you know their names or how old they are by any chance?" he enquired, not really expecting to know them.

"Biedermann: two brothers: Ernest and Leopold I think they're called."

Henry looked surprised. They can't be, he thought: not the two little fellows at his wedding! If it is, then they must now be in their twenties, and probably here with their wives. He remembered that soon after they had moved to Earl Street, Augusta had received word in one of her letters from home that their friend, Paul Biedermann, had died suddenly. It was soon after some of the German banks had collapsed, and they had been told earlier that Paul had been made bankrupt. These could be his sons. If they are who he thinks they are, he would naturally like to meet them.

"Where can I find them?" Henry asked.

His friend looked at the clock. "At this time they could be in the 'Queen's Head' in Commercial Street. Do you know it, Henry?"

Henry knew the area all right, but it was not in a very salubrious part of Bishopsgate to say the least. "It's a bit too close to a pretty rough quarter for my liking, but you've made me curious and I think I'll go along to see if they are who I think they are."

Henry walked past the house where he used to live, noting that the property was still standing although empty and derelict, and made his way along White's Row into Commercial Street. He noticed that the area on the other side was still a labyrinth of slums, as bad as when they had left their house nearly thirteen years previously. He glanced down Flower and Dean Street that was noted for its overcrowded houses. Criminals and prostitutes occupied much of the property: he hoped that

64

none of his friends would see him and draw the wrong conclusions as to why he was there.

When he arrived at the 'Queen's Head', the two men he was seeking were not there.

"I fink I do know who ya mean," the landlord told Henry, "and if ya wanna leave a message for em, I'll see they ge'it."

Henry was disinclined to hang about, so he left his address and a message should they wish to contact him.

When Henry got home, he told his wife about what he had learnt about the two men, and said that they could arrive at any time. After three or four days had passed without even an enquiry, Amelia gave up hope of seeing them. However, the following week, she answered a knock on the door, and the two young men stood there looking slightly embarrassed.

Amelia was the first to speak. "You are not Paul's sons by any chance, from Riestedt?"

They both grinned and nodded their heads.

"Now which one are you?" Amelia asked the taller of the two men as she led them into the living room.

"I am Leopold, the eldest," "And I am Ernst," the other intervened, "or perhaps I should call myself Ernest now I'm in England," and then added with a chuckle, "I am the handsome one with the blonde hair and bushy moustache."

Amelia smiled at his joking, but looked closely at Leopold who was much darker. His moustache was longer, and came to a point at both ends. She thought what good-looking boys they both were, but did not look a bit like brothers. Leopold said that they had been given the message by the landlord of the 'Queen's Head' that Mr Rolfs had left, "but it's taken this long for us to pluck up the courage to come," Ernest admitted.

"Never mind, you're here now. Come and tell me all the news from back home. How is your mother? Did you see anything of my mama and papa before you left?"

Ernest gave her all the news from back home, and explained that their own mother had died earlier in the year. This was one of the reasons for their coming to start a new life in London. Leopold told her that he was shortly to be married to a girl from Sangerhausen, who had come over with them.

Hearing strange voices, and naturally curious to see who had been invited into their house, Otilia and Bertha came into the room. As their mother introduced the two young men, she told them, "Your Aunt Augusta used to baby-sit for the parents of these two boys, but look at them now: two fine young men."

Ernest did not hear the introduction too clearly; he was looking at Otilia and was completely enchanted by her. When he stood up to shake her hand, his legs felt weak, and the touch of her soft skin left his mouth dry. Tilly dropped her eyes, aware that this blonde handsome man was still looking at her, long after he had released her hand.

"You girls can go back to work now;" Amelia told them. "They won't go without saying goodbye."

She explained to her visitors that she did not expect Henry to be too long before he returned. "He'll be thrilled to see you; we often used to talk about you and the other children who were at our wedding, wondering what had happened to you all. We never dreamt that we would ever see you here in England."

While Amelia sat listening to Leopold telling her all the news from back home and about the friends that she and Henry had known, she was wondering what she could do to help these two young men who had lost both their parents.

"And when are you getting married, Leopold?" she asked. "Have you arranged a date yet?"

"As a matter of fact I'm getting married very soon, next month in fact. You must come and join us after the wedding."

"And bring your daughters too," Ernest added quickly.

Amelia turned towards him. "And what are you going to do, Ernest, after your brother marries? Do you now both live together?" She was still wondering what she could do to try and help either of them.

"After Leo leaves, I will move. I have found some new lodgings in Bell Lane...."

Amelia interrupted him, "Oh no, that's an awful area! We know, because we used to live close by. Why don't you come and live here? We have room. One more will make little difference. I can make up a bed in one of the rooms we have on the top floor, and you can stay with us until you can find somewhere better than Bell Lane to live." Amelia thought that as well as helping this young man, the extra money would help with the family's budget.

Ernest could not believe his luck. He thought that he had met the girl of his dreams only a few minutes before and he was already longing to see her again if only for a second. Now he had been invited to come and live in the same house with her! He did not want to show too much enthusiasm for fear of giving himself away, but would liked to have asked if he could move in immediately.

"But firstly, I'll need to ask my husband if he agrees," Amelia added as an afterthought.

Ernest took in a deep breath as he imagined he could hear Mr. Rolfs saying that he did not agree, but then his fears dissipated when Amelia added, "But he usually leaves those sort of things to me. Would you both like a coffee while you wait for Henry to come back?"

There was no disguising the look of delight on Ernest's face when it had sounded as though there would be no problem in him staying there.

Leopold looked hard at his younger brother as Amelia left the room. "I know what you're thinking, Ernest, you've got your eyes on that eldest daughter of her's. What was her name now? Oh yes! Otilia, that was it. I bet you can't wait to get your hands on her. She's not one of your usual kind. You won't be able to treat her like the others you've known"

Ernest chose to ignore what Leo was saying, but realised that his brother had guessed quite rightly that he had an ulterior motive in wanting to move in to the house.

"I think I've fallen for her already, Leo, but not in the way that you're thinking. I realise that she's not the 'usual kind' as you put it, and I doubt at her age, if she's had any experience of men. Anyway, you mind your own business. I reckon that I'm going to do all right here. She seems a nice girl, so let's leave it at that, shall we?"

Leopold was a little surprised at his brother's reaction to what he had said, which had meant to be more in the form of a leg-pull than a serious comment. He decided not to pursue the matter any further.

When Mr. Rolfs arrived home, he was thrilled to meet the boys, and would hear of nothing else other than that Ernest should stay with them. "If Amelia says it's alright, then it's alright with me," he said, and then added in a quiet voice intending that only Leopold should hear, " After you are married, you'll find it less of a problem if you agree with your wife's decisions rather than disagree."

Amelia overheard what Henry had said. "Hm! Henry's giving you very good advice there, Leopold. You should take it," and she pretended to box her husband's ears.

Leopold, however, thought that maybe Mr. Rolfs had a point and decided to try and remember the advice he had been given. After all, his parent's old friends were obviously very happily married and perhaps this was one of the recipes for a quiet life!

"I'd like you to meet Eva, Mrs Rolfs. Perhaps I could bring her round to see you before we get married."

"Of course you can, Leopold, I would love to meet her. Would we know her family?"

"She is Klaus and Helga Neumann's daughter from Sangerhausen. Her father had the pork butcher's shop in the town."

"I believe that I do remember the shop, but I don't think we knew the Neumanns, did we Henry?"

Henry shook his head. "If you lads have finished your coffee, I'll take you to the tavern on the corner for a pint of ale to celebrate this event. Are you ready?"

Otilia peeped into the room when she heard that they were leaving, her cheeks taking on a crimson glow as the two men said their goodbyes. She blushed even more when Ernest gave a little courteous bow especially for her and their eyes met briefly.

As soon as they were married, Leopold and his bride went to live in a house in Greenwich where he had managed to acquire two rooms on the second floor. Ernest moved in with the Rolfs at the end of June.

It was not the warmest or driest of summers that year but, in spite of the weather, Ernest took Otilia and her sister to Regent's Park Zoo and Madame Tussaud's, and other places they hadn't seen before. In the grounds of Alexandra Palace on a dismal Bank Holiday Monday, they watched with thousands of others, the breathtaking spectacle of Professor Balwin parachuting from his balloon. However, despite the inclement weather they all enjoyed the day, and Ernest took advantage of the conditions by using his coat to wrap around Otilia's shoulders to protect her from the light rain. He knew that he was winning her affections, and promised himself that when she was eighteen he would tell her how much loved her and would then ask her to marry him.

Otilia looked forward to every outing, but her happiness was interrupted the very next day when everyone was talking about the mutilated body of a woman being found. She had been murdered in a yard close to Osborne Street, not far from where Ernest and his brother had lodged previously.

Amelia had no inclination to read newspapers, and always relied on her husband to keep her informed of the events that would interest her. She was aware that murders were fairly commonplace, but rarely made the headlines as the murderers were usually quickly identified. She had heard about an unsolved murder earlier in the year, but this one was much nearer to home and, for the next day or two, it appeared to be causing a great deal of unrest.

Henry thought it best to tell Amelia a little of what was going on. "It appears that she was stabbed many times, but she was only a woman of the streets, so there is nothing to worry about," Henry told her, trying to relieve her from any anxiety that she may have had. However, he had a few reservations himself about what had happened. "According to the evening papers....." he said, sounding somewhat perplexed, ".....the police seem to have no idea who might have done it. I suppose that it could have been one of her many, er..., so called, 'clients'."

Amelia looked hard at her husband who was frowning.

"Hermann Wilke has invited me to attend a meeting which is going to be held next week if the murderer had not been caught. People are concerned because of the terrible way the girl had been butchered." He thought it best not to go into any more details about what had taken place.

"Are you sure that there is no danger to the girls?" Amelia asked, looking worried.

"Good Lord no! The woman was a prostitute and the murder was committed in the early hours of the morning, so there is nothing to worry about. The main concern that people have is how she was murdered, especially as it appears to have been sexually motivated."

Henry went to the meeting with Herman, and they heard that a Vigilance Committee had been formed to watch the streets late at night, in case the murderer turned his attention to other girls or women. Amelia was anxious to know what went on at the meeting and was waiting up for him when he arrived home.

Henry told her what they had decided to do. "Some people think that it might have been one of those Grenadier Guards who did it. I told you I didn't trust them. We must tell the girls not to go anywhere near those barracks until this man's been caught!"

Amelia could not believe what she had just heard. She had never agreed with her husband's views about the soldiers being untrustworthy, and could not believe that one of them could have been so violent. She had always found them to be most polite and kindly to her when she had met them whilst shopping. "I don't think that it could be one of them, Henry," she exclaimed, slowly shaking her head in total disbelief.

"We will see," Henry retorted, looking very knowing and certain that his suspicions would prove to be correct. He was aware that many of the soldiers indulged their pleasures with the prostitutes that lodged in the houses in and around Flower and Dean Street, and would not have put it past one of them to turn sadist in order to indulge in his sexual desires.

He was more than a little concerned for the safety of his daughters should they be out at night, in case the murderer could not control himself and attack anyone whom he happened to meet. However, he would not let Amelia know of his concern or what he had heard about many of the soldiers' reputations so as not to worry her.

The papers led with the story of the brutal murder for over a week, and there were rumours that the murderer would soon be caught, but after intensive enquiries at the barracks by the police, all suspects were cleared of any connection with the murder. However, Henry remained unconvinced until at the end of the month, the papers carried the story of another even more brutal murder that had taken place close to the Jews' cemetery in Whitechapel. This time, Henry told Amelia even less about the murder because he considered that the details were too gruesome for her to hear. However, his daughter, Otilia, heard about it from her friends, and asked her father whether it was true that Jack Pizer had done it, as the 'Star' newspaper had reported.

Jack was a well-known slipper maker, and was often seen in Petticoat Lane still wearing his leather apron. A great many stories about Jack circulated among the girls, and many women feared him. It was well known that he made fun of and bullied the prostitutes because of what was, in his view, their objectionable way of life.

"Well, I suppose it could be him who has done the murders but I very much doubt it," her father told her. "He's probably being questioned because of his hatred of the women who walk the streets, but I personally would not think him capable of doing what the murderer did to that Polly Nichols, and if you don't know what happened to her, then don't ask me." He considered that his daughter was taking too much of an unhealthy interest in the murders.

Henry had learned that Charlie Cross had found Polly's body, lying across the entrance to his stable yard when he went to harness the horses very early on the Friday morning. Henry knew Charlie very well as the driver of the horses that pulled the large wagon belonging to Pickford's removal firm. He had told Henry how the woman lay there covered in blood with stab wounds, her throat cut, and her abdomen ripped open.

Henry was certainly not going to go through the details of the murder with Otilia. "Now let's forget it, Tilly; there are many more pleasant things to talk about. What do you think about Ernest?"

Otilia felt the blood come to her cheeks at being asked the question. On a number of occasions when Ernest had made advances towards her, she had felt excitement when he had touched her. There had been one instance when he had put his arms around her, and she had felt her heart beat faster as his body pressed against hers his strong arms holding her close to him. She had turned her face away as he tried to kiss her, but then afterwards she had regretted not letting him do so. She had never told anyone about the incident, and she certainly was not about to tell her father about it now, but wondered whether her blushes might give her away.

"I think he is very nice," she answered truthfully. She would have liked to have told her father how much she liked being with Ernest, but he interrupted her thoughts.

"You do know that he's a bit of a ladies' man, and you are not yet eighteen? I hope that you know what you're doing, Tilly. Have you had a word with your mother?"

With her father talking about Ernest in this way, Otilia felt a little embarrassed, but she was aware that he only had her welfare at heart. However, because he had spoken to her in this way, she had wanted to tell her father that she had fallen in love with the man he was warning her about. She wished now even more that she had let Ernest kiss her when he tried to.

A week later everyone was talking about yet another woman who had been brutally murdered, this time in Hanbury Street, and the details of the way she had been attacked were even more gruesome and sadistic than the previous ones, but like the others, she too had been a notorious prostitute.

"Didn't we know her, Henry?" Amelia asked. "I seem to recall the name of Annie Chapman. Wasn't that the woman who lived somewhere in Dorset Street, and we used to see her pass by our house occasionally before we moved here? If it is the same person, she was quite plump I recall, and nearly always wore a straw bonnet with fur round the brim. I believe that I saw her only a few weeks ago in Petticoat Lane. She was beginning to look older and still looked an awful mess, but I'm sorry if she's the one who's been murdered."

Henry tried to think of whom his wife meant, but he was not in the habit of looking at prostitutes. However, he did recall a person who could have been the woman his wife had in mind. The description also fitted a person everyone knew as 'Dark Annie'. A lot of these women were well known to both respectable women and men - after all, they were always hanging about the streets and stood out amongst the rest of the community with their low cut dresses and almost naked uplifted breasts.

"I suppose it could have been her," Henry agreed. "According to

Herman, the murders are certainly causing some panic around Whitechapel, especially among the prostitutes."

"I suppose we should be thankful that he only appears to be murdering those sort of women, but is he going to attack anyone else?" Amelia asked nervously, and then added impatiently, "and I can't understand why he has not been caught! I have been told that some of the women who work at the match factory in Stratford are also frightened for themselves as well as being concerned about their daughters. They work until nine o'clock and then dread coming home at that hour with a murderer loose, especially now that it is getting dark much earlier."

"Well, so far the murders have all taken place in the early hours, and I still don't think that anyone other than these loose women are in any danger," Henry said reassuringly. "There is also no need for you to worry as far as any of our girls here are concerned. They are never out late and, in any case, we live some way away from where the murders have taken place," he added dismissively.

Amelia knew that Henry was only trying to put her mind at rest, and she did not think that half-a-mile was, as Henry put it, "some way away" from where Annie Chapman had been recently stabbed to death.

The London evening newspapers were displaying such headlines as, 'REVOLTING MURDERS', and 'HOMICIDAL MANIAC AT LARGE', and Henry thought it best not to bring them into the house for fear of upsetting the household.

A few days later, Herman told him that he had noticed that there were fewer people about late at night, especially those types of women which was all to the good. As the late September days passed by, the stories disappeared from the newspapers and everyone tried to forget about the murders.

Ernest Biedermann now began to work quite late most evenings so Otilia saw little of him except when he had time off, and then she herself would be busy sewing with her mother and sister. The occasions when she and Ernest could talk were usually early in the day before he went off to work in the hotels. He never let her see that he took the murders seriously, and once he made her screech with laughing when he chased her around the kitchen, knife in hand, saying, "I'm Jack the Ripper coming to get you." Otilia allowed herself to be caught just as her mother came into the room, but she would have been cross with Ernest had she known what he had been joking about.

"Why don't you young people have an evening out sometime now that things seem to have quietened down, go to the Music Hall in

Whitechapel or something: you'll enjoy it."

Otilia looked at Ernest, longing for him to say that he would take her. Some of her friends had been and had told her what a good time they had had. She had also heard that some of the artistes and their songs were a little risqué, and that the Effingham Theatre was not perhaps the best place to go, but nevertheless it would be fun.

"Would you like to go?" Ernest asked her.

"Like to? I would love to," and then she asked eagerly, "When can we go?"

"I believe there is a new performance on Saturday, and I'll arrange to get time off work, so make sure you look your best," he teased.

Ernest held Otilia's hand in the cab as they came home after spending an evening listening to the popular and cheeky songs of the day, and marvelling at the artistry of the performers they had seen doing their 'turns' on the stage in the Whitechapel Music Hall. She was still humming 'Ta-ra-ra-Boom-de-ay' as they entered the house, and putting her hands on her hips, as she had seen Lottie Collins do, she took a few steps and sang the chorus line quietly.

"I have had a wonderful time, Ernest. Thank you so much." She stood on tiptoe and gave him a kiss on the cheek.

Ernest wanted to hold her tightly in his arms and kiss her properly, but when he touched her he felt her shaking.

"Tilly, I want to kiss you, and I love you."

Otilia gasped at Ernest's forthrightness, and felt her face go bright red. "Ernest, no! You must not say things like that. Mama and Papa are in bed and I must go too."

As she began to move away, he pulled her towards him, took her into his arms, and kissed her passionately. She felt a warmth and excitement that she had never experienced before going limp in his arms. When his lips released her, she broke away from him in the realisation that she had succumbed to his embraces too readily. "No, Ernest, no, we mustn't. Thank you for a lovely evening," she said quietly, and with that she turned away from him. Otilia felt that her heart would burst as she hurried to her room where Bertha was sleeping soundly. She wanted to wake her a shout out how much she loved this man but instead crept quietly into bed alongside her sister whispering his name a hundred times before she fell asleep.

Ernest had stood motionless as he had watched her going away from him, but as she had not turned to look at him before moving out of sight, he became worried in case Otilia should tell her parents about what he had done. He thought that they might conclude by his actions that he was taking advantage of their young daughter's innocence and acting improperly towards her. He did not want to do anything that would jeopardise the way that the family regarded him. However, he was still unsure as to what Otilia's feelings were towards him. As he went to his room, he put these thoughts out of his mind and felt confident that sooner or later he would win her over to become his bride.

Nothing was said the following evening when Ernest returned from work, but was surprised when Otilia's mother asked him whether he had enjoyed the evening. "We know Tilly did, because she was so excited about it when we asked her this morning."

Ernest breathed a sigh of relief. Otilia had obviously not told her parents what had happened when they arrived home. He smiled to himself as he contemplated what Otilia had been excited about: the show, or the kiss in the hall?

Very early on the Sunday morning on the last day of September, two more terribly mutilated bodies of women prostitutes were discovered in the Whitechapel area. Details of the horrible way that they had been murdered were in the 'Star' newspaper the next day. It also reported that Isaac Kozebrodski, together with another man who was a steward of a club where Isaac had spent the evening, had found one of the bodies. As soon as he read this, Henry put on his hat and coat and hurried down to Middlesex Street to call on his old friend Abraham Solomon.

"I could not believe it when I read that Isaac found that murdered woman in Duffield's Yard," he announced, as soon as Abraham opened the door. "Is he under suspicion, do you know?"

Henry had met Isaac on many occasions. Being Jewish, he often did some work for Abraham, and Henry knew him to be an excellent tailor as well as a very quiet and inoffensive little man. It was for these reasons that he worried in case the police might think that Isaac might be in some way involved. He also was concerned for both him and Abraham in regard to the anti-Semitic outburst that had followed the murder of Annie Chapman. Although the police had dismissed any suspicion by some of the local people that a Jew was the murderer, he was particularly concerned for his friend and his wife, Esther, should these latest murders spark off another bout of racial hatred or unpleasantness towards them.

"No! I am sure he isn't," replied Abraham, "and following the last trouble we had, the Rabbi from our Synagogue has explained to the police that there would be no way that a Jew could do such horrible murders. He told them that it was against all our religious teaching to do anything as horrible as that to a fellow human being, even if they were women of ill repute. But thank you for coming, Henry; come and join me in a glass of wine, won't you?"

Esther greeted Henry when she came into the room where the two men were talking. "Henry was concerned for us, and that is why he's here," Abraham explained to her. "Not that he needs an excuse to come, as we both know, but about the latest killings he's very worried."

"As we all are," Esther said, "but I have Abraham to protect me, Henry." She laughed, trying to make light of the serious situation as she cuddled up close to her husband and put her arm through his.

"Thousands of handbills have been printed already, asking if anybody has information as to the identification of the murderer," Abraham explained, "and we are all helping to distribute these. Tomorrow evening, there are going to be a number of meetings to enable groups to be formed. The men will carry whistles and clubs and patrol the streets during the night, with the sole purpose of trying to catch the brute."

Esther said, "I hope that they do soon," and she left the men talking, not wanting to hear any more about it.

"Like you, my friend, I don't let Esther see the newspapers," Abraham said quietly. "They give too much detail about the butchery. The second murder that night took place in Mitre Square not far from St.Botolph's Church, and the police think that it was the same man who did both. I do not understand it, Henry. He must have been covered in blood when he did that killing, yet no one heard any screaming or shouting out by the victims, neither has anybody reported ever seeing anyone running away."

"I don't understand it either," said Henry. "All we can do is leave it to the police." The two friends talked for a while and then changed to more pleasant subjects, before Henry said that he must get back to Amelia.

"I hope you will be taking a cab, Henry Rolfs," said his companion sounding concerned for his safety. "There's another dense smoky-fog come down again tonight, and the sooner you get home the better."

"I don't think the murderer would ever take me for a woman of the streets, Abraham," Henry quipped as he left. Henry did as his friend had suggested and Amelia was glad to see him return safely. She made him some hot soup from the leftovers she had saved from the meal they had had that day then sat down to hear his news.

"What did Abraham have to say?" she asked, as she put the hot dish in front of him.

"Oh, he is confident that Isaac is not under suspicion and doesn't appear to be worried, but he is as baffled as I am as to why the murderer has not been caught."

"Well, let us hope that they catch him soon before he does any more murders," Amelia stated firmly.

"Oh let's not worry any more about it, Amelia. I'm sure that the police are doing everything they can to try and catch the brute. Let us change the subject and talk about much more pleasantries."

But the unrest in the East End didn't go away and, a few weeks later, Henry told his wife that there was so much unrest in the area, even though there had not been any more murders reported.

"People have been flocking all over the sites where the murders took place," he said, "hoping to be in the right place, it is said, should the murderer do another. The police seem to be no nearer catching him, but some good is coming out of all this, thank goodness."

Amelia looked surprised at what he had just said and waited for him to explain. "The local costermongers have done a roaring trade with the sightseers," he added with amusement.

His wife was not amused. "I just don't know where it's all going to end, Henry," she said in despair, and then wishing to change the subject asked, "Do you realise it will be Tilly's eighteenth birthday on Monday? It doesn't seem long since she was born!"

Otilia celebrated her eighteenth birthday in fine style with all the family present. Ernest made a lovely fruit cake covered in marzipan and icing, which he had decorated beautifully with his expert hand. "What did you wish for?" Bertha asked as her sister blew out the candles.

"If I tell you, it won't come true," she told her, and glanced at Ernest then looked away quickly, afraid that someone might have seen her and read her thoughts. Ernest had not missed it, and had already laid his plans to capture her heart. He thought that he had read the meaning of her look correctly.

Later in the evening, as they stood in the small kitchen making the coffee for the family, he asked, "Can I guess what you wished?"

"You can try."

Ernest hesitated. Before this moment he had been certain what she would reply, but now, doubt was in his mind and he did not want to ruin his chances. He decided to choose his words very carefully.

"Am I part of your wish?" he said cautiously.

"You might be."

"Then dare I guess, and ask if you love me." He was suddenly aware how conceited that must have sounded and added quickly, "I told you before that I love you, Tilly," and he took hold of her hands and looked into her eyes, trying to read whether he had been right to declare his love.

"Now you can guess my wish," she said shyly. She had never had the sort of feeling she was experiencing towards anyone before and thought that this must be love. Otilia had not known of any other kind except that of her parents, sisters and brothers. She felt fear of being alone with him, but at the same time wanted to feel his arms around her, and be with him for ever and ever. Leaning towards him, he put his cheek against hers. She suddenly found it easy to say what she had practised saying on her own many times, "I love you too, Ernest."

He held her face gently between the palms of his hands and kissed her tenderly.

She felt his hands on her shoulders, then down under her arms as he pressed them gently against her breasts. Somewhat reluctantly, she pulled away from him and drew in a deep breath. Moving his hands from her bosom she leaned towards him. "No, Ernest. I don't think you should."

"But, Tilly, I love you and need you, and it isn't wrong to....."

Otilia put her fingers against his lips to stop him from continuing. "Mama will be wondering why we are being such a long time."

"Come on then, we must tell your mother and father," Ernest said boldly, but Otilia held him back as he tried to move towards the door.

"No! no! Please let us keep this to ourselves until tomorrow. I want it to be our secret tonight," Otilia pleaded. "Only we should know how we feel towards each other now, and then you can tell mama and papa tomorrow." She gave an excited giggle and kissed Ernest briefly on his cheek. "We'll take in the coffee now and pretend that nothing has happened."

Bertha looked at them suspiciously when they returned to the living room. "You have been a long time making that coffee." She gave a little titter and grinned at them, already knowing, of course, how her sister felt about Ernest. Henry was asleep in his favourite chair with the evening paper partly over his face, Charles and John were in their room upstairs, and Amelia had just taken Clara to bed.

"It appears we wasted our time in the kitchen making coffee, Tilly," said Ernest, stating the obvious, as he put the tray down on the table.

"I don't think we did," Otilia whispered, somewhat boldly.

Ernest wondered what Otilia was thinking, and wanted desperately to get her on her own. He wondered how she would look if she removed the pins in her hair which she always had in a bun, and let her long dark hair fall over her shoulders and down her back. He wanted to hold her in his arms and make love to her.

Henry had roused himself, said 'goodnight' to them both and took himself to bed. Bertha had left at the same time with a cheeky glance in her sister's direction. Otilia felt nervous and thought she too had better leave, yet wanted to stay. "I think I'd better go, Ernest," she said a little unconvincingly.

"Not yet, Tilly, stay and talk to me a while," Ernest urged. "Come and sit next to me."

Otilia did as he requested and, putting his arm around her shoulders, he pulled her towards him. With his other hand against her cheek, he turned her head to kiss her, gently at first and then with passion, as she suddenly felt his hand again touching her breasts. She pushed him away. "No, Ernest, no," she said firmly. "Do you really want to marry me or is this all you want from me?"

"Of course I want to marry you, Tilly, but isn't it normal for me to touch you, hold you, to feel your body close to mine? Don't you have the same feelings for me?"

His hand against her breasts had excited her: she had experienced sensations which had left her breathless, but she was confused. She had had no experience of men, and although she felt in her heart that Ernest was the man for her, she had no desire to go beyond what was recognised as decent behaviour. To give herself to him in any form, even by touch, she considered would put her into the same class as a whore.

"Please do not ask me for an answer to your questions, Ernest. All I know is that I want to wait until we are married. Please promise me..." she left her sentence unfinished, hoping that he would understand.

Ernest felt a little annoyed that she had rejected his advances. He had been used to girls agreeing to his every whim. Although he was aware that Amelia was a different kind of girl and more respectable than the ones he was usually associated with, he had not expected that she would not succumb to his wishes. He could see that he would be unable to get anywhere this time and concluded that he would need to marry her as soon as her father would give his consent. He pulled her to her feet and kissed her two or three times on her lips. "Alright, Tilly, I'll see you in the morning and when I come home in the evening I will have a word with your father, and hopefully be able to break our news to everyone."

But the announcement of their engagement was not made the next day as they intended, indeed Otilia's parents did not learn about their daughter's and Ernest's declared love for each other for some time. That morning, a letter arrived from Germany that Amelia was thrilled at first to receive. Immediately recognising her sister Augusta's handwriting she opened the envelope eagerly and began to read.

"Oh! no," she cried, and sat down heavily on a chair, her hand to her mouth and taking in a deep breath. She thrust the letter down at arm's length and closed her eyes, not bearing to read any more.

Everyone stopped working, and Henry, hearing her gasp, came over to where she was sitting. "What is it, Amelia?" he said, quietly taking the letter from her.

"My dearest Amelia," he read out loud, translating the letter to English, "It is my painful task to tell you that our very dear papa passed away yesterday. I cannot tell you how much of a shock this has been to us all, and for mama in particular. It all happened so suddenly...." Henry read the rest of the letter to himself.

Her sister went on to explained how papa had been working in the fields, when, according to his workmen, he suddenly complained of a tight pain in his chest, collapsed, and his heart stopped beating. There had been nothing that anyone could do. Henry began to read the contents of the letter out loud again as Augusta informed them that the funeral had been arranged for Thursday morning, "...and as mama did not want you to travel all this way, we thought that you might like to arrange your own little service that day at your local church."

The letter concluded, "Bertha is still at home, and Johannes and I are still at the next farm, so we are all looking after mama. It is too early to make any plans about the farm, but I will write to you again after we have sorted everything out."

"Oh! my poor papa," Amelia kept repeating between sobs, then suddenly realised what day it was. "But it's Thursday tomorrow!" Henry took her to the other room, announcing that work must stop, and that there would be no more done that day. He would need to go out and see the vicar of St.Leonard's to ask if it would be possible to hold a brief service in the morning at about the same time as the funeral in Riestedt.

After he had gone, Amelia recalled the last time she had seen her father on the day they left for England. She took out a neatly folded handkerchief from a little wooden box on her dressing table, the same one that her father had given her that day to dry her eyes. She had kept it all this time, and, strangely, it seemed to give her the strength to bear her grief as the morning slowly wore on.

Otilia stayed close to her mother trying to understand the extent of her grief, her own news that she and Ernest had planned to give her mama and papa was postponed for the time being. She knew that she would have to wait until the right moment before she could tell them that she and Ernest wanted to marry, and this was not it. She had never known her grandfather, of course, but she tried to understand how her mother was feeling by thinking how she herself would have felt if it had been her own father that had died. Her eyes filled up with tears at the thought. Henry came back after an hour and told Amelia that everything had been arranged and that the Reverend Buss had been very understanding about it all. "He will be coming to see you later this afternoon to go over the details with you. I hope that I said the right thing by telling him that you wouldn't mind."

And so it was that the Reverend Buss led appropriate prayers for the Rolfs family and their friends, who occupied the first two rows of pews in the parish church of St.Leonard's the following morning. Amelia's thoughts and prayers were for her mother and sisters whom she knew would be in the little church in her home village of Riestedt attending the funeral of her father.

As they walked home arm in arm in the cold, damp and foggy November day, Ernest and Otilia said nothing about their unofficial engagement to anyone, and they agreed to wait until towards the end of the following week before Ernest would ask her father for his daughter's hand in marriage. Otilia wanted it to be a happy occasion, and Ernest too felt that it would be wrong until her mother had recovered from her grief, and hoped that the announcement would have the desired effect of helping her to overcome her sadness.

It was the second time that the announcement had been delayed, and Ernest found that he could hardly bear to stay in the house longer than was necessary in the atmosphere created by the bereavement. Otilia hardly spoke to him and there was little or no conversation in house. Ernest made the excuse to Otilia that he had to work late that week and would probably find it more convenient to sleep at the hotel where he worked for a night or two. "Leopold will also be in the kitchen with me, so we might even have a bachelors' night out," he joked.

"Well, don't you forget that you are engaged to me," Otilia whispered, looking at him seriously as she did so.

The following evening, the two brothers worked at the hotel in Whitechapel Road until after midnight.

"Where are we sleeping tonight, Leo?" Ernest asked his brother.

"I thought that you ought to have a final fling now that you're going to be tied down soon, alright? I'll take you for some special entertainment!" he said, wagging his finger and laughing.

"Where are we going?"

"Ah! wait and see," replied Leopold, and he laughed again.

Ernest suddenly realised his brother's intentions. "I think I can guess where you're taking me."

"Are you sure you want to come?" Leopold did not want to pressurise his brother into doing something that he did not want to.

"Why not? As you say, it'll be my last fling before I get married, and everybody at home is as miserable as sin at the moment."

Having first called in to the 'King's Head' for a few large measures of Scotch whisky, it was after one o'clock before they reached 'The Cross Keys' in Gracechurch Street.

"Now this is the famous night house of Kate Hamilton," Leopold explained to his brother as they entered though the door at the back of the building, "and here she comes."

A lady of huge proportions about fifty years of age, but trying to look about thirty with the liberal use of make-up, greeted them warmly. "Who's your friend, Leo?" she asked.

"Call him Ernie - he's engaged to be married soon, so I've brought him for a night out before he loses his freedom. Can you fix him up?"

"I can find someone who can," she chuckled, and her huge frame wobbled like a large pink jelly as she laughed. Ernest thought that her huge breasts were about to jump out of her low-cut dress and was certain that the reason why she put her hand across her deep cleavage was to prevent them from doing just that. Leopold bought a bottle of Burgundy from Kate and he poured out two large glasses.

"Follow me," she said, beckoning the two men with a fat finger. They followed her to another room where a number of her girls were lolling about on chairs. The room was very warm and his head was beginning to spin with the amount of alcohol he had consumed. Looking around, he saw that the girls were only partly clothed, and his bleary eyes alighted on a pretty young brunette who looked remarkably like Otilia.

"That's Lily," Kate remarked, and, walking over to her, lifted up her loose chemise to give him a good view of her voluptuous white buttocks, and everything else that she wanted him to see.

Ernest gulped his wine as he stared at the young girl.

"She'll give you a good time. Half a crown for the night, and if you

81

include a bottle of wine, three and six."

Ernest thought that it sounded a bit expensive, but as it would probably be the last time he could have his fling, he nodded his head without taking his eyes off her. "I'll have the girl and the wine," he blurted out.

Ernest nudged his brother as he drained his glass and put down the empty bottle.

"You'll do alright there, Ernie!" his brother told him. Mind you keep awake.

Ernest filled his glass again from the second bottle and carried the glass in one hand and the bottle in the other, as he followed the girl to a room. She had to remove his shoes because he fell over twice trying to undo the laces himself. He fell over yet again in trying to remove his clothes. Gulping down another glass of wine, he dropped the empty glass, pushed the girl down on the bed and ripped off her chemise. As she lay on her back, he kissed her firm white breasts.

"I love you, Otilia," he murmured as he caressed her naked body.

"I ain't Otilia, I'm Lily," she told him coldly.

"You're my Otilia," he gasped, his heart pounded with the fury of his actions, unable to wait any longer.

"Cor, you don't mess about, mister, do yer?" Lily said, as the well-used bed bounced up and down with all the energy he could muster. Lily felt his heavy weight on her body when his movement ceased. "That didn't last long. It's one of the quickest I've ever 'ad."

Ernest didn't hear Lily's final remark because he was sound asleep.

"I 'ope your Otilia, 'oo ever she is, ain't goin' to be disappointed," she said, slipping out from under him and grabbing the half-full bottle of wine.

Ernest's head was still spinning next morning when met by Leopold.

"How was it?" Leopold asked.

Ernest put both his hands to his head. "I wish I could remember."

Leopold thought that his brother sounded disappointed.

"I think she was a bit of alright - but I thought I was with Otilia all the time until I woke up this morning!" Ernest admitted, but there was no one there, and then as an afterthought he added, "Perhaps I'll do better next time."

"Well, Tilly won't be expecting you back until the weekend, so you'll have more time to practice and recover," his brother observed.

The week that Ernest had been away had seemed an eternity to Otilia. She did not question what he had been doing as she had no reason to suspect that he had not been working all the time. In any case, to question him would not have been right and proper. It would have shown that she didn't trust him. Ernest had relied on this and it also saved him from lying to her, although he would not have had any conscience about doing so. Otilia was anxious to talk to him about announcing their engagement and they agreed that the next weekend would be about the right time to tell her parents and for Ernest to ask her father's permission to marry her.

Friday was the day of the Lord Mayor's Show. They walked to Fleet Street arm in arm looking for a suitable place to watch the procession. Otilia could barely contain her excitement at knowing that they were to break their news that very evening.

"I'm asking your father first, of course," Ernest said solemnly.

"And I know that everything will be alright," Otilia said with confidence. "He's never ever said a word against you, so I'm not at all afraid that he will disapprove."

She had so little opportunity to be alone with Ernest, and Otilia was thrilled at the thought that she would have him all to herself for the rest of the day. She hung tightly on to his arm as they stood patiently on the pavement waiting for the new Lord Mayor, the Right Honourable James Whitehead, to drive in State from his court and office in the Mansion House to the Law Courts. From where they were standing, they would have an excellent view, but as the procession came from Ludgate Circus into Fleet Street, there was a disturbance in the crowd. What began as a murmur soon became a loud rumbling, as people passed the message along that the badly mutilated body of another woman had been found in Dorset Street. Thousands began leaving the pavements and running towards Bishopsgate. A large number of police followed, who possibly thought that they would be needed more at the scene of the murder to control the crowds, than in Fleet Street to deal with the procession. Otilia put her hands over her ears as word spread of the details of the mutilation.

"She was only a young girl," she heard one woman remark to another.

Ernest thought it best that they should get home as quickly as possible, even though it meant moving in the same direction as the crowds were going. Some of the details of the murder were already spreading through the crowd.

"Her guts are all over and he's cut her tits off," someone shouted with morbid enthusiasm.

"It's horrible, it's horrible," Otilia repeated as they made their way back to Earl Street, "and all these awful people are going to the scene." Otilia began to shake with fear, the thought of what the people would see when they got there making her shudder.

Amelia met them at the door. She had seen them both coming before they got to the house, and could tell by her daughter's face that she had heard the dreadful news.

"I am so glad that you've brought her home, Ernest. I was worried for you both. Your papa has gone to see Mr Wilke and Abraham Solomon as soon as the news reached us earlier. It's terrible, and such a young girl too?"

Ernest said nothing not knowing what Mrs Rolfs had heard, and not wishing to discuss the matter further anyway. He looked towards the others in the house. They were all working in silence and trying to concentrate hard on what they were doing, but he noticed that young Bertha's hands were trembling.

"I'll go and make a cup of tea for everyone," Ernest announced, "It looks as if everyone could do with one." He took hold of Otilia's hand and added in a quiet voice, "Come and help me, Tilly."

"Well, that's ruined our happy day again, Ernest," Otilia said with a slight croak in her voice when they were alone in the kitchen.

"You are not to start to cry now," Ernest said with authority. "Whatever happens tomorrow, first thing at breakfast, we're going to tell your mother and father about us."

"What about asking papa first, like you said you were going to do?"

"I thought that it might be a good idea to ask him in front of your mother. There will be less chance of him saying no," Ernest suggested. "We'll take them by surprise. After today I think that they will be only too pleased to hear something to rejoice about."

"I hope you know what you're doing, Ernest."

"So do I," he laughed, and he put his arms around her. "Don't worry, everything will turn out all right. I know it."

Next morning at breakfast, Ernest began with confidence with the words, "Tilly and I..." but then became completely tongue-tied as everyone stopped eating and looked at him solemnly.

Otilia's mother broke the silence by saying, "And about time too. I've been expecting you both to tell us for long enough."

Her father expressed his approval and Bertha gave her sister a hug and kissed her. The two boys, John and Charles, carried on eating their breakfast completely disinterested in what was going on, but little Clara, always ready to find an excuse to dress up in fine clothes, said, "Now that I'm seven, please can I be a bridesmaid?"

CHAPTER SEVEN

1888-1891.

The news of the engagement of Otilia to Ernest Biedermann was received with joy in the small village of Riestedt, especially by Otilia's grandmamma and her aunt Bertha. Since her husband's death, Isabel Bansmer had been considering whether to go and live with her widowed sister in Neustrelitz, but she worried about leaving her daughter, Bertha, who did not want to move from the family home in Riestedt. When she read the letter from her granddaughter, she wondered whether Bertha would have liked to go to Otilia's wedding in England. Isabel also thought that the main reason Bertha was reluctant to leave home was because of leaving her on her own. At twenty-six years of age her youngest daughter ought to be married, and if she had been, it would have left her free to go and live with her sister in the north, which was what she wanted to do.

"Why don't you go to Otilia's wedding when the time comes?" she asked Bertha.

"And leave you here all alone, mama!"

"Augusta and Johannes are still in the village and they would see that I'd come to no harm." She then took advantage of the situation to add, "...and if you should decide to stay in England for a while, I could always go to stay with my sister, Louisa, in Neustrelitz."

Bertha thought hard about what her mother had said, and realised that her own selfish desires not to leave were obviously preventing her mother from doing what she wanted to do. After all, if her mother were to die she would not stay in Riestedt, so perhaps she ought to go and visit her sister in England as her mother had suggested.

"Are you sure that you want to leave here, mama? What about Augusta?"

"Oh, she and Johannes are busy with the farm, and I would like to spend my last days with my sister. You have stayed here looking after me for far too long. Go off and enjoy life while you're still young." As she spoke, Isabel dismissed her daughter with a wave of her hand.

"We'll see," Bertha said. Otilia's letter had suggested that the wedding was unlikely to take place for at least a year, so Bertha thought that the intervening period would give her sufficient time to decide what to do.

Otilia's father thought it best for the wedding to be delayed until after her nineteenth birthday. Although he had given his approval, he was not sure that his daughter had made the right decision. Ernest had been the only man she had known and he had heard a few unpleasant rumours about his lifestyle. Her mother too wanted her to wait until they had found somewhere to live. As she waited to marry Ernest, the eighteen months since their engagement seemed an eternity to Otilia, but during that first winter following the murders, the districts close to Whitechapel and Bishopsgate were rife with rumour as to the identity of the person who had murdered the six prostitutes. Many suspects were questioned, including a forty-year-old German hairdresser. However, he had been released at the end of September - not least because he was in police custody at the time the last two murders took place - but his arrest caused many Londoners to look with suspicion on all foreigners, especially Germans.

Although things had quietened down by January and the police presence reduced, people still boarded up their windows at night and put stronger locks on their doors. But then July was marred by yet another brutal murder of a similar nature to the others, causing most of the immigrants to continue to keep a low profile for some time afterwards.

It was not until the following Spring that Henry found rooms for his daughter and so, in the May of that year of 1890, the Reverend Stephen Buss, Vicar of St. Leonard's Parish Church of Shoreditch, married Otilia to Ernest Biedermann.

Little Clara, who was now eight years old, got her wish to be a bridesmaid, and Otilia's Aunt came to England from Riestedt for the wedding.

"What are you going to do?" Amelia asked her sister after the wedding. "Are you going back to Saxony?"

Bertha had no desire to return. Their mother had finally decided to leave the village and go to live with her widowed sister in Neustrelitz as she had always wanted to do ever since her husband died.

"If I went back, there is now only Augusta left in the Riestedt, and she and Johannes are fully occupied running the farm, so I would have to find somewhere to live, but if I stayed here what could I do?" Bertha asked.

"You could sleep in Tilly's bed now that she has left, and as Mary has gone back to look after her mother, you could take her place in preparing and cooking the meals, and then I will have even more time to help Henry." Amelia appeared to have already thought all this through, and as her sister said nothing she added, "Well, that's settled then."

Henry listened to this conversation and wondered whether he ought to give his opinion on the matter. He had mixed feelings about it all. It was a question, he thought, of balancing one option against the other. They earned so little in what they did: the more finished clothes they turned out, the more orders they could deal with and the extra money would be useful. On the other hand, he would not be getting his meals cooked by Amelia. However, if Bertha's cooking was as good as his wife's, then he considered that he would have the best of both worlds! After a few moments contemplation, he decided that it was best to say nothing.

The rooms that Henry had found for Otilia and Ernest suited them perfectly, being close enough for Otilia to be able to continue to help her father during the time when Ernest was at work. She was very happy in her new home and soon looking forward to raising a family. During a visit to Ernest's brother's wife, Eva, she had confided these thoughts to her sister-in-law, telling her that she was longing to have children to love and to care for.

"I know exactly how you feel, Tilly," Eva had agreed, and then became excited as suddenly she had an idea.

"Wouldn't it be marvellous if we could both have a baby at about the same time? We would be able to compare notes and help each other."

After three months, Otilia again visited her sister-in-law, but said nothing about what they had both hoped would happen until Eva could not bear the suspense any longer. "Well!...are you?"

"Am I what?"

"Oh don't be so infuriating, Tilly. Are you pregnant?" Eva asked.

Otilia smiled and said nothing, keeping her guessing, then suddenly leant forward to take Eva's hands into her own. "Yes, yes, yes! Please tell me you are too."

Eva gave a shriek of delight. "Our wishes have come true Tilly. We're both going to have a baby. Tell me when, when!"

They were both so excited at the thought that their babies would be born so close to each other.

At the beginning of August, Amelia received a letter from her mother in Germany.

"What does she have to say?" Henry asked. "Has she settled into her new home with her sister?"

"They want to come here, and mama wants to know whether we could put them up until they find somewhere to live."

"It's only been a few months since Bertha told us that your mother would not come to Tilly's wedding! Now she wants to come for good! What are you going to tell her?" Henry asked, sounding concerned. He visualised that with more people in the house, especially those too old to help with the work, would cause a disruption in the household.

Amelia was holding the letter tightly in her hand and not listening to what Henry was saying. She spoke her thoughts out loud. "I've never met my aunt and I can only remember her being mentioned once or twice, but it will be lovely to see mama again after all these years."

"I can remember you mentioning your Aunt Louisa and her husband once at your house. What did he do?" Henry asked.

Amelia explained that Joseph Bochnest had had a farm at Neustrelitz in Northern Germany, and had married her Aunt Louisa some years before her mama had married her papa. "My aunt must have got in touch with mama when Uncle Joseph died. Bertha told me that she was a widow, but she did not know for how long. They must be getting on well together, otherwise mama would not have written to say that they both wanted to come here." She suddenly had an idea. "Bertha told me that there are some rooms coming vacant across the road in a couple of weeks time. She said the other day that she was looking for somewhere to live and had considered moving there with our own daughter Bertha for company. They do get on well together, Henry as you well know. Mother and my Aunt could then come here. What do you think, Henry?"

Henry was trying to take in all that his wife was saying but expressed surprise at the suggestion that his daughter would be leaving. "Our own daughter Bertha to move out as well as your sister? But I thought it was all arranged that your sister Bertha would continue to help you in the kitchen."

Amelia gave a little shrug of her shoulders. "Well, perhaps that had not been a very good idea after all. Two women in one kitchen does not always work out very well Henry, especially sisters. We have had one or two slight disagreements already."

Henry had sometimes heard raised voices coming from that direction and had wondered at the time whether there might have been some friction between the two women but had thought it best not to interfere at the time. He had recently lost one daughter, albeit for a very good reason, and now his wife was suggesting that his other daughter should move out with her aunt. He was not particularly overjoyed at losing both his sister-in-law and his daughter: he would miss their company, especially now that Otilia wasn't here. Why shouldn't Amelia's mother and her sister move over there instead? he thought. Would it not be more sensible for his daughter and her sister-in-law to remain, and for his wife to try and overcome the differences with her sister? He would suggest it.

But before he could speak, and as if his wife had read his thoughts, Amelia began to explain the reasons for suggesting her solution to the problem. "I don't think it would be fair to let mama and auntie to have those rooms over there. They would have difficulty communicating with the other tenants as neither of them know a word of English."

"How do you know that?" Henry was astonished at her presumption.

"Mama wrote to Tilly in German didn't she? How could either of them have learned English? .... and in any case, it does not appear that they had any intention to come here until recently......."

She didn't wait for her husband to respond so she quickly went on "........so if you agree to Bertha moving over the road with my sister, then we'll have room for mama and Aunt Louisa to come and live with us as soon as they arrive, and then we can see what develops later."

Henry knew when he was beaten, and nodded his head in agreement, but could not help wondering what his wife had meant by the phrase, "then we can see what develops later!"

*

Isabel Bansmer and her sister, Louisa Bochnest, arrived in London in September. Henry met them at the East India Docks and brought them to Shoreditch by open coach. Both were now in their sixties and Henry admired their courage for attempting such a difficult journey all the way from Northern Germany. However, while he chatted to them they did not appear to be listening, instead, they held their hankies to their mouths as they surveyed the scene outside. The two women had been looking forward to coming to London, but were so disillusioned when they saw the East End of the city. Back home, they had left the quiet lakeside town of Neustrelitz, with its delightful Schlosspark and Baroque buildings, the lovely surrounding countryside of lakes and open fields, and the woods of mixed oak, birch and conifer. This all contrasted sharply with what they saw on their journey from the docks.

Arriving at the house, Amelia met them at the door and she threw her arms around her mother in an emotional greeting. "It's been so long, mama."

Henry brought in the small amount of luggage they had brought with them, and they explained that they had left the rest at the docks to be picked up later. Little Clara had come running to the door to meet her Grandma, followed by the children.

"These are the boys. John who is fourteen, and Charles is twelve," Amelia explained to her mother, and a small voice added quickly, "And I am Clara, and I'm nearly nine and a half."

Amelia translated what she had said, and everyone laughed except Clara, who did not think that there was anything to laugh about. Amelia introduced her mama and aunt to the other people who lodged and worked in the house: John Ziesemir, Charles Bender and his daughter, Dora, and Matilda Huller.

"It seems that you are doing quite well for yourselves, Tilly," her mother remarked.

Henry smiled, "Well, we all work very long hours and the pay is not good, so we will never make a fortune, but we get by."

Amelia's mother looked round, as if missing someone. "I thought that Bertha would be here. Where is my baby?"

Amelia laughed recalling how her mother had often referred to her younger sister as baby Bertha.

Amelia explained that she was living in rooms across the road with her own daughter Bertha.

"I hope they have not moved out because of us." Isabel looked concerned.

"No, mama. They wanted to have some independence, and they do get on so well together. They will come over to see you as soon as they know you are here."

"When do we get to see Otilia? Your papa and I were so happy to receive your letter to say she had been born. It seems as if was only yesterday." Tears came to her eyes as she recalled how wonderful both she and her husband had felt at the time and that Karl had been so looking forward to seeing his first grandchild. It had also been the day when they had learned about Augusta's intention to leave Germany, but her eldest daughter and her husband had returned home, and now it was she herself who had left.

"We will go to see Otilia tomorrow morning after you have had a good night's rest," Amelia assured them. "You must both be tired after your long journey."

Otilia could not wait to meet the grandmother whom she had never seen and they greeted each other warmly. When Otilia told her that she was pregnant, her grandmother was delighted.

"I was so far away when you were all born and longed to see you all when you were babies, "Isabel said, "but I won't miss out on my first great-grandchild. How long will I have to wait?"

"It will be in early April and, luckily, my baby will have a cousin about the same time if all goes well, because my sister-in-law, Eva, is also pregnant."

Amelia had to act as interpreter during this conversation and she also explained to her mother that Ernest's brother, Leopold, had married Eva, and were living in Greenwich. Otilia smiled to herself as she remembered the conversation that she and her sister-in-law had had the previous year.

The following March, Eva gave birth to a daughter, Kate, and just a month later, Otilia had a son whom she named Henry after her father.

CHAPTER EIGHT

1893-1894.

The winter of 1892/3 had been a hard one in Saxony but now that Spring was approaching, Johannes Weinerlein's farm workers from the village had begun to prepare the soil for the sowing of the sugar beet. His father had died during the winter and with Augusta's help he was determined to keep the farm going and make a success of it.

"I'll take the cart into Sangerhausen this morning to get some seed and while I'm there, I'll probably call in at the friseur's and get them to relieve me of some of this hair that's grown during the winter. If my crops do as well this year as my hair has during these last few months, we should have a good harvest," he quipped.

Augusta laughed at the way her husband had drawn a parallel between his hair and the harvest. "I think I'll come with you, and get myself something new: a pretty blouse perhaps."

He was about to protest, but she put her arms around her husband's neck and gave him a kiss. "I still love you so after all these years, Johannes, but I do believe that you are keeping something from me, and that you have another reason for going into that barber's shop that you don't want to tell me about."

"Well, I do want a hair cut, but Friedrich Siebenhüner asked me if I wouldn't mind going to see his lad Oswald who works there with Carl Matzke's son, Gustav. It seems that the two lads have made their minds up to go to England and he asked me to try and talk them out of it."

"I knew that there was another reason, but why you?" She pinched his nose.

"Well, their fathers don't want them to leave, and Friedrich asked me to tell them how disillusioned we were and how foolish it would be if they went there."

"But that was well over twenty years ago! Maybe things have changed since then. If you manage to talk them out of it you will get the blame if things go wrong. I think that you're taking on too much responsibility, Johannes."

"I'll be very careful what I say, but I did tell Friedrich that I would speak to them, so I'd better keep my promise. I can only tell them what it was like then. I'm not going to persuade them; it will be up to them to decide what to do. If they change their minds it'll be their decision. In any case, they may have a sound reason for wanting to go which their fathers do not even know about."

Augusta gave her husband a hug. "I don't want you to get into trouble. If the lads don't go they might regret it later and blame you. If they go, then it'll be your fault that you were not able to talk them out of it. It seems to me that you can't win whatever the outcome." She sounded very concerned.

Johannes told her that he had always thought that Friedrich wanted his son to follow him into the mines. "He is a qualified colliery engineer now and Carl is an inspector of mines; they've both done very well for themselves."

"And I suppose that they're both disappointed that their boys have only turned out to be barbers!" Augusta concluded.

"No doubt that's true, but I'll talk to them and listen to what they have to say." Johannes went to the stables to prepare his horse for the journey into town and to hitch him securely to the cart.

Eventually reaching Sangerhausen, Augusta hurried off towards the shops while Johannes went straight to the friseur to see the young men and to try to discover why they were so intent on leaving Saxony.

"Good morning, Mr.Weinerlein," the two lads chorused as soon as Johannes walked into the shop. "Please come to my chair," said Gustav, giving him a military bow. Gustav was neat in his appearance. His black hair, parted meticulously down the centre, was straight and flattened down firmly with the shop's own brand of hair lacquer. The immaculate greased spikes on his butterfly moustache protruded horizontally for a couple of inches either side. He rolled one end gently between his finger and thumb as he spoke.

"The last haircut he gave," Oswald told Johannes, partly under his breath but loud enough for Gustav to hear, "was so terrible that the man took one look at what he'd done, then ran out of the shop without paying!" Oswald screwed up his face, opening and closing his eyes rapidly in a kind of nervous twitch, as was his habit, gave a little chuckle at the same time and turned his chair round to face Johannes inviting him to sit down.

Johannes sat down gingerly fearing that he may be the victim of a prank. Oswald smiled as if reading his thoughts and put the chair back to its original position facing the mirror on the wall. Johannes gave Gustav a dismissive hand gesture, "I'm sorry, Gustav, I'll come to you next time."

"There may not be a next time," Gustav answered decisively.

Johannes wondered whether he should take this opportunity to broach the subject about their leaving.

"Do you mean you may not be here?" He said it trying to sound as if he knew nothing about their impending departure.

Oswald leaned over to whisper into Johannes's right ear. "He's got a girl into trouble and he's running away," and gave that same little chuckle as he placed a cloth over Johannes's shoulders with a flourish, tying it loosely around his neck. Through the mirror Johannes saw a twinkle in Oswald's eyes and a broad grin beneath his neat moustache.

"Do not believe a word he tells you, Mr Weinerlein," protested Gustav. "He'll get me sacked before long with his wild stories."

Oswald snipped away at Johannes's hair for a while with his long-bladed, pointed scissors, before he volunteered the information that he and Gustav were seriously considering going to England.

Gustav leant against his empty chair, arms folded, listening to what Oswald was saying. "You've been to London, Mr Weinerlein. What was it like?"

Johannes had prepared something to say, but had not expected to be questioned.

"It depends, I think, on what you plan to do when you get there."

"Cut hair!" they said together, then burst out laughing. "What else can barbers do?" Oswald asked, and then added as an afterthought, "What are the girls like over there?"

Johannes was surprised that they appeared to be treating the decision of whether to go or not so lightly.

"Why can't you continue cutting hair here in Sangerhausen?" he asked, quite seriously. "What makes you think that you will be more successful in England? - and I don't mean with the girls!"

Oswald's smile left his face. He stopped cutting and looked at his customer through the mirror. "The answer to your second question is that we don't know, but to the first it is......" Oswald looked around the shop as if fearing that someone else may have been listening to their conversation, "......our beloved Emperor, William II."

Johannes quickly observed the sarcastic tone in Oswald's voice. "The implications of that remark being.....?"

Gustav intervened, "We are a military nation, Mr Weinerlein. Look at William's record so far. First he dismisses Bismarck and then takes over the direction of German policy himself....."

"Which means," interrupted Oswald, "that he wants to build up an even bigger army than Bismarck had.... for what?"

Gustav came in again. "Then he's always making martial speeches to the troops, maintaining belief in his own rule by divine right. Germany has lost so many young men leaving to go abroad that he needs to enlist more and more men in order to keep his army at the same strength as Bismarck's."

"Then he'll start another war and the men left will be sacrificed as others have been before." Oswald concluded.

"We have been lucky so far," Gustav observed, "but will our luck hold out? We've heard of some other men in their twenties being called to serve and we want none of it, so we're off!"

At that moment another customer came into the shop and Gustav invited him to sit down in his chair. Johannes remained silent as Oswald returned to cutting his hair and trimming his beard. The two men had put up a fairly convincing argument and their points had been valid. He remembered, as if it had been yesterday, his own experience in the army some twenty-two years earlier during the battle near St.Quentin and felt the pain in his leg where he had been wounded. He recalled the stench of rotting dead bodies, both of horses and soldiers, the sounds of wounded men screaming and calling out for help after losing limbs, and the blood - spilled human blood, thickening on mounds of mud and congealing around the edges of deep red pools between the bodies. Johannes shivered as these thoughts went through his mind, as they often did - nightmare thoughts, memories which he tried hard to forget without any hope of succeeding. How could he tell these two young men to respond to the call to fight for their Fatherland if needed?

"If you have both really made up your minds," Johannes told them as he was leaving, "come and see us before you go and my wife will give you her sister's address as a contact when you get to London. I'm sure she will be able to help you find somewhere to stay."

Augusta was waiting for Johannes in the Marktplatz where they had arranged to meet. "Did you manage to persuade them?" she asked.

"No I did not! In fact I told them to come and see us before they go so that we can give them your sister's address."

"They are going then?"

"Almost certainly, and with my blessing."

Augusta could see that Johannes did not wish to discuss it any more and would probably tell her what happened in the shop in his own time.

When both Oswald and Gustav arrived to their respective homes later that evening, they were questioned by their fathers as to what their intentions were. Neither Friedrich Siebenhüner or Carl Matzke blamed Johannes for his failure to persuade their sons not to go, but they were disappointed that they had made up their minds to leave, and that no argument would make them change their decision. The young hairdressers had agreed not to tell their parents about the promise that Johannes had made about giving them his sister-in-law's address in case they thought that he had encouraged them to leave their homeland. However, the young men occasionally had doubts as they waited to find out about their passage, knowing that upon leaving their country it would probably mean relinquishing their German citizenship after they had arrived in England. But when they saw other young men being called to serve the two or three years compulsory military service, it made them more determined than ever to go away from their village and to find a new life for themselves in the city of London. So, with the enthusiasm of youth, they set about making their arrangements to leave.

A few months later the two men arrived in London to be warmly welcomed by Henry and Amelia when they arrived at their house.

Amelia had been very much looking forward to their visit, having previously received a letter from her sister telling her that they were coming. Augusta had explained that the two men would be seeking employment as hairdressers and wondered whether they could find them somewhere to stay.

"I can just remember you as a baby," she told Gustav. "Your mama brought you to the church on the day of our wedding, and you cried and cried during part of the service."

"And he's never stopped crying since!" Oswald added.

Amelia laughed. She thought how much like his father he was and took to him straight away. "We received a letter from your mother when you were born and I remember Henry joking about you then, but please tell me about our old friends." She was enjoying meeting these two young men so much with their refreshing sense of humour, but she was also anxious to hear what they had to say. For the next hour or so the young men told them all the latest news from their homeland as well as answering questions about the people that they had known all those years ago. Everyone had been so friendly together when they were young, and Henry was shocked to learn that Carl Matzke, Gustav's father, had been killed in the mines just before they had left.

Amelia gave them both a good meal and found them somewhere to sleep for the night. Next morning they visited hairdressers' and barbers' shops in Bishopsgate and Whitechapel looking for work. Both soon found employment working together in a shop in Middlesex Street, owned by a Charles Ludwig. He was also of German origin and welcomed the two experienced fellow countrymen, soon realising that their presence would give him more time to spend in the many taverns in the area, an obsession which had frequently in the past, caused him to be incapable of carrying out his duties afterwards.

"I am so pleased that you boys have managed to get a job so quickly," Henry told them when they returned. "While you've been away, Amelia's been busy getting you some lodgings. Unfortunately we do not have enough room for you here, but I believe that my wife has something organised for both of you if you agree."

When Amelia returned she told them that there was only one room she had been able to find at present in a house across the road. It was the same house where her sister and daughter lived but on a different floor.

"There's a single bed there, in rooms shared by a Felix Wagner and a Richard Keul, who have recently moved in. My other married daughter is expecting her second child, but she is also prepared to take in one of you. So if you think that those arrangements are all right, I'll leave you to decide who goes where."

"I think that's a bit unfair," Gustav whispered to Oswald after Amelia had left them to discuss what she had suggested.

"What is?"

"To have to decide who goes to live with the married one, and who lives in the same building as her unmarried daughter. I wonder what she's like?" Gustav closed his eyes and imagined that he was about to meet the prettiest girl in London. Then, before Oswald could make any remark, he concluded, "I think I'll take a chance and go and share the rooms with those two that Mrs. Rolfs mentioned, and I will let you have the home comforts of the married one. Anyway, she mentioned that her husband was Ernest Biedermann. I remember him from back home in Sangerhausen, if it's the same man. I didn't like him very much then." Before Oswald could speak, he added, "In any case, I can't stand babies - and she's got one and having another!"

"Well, thanks a lot for sorting it out," Oswald remarked sarcastically. "You make my lodgings sound very attractive. Now, only because you are my friend, and therefore prepared to sacrifice everything for you.." (Gustav began to play an imaginary violin as Oswald continued...) "I'll go and live in the unpleasant surroundings of screaming babies."

Secretly, Oswald thought that he had the better deal, as he would no doubt be well looked after living with a family and with someone to prepare his meals, but he was not about to inform Gustav of his conclusions.

"You are a pal, Oswald. I'll never forget you for this."

"Even if she has a face like the rear end of a donkey?" Oswald chuckled, "or that her aunt discovers your reputation and protects her from you?" he added jokingly.

They were both laughing when Amelia returned. "What do you both find so amusing?" she asked, and then not waiting for an answer, added, "Have you decided who is going where?"

"Gustav's decided," Oswald said quickly, and before Gustav could say that it was he who had decided. Oswald could see that if Gustav was not happy in his lodgings, then he would have had an excuse if Amelia thought that Oswald had made the decision.

Gustav gave his friend a quizzical look wondering what his friend was up to.

Henry took Gustav across the road, introducing him to the two Germans who were already living there.

"You'll no doubt meet my daughter and sister-in-law tomorrow," Henry told him. "Now I must get back to take Oswald to my other daughter's. Otilia may be in bed early."

When they reached the house, it was as her father had predicted. Ernest greeted his new lodger. "I'm afraid that Otilia is not feeling very well, so she sends her apologies for not meeting you and said that she will see you in the morning."

Oswald thought that he had said it in a matter of fact sort of way, which gave the impression that perhaps all had not been well in the house before they arrived. He hoped they had not had a disagreement about him staying there.

"I've been trying to recall whether I knew you before I left Sangerhausen," Ernest said, "and now that I've seen you, I've just remembered. You were only a young lad when I used to go into the Friseur Salon in Sangerhausen where you and Gustav Matzke worked. You've swept up the trimmings of my moustache many times."

It occurred to Oswald that probably the reason he had not continued to frequent the shop was because of what Gustav had said earlier about him. "Er..yes, I think that I remember you too," Oswald replied politely, "and I'm very sorry to hear that your wife is not feeling well."

Oswald's condolences went unnoticed. "It's just that she's expecting our second child in about a couple of months and she's not feeling up to it. She usually gets a bit distressed when she is pregnant."

Oswald furrowed his brow feeling a little embarrassed and that he might be in the way by being there. Also, this man who he only just met, appeared to have little respect for his wife by telling a complete stranger how his wife was apparently not coping very well with her pregnancy. He either had little respect for his wife or had no understanding or compassion for her in her present condition. He could see why Gustav had not got on with him previously, and immediately summed him up to be arrogant and too full of his own importance.

After Henry had left Oswald with his son-in-law, he walked home feeling pleased with the way the two young hairdressers had settled in their lodgings, but somewhat concerned at the way that his Ernest had changed over the past year or so. He worried about his daughter, wondering if she was as happy as when she was first married. There was nothing to suggest that her marriage was going through a difficult time - indeed Otilia was soon to have her second child within three years - but he had noticed that the forthcoming event did not appear to be bringing Ernest the happiness that his first child had brought. For some reason also, he was not spending as much time at home as he used to. Henry had agreed with his wife's arrangements of where the young men should sleep, especially about having one of them to stay with their daughter in the belief that having somebody to talk to when Ernest was not there would be company for Otilia. Now that it was done, it appeared to have been a good idea. Oswald Siebenhüner was about the same age as his daughter and seemed a jovial fellow, full of fun, and just what his daughter needed at this time he thought.

Next morning Oswald was up early in order to get to his place of work in plenty of time. Otilia had also got up earlier than usual in order to get him a breakfast.

"I'm Tilly," she explained, "and this little fella is my two year old son, Henry. We named him after my father. Ernest has already gone off to work, as you must have guessed. You met each other last night, of course."

Oswald thought that she looked a little sad, and it confirmed his suspicions of the previous evening when he had thought that perhaps they were not in full agreement to him staying there. He had to ask in order to feel comfortable. He could always make an excuse and find somewhere else.

"Do you mind me being here? I could always..."

Otilia interrupted him, "Oh no! I am going to love having you. My husband is a cook and often works late at the hotels so I see little of him in the evenings. You'll be good company for me after I've put little Henry to bed. I hope you're not thinking of leaving so soon."

Oswald was immediately reassured that if there had been any discourse at all over his presence, it had certainly not been because this dear lady had objected. He saw how she had changed suddenly when she thought that he might have been leaving. He smiled at her and she gave him a sweet smile in return. She did not give him the impression of a lady in distress as her husband had suggested the previous evening. Indeed she had a glowing appearance and full of life.

Half an hour later, when Oswald met his friend outside the chapel in Wilson Street, on their way to work, he could see that Gustav was bursting to tell him something even before he reached him.

"She is gorgeous!"

"Who is?" Oswald asked, knowing all the time whom he had meant.

"Why Bertha of course! Who did you think I meant, dumb-head?"

Oswald laughed. "You think all women you meet for the first time are gorgeous. I bet she thinks differently about you!"

Gustav was not listening. "Her eyes! her eyes are like blue fountains...."

"What do you mean," Oswald interrupted, "Have you made her cry already?"

Gustav ignored Oswald's joking. "She is a dream. I'm in love."

"What again! You always fall in love with every girl you meet for the first time."

"But I think she's in love with me, Oswald. She blushed when her aunt introduced me to her, and couldn't look at me full in the face. She was so shy."

"I'm not surprised that she couldn't look at you. I find it hard to do that!"

"I can't wait to get her on her own," Gustav added, without even hearing what Oswald had said.

Oswald turned to look at his friend. "Ah! now the truth is coming out. You mean you can't wait to get her into bed."

Gustav grinned. "You can think what you like, but I'm pleased that you are living with her married sister and not here! By the way, what is her sister like, apart from fat?"

Oswald usually enjoyed a joke, but this time he thought that Gustav's last remark had been in bad taste, and he told him so. "She's very nice as a matter of fact and her little boy took to me straight away.

Gustav looked closely at his friend. "And Ernest?"

"Well, I'm not too impressed by what I've seen of her husband so far, but he was probably in a bad mood when I arrived last evening, and perhaps he....."

Gustav interrupted him, "I told you so. I never liked him back home. He's a good cook and that's about all. I'm three years younger than Ernest," Gustav's mood had changed and he was now quite serious. "and I always remember him back home, boasting about his conquests, and what's more I've been making enquiries about him - and between you and me," Gustav lowered his voice, "I've already heard from the two fellows where I'm living, that he's often been seen at a brothel in Whitechapel Road, wherever that is!"

Oswald looked shocked.

"Mind you, it could only be rumour, or a case of mistaken identity, but I dislike the fellow so much I would like it to be true," Gustav added.

"I think it's a case of wishful thinking on your part," Oswald chuckled, wanting to make light of the conversation, "or maybe you're just jealous." They then had a good laugh about it as they approached the shop where they both worked.

Throughout the morning, Oswald continued to think about what Gustav had told him. He found it hard to believe that the man he had met briefly the evening before could be so unfaithful to the attractive woman he had met at breakfast. As the weeks went by, he looked at her differently and felt very sorry for her, but she gave him no reason to suspect that she knew what her husband was up to, even when Ernest came home very late from work, which he did frequently.

Otilia's second baby was born in the early hours. Oswald could not sleep with all the activity going on, and the sound of the baby's first cry was, he thought, unusually loud in the middle of the night. Not that he knew how a baby should sound after coming into the world, as he had never been near to one so young. It was not until the evening that he saw the tiny bundle in a cot who was to be known as Marie, and marvelled at the perfectly formed minute nails at the end of her tiny fingers. He smiled at Otilia as she lay propped up on her pillows in the bed, looking extremely pleased with herself.

"I've never seen a newly-born baby before," Oswald said. "She's a beautiful little thing," then added with a grin, "just like her mother."

Oswald had joked with her on many occasions and she often reciprocated in an equally humorous way. They had laughed together many times, Otilia once telling him that she had never met anyone so full of fun. Oswald in turn had said to her that he thought Ernest had married the prettiest girl in London. She had felt the colour rush to her cheeks, but then he had added with his usual chuckle, "But I haven't

101

seen many of the others yet."

She had thrown the crocheted shawl she had been working on at him and he had thrown it back. It was the sort of silly things they did when Ernest was not there.

Gustav, meanwhile, was having little success with Bertha.

"She is such a tease," he said, when Oswald had asked him how he was getting on with his love life. "She seems to like me to talk with her and even lets me hold her hand, but when I've tried to kiss her she pushes me away and makes some excuse or other. That aunt of hers clings to her like glue. If only I could get her on her own."

"Then her reputation would be lost!" Oswald remarked, tongue in cheek. He wondered whether he had better take some sort of control of the situation before it got out of hand. "I don't know why I'm suggesting this, but why don't we arrange to go to the Music Hall next week? We can invite Bertha, and I'll ask her aunt if she will join us. You'll then have the chance to be with Bertha on your own, while I look after the aunt and at the same time keep an eye on you."

"Oh, I like the first part of what you said, Oswald, but not too happy about the second." Gustav looked a little disappointed. "But I suppose it's the best I could hope for with you making the arrangements."

"Leave it with me then."

It was the first of many evenings out they all had together, Bertha's aunt and Oswald eventually withdrawing from the scene. After a few months it became obvious to them that the couple had fallen in love.

"I hope you're keeping your instincts under lock and key and not destroying that young lady's reputation," Oswald enquired of his friend.

"I know that you'll find this hard to believe, my dear Oswald," he replied indignantly, "but I don't think of her in that way."

Oswald looked at his friend suspiciously, trying to see if he was telling the truth. Gustav possibly had that something that ladies did find attractive, in spite of his spiky moustache and straight hair flattened down on either side of a wide parting. He concluded that Bertha had probably been won over by his charm, and was about to tell him so, when suddenly Gustav announced, "You will be surprised to know that she's promised to marry me soon after her 21st birthday next year."

Oswald realised that Gustav was being serious, but was concerned that perhaps he was taking things for granted, and might upset the good relationship that they had with the Rolfs.

"Have you said anything yet to her father?"

"It's with his blessing that we are to be married and I'm relying on you to be my best man."

Oswald was taken aback by it all. He had never known how far the relationship had progressed or realised how serious Gustav had been, but was pleased for him nevertheless.

Less than two months after celebrating her coming of age, Bertha was married to Gustav Matzke in St.George's Lutheran Church in Whitechapel. It was a big wedding and the reception was held in Toynbee Hall in Commercial Road. Henry and Amelia felt proud to see such a large gathering and memories of their own wedding came flooding back.

"Bertha reminds me of you when we were married," Henry whispered to Amelia.

"And she's marrying one of the babies who was there at our reception. Can you believe it, Henry?"

"It's all your fault, you know." Henry pointed to their two small grandchildren, Henry and Marie, sitting with their parents. "Look what you've done!"

Amelia gave her husband a light tap on his hand, "It's just as much your fault as mine." They were still laughing as Oswald came towards them.

"What are you two laughing about? This is supposed to be a solemn occasion. You are losing a daughter and I'm losing my best friend."

"But we're gaining another son," Amelia reminded him.

"If you think that's a gain, then I feel sorry for you," Oswald joked. "I know him better than you," and he twitched his eyes in his usual manner walking away chuckling to himself.

"I think that Oswald is such a grand fellow, Henry, and such fun. He is such good company too for Otilia. I do hope he finds a nice girl to marry," Amelia said with feeling.

CHAPTER NINE

1894-1896.

Oswald felt very content living with the Biedermanns and always looked forward to going home after a long day at the barber's shop. Often he would find Otilia sitting alone when he came in from work. The children would usually be in bed and, as soon as he came in, she would put down her sewing to give him his supper. It made him feel that he was part of the family. He was good company for Otilia, especially when Ernest remained supposedly all night at the hotel working. Oswald did not want to hurt Otilia by telling her about the rumours he had heard about her husband in case they were untrue, but it was obvious to all that Ernest appeared to be taking take less and less interest in his wife. Oswald also listened in disbelief when she told him the reasons Ernest had given her for not coming home some evenings.

In view of his absence, Oswald found that he was spending more time alone with Otilia, and they would sit for hours reading or talking. He enjoyed helping her with the children, sometimes reading a little to them before she put them to bed or, on the days he wasn't working, taking them to play in the field on the far side of City Road. She rewarded him by teaching him English, but gave up trying to get him to pronounce the letter 'w' correctly, as well as the combined letters of 't' and 'h'. After many unsuccessful attempts, she would smile, shake her head, and mutter "Oh Oswald!"

He would twitch his eyes two or three times, then give his usual chuckle, causing Otilia to burst out laughing at him.

When she gave birth to her third child at the end of August, Oswald stayed close at hand as the midwife delivered the baby in case he might be needed. He had known nothing about babies before coming to England, but now with Otilia's third child, and the second to be born since he arrived, he was experiencing a feeling that he had never had in his life before. It was a burning desire for the baby being born to have been his.

Oswald lay on his bed unable to sleep. Ernest's and Otilia's happiness or marriage was nothing to do with him, but he could not get either of them out of his mind. He tried to answer the many questions that prevented him from sleeping. Was he feeling sorry for her, or was it jealousy? Was it because Ernest had not been present at the birth? Her husband had not been there to hear the baby's first cry or see the look of joy on his wife's face, radiant and proud, as she held her newly born baby in her arms. Ernest usually made quite a fuss of the children, but appeared to be so indifferent to Otilia. Oswald sometimes felt angry about Ernest's attitude towards his wife, as he did not like to see her hurt. Was it really just a fondness for her he felt, or something else? He had no right to feel anything other than that but knew that he was really desperately in love with her. As he closed his eyes, he imagined lifting her up in his arms and taking her and the three children away from her uncaring husband to start a new life with him in a different city, far away from London.

Gustav greeted him the next morning as they met on their way to their shop. "You look dreadful, Oswald, more dreadful than usual!"

Oswald smiled weakly at the joke. "I didn't sleep very much last night. Mrs. Biedermann had her baby soon after I got home from work. She's a nice little thing: she's going to call her Emily."

Gustav looked closely at his friend. "What's wrong? Come on, tell your old pal Gustav."

Oswald remained silent for a little while wondering if it would help to explain to Gustav how he felt but then he thought better of it and decided not to tell him.

"It's just that her good-for-nothing husband didn't come home again. I'd like to tackle him to find out just what he's doing when he stays out all night."

"You know my feelings about him," Gustav remarked, "but their problems are really not your concern, are they?"

"Perhaps not, but..." Oswald hesitated again.

Gustav finished his sentence for him. "You don't like to see his wife hurt. Is that it? You be careful you don't fall in love with that woman."

Oswald could feel his heart beating fast. "I think I have already," he said quietly, his voice breaking, "and I don't know what to do."

Gustav saw that Oswald was visibly shaking. "You need a stiff drink when we get to the shop and we'll talk about it there. Don't be a fool man. You can't fall in love with her Oswald, she's a married woman!" he said sharply, and without any sympathy for his friend. He then decided not to mention it again as it appeared that what he had said had brought Oswald to his senses.

Oswald ignored the advice his friend gave him and on the way home that evening he rehearsed a hundred times what he was going to say to

Otilia. He would ask her if she still loved her husband, then, if she said that she didn't, he would tell her how much that he loved her and that he wanted to take her away from the wretched man to start a new life with him. He would never see her unhappy again and they would live together until she could get a divorce. At first it did not enter his mind that she would refuse his offer, but as he neared home he had second thoughts. What if she said no and laughed at him believing him to be only joking, or, worse still, become angry with him when he declared his love for her.

He dismissed those thoughts from his mind, as he got nearer to the house on that cold October evening, confident that she felt the same way about him as he did for her. He recalled the many conversations he had had with her during the last two years. They were always so happy in each other's company and got on well together. When Ernest was at home Otilia hardly ever smiled and he often saw sadness in her eyes, especially when he said something which hurt her feelings. He was sure that she loved him and he wanted desperately to hold her in his arms and to feel her cheek against his. He began to shake a little in anticipation as he reached the door of the house.

Oswald's heart fell when he saw Ernest in the room. He was sitting down with the baby cradled in his arms.

"What do you think about our new daughter, Oswald?" he asked. "I heard that you only got a little sleep last night."

Oswald was completely taken aback by his presence. Ernest shouldn't have been there. He stopped shaking when he realised that all his plans had been ruined. He could not even go into the bedroom to see Otilia, otherwise Ernest might have suspected that he was taking more than a just a casual interest in her. Ernest had spoken to him but what he had said he had not really taken in.

"How's your wife?" Oswald enquired politely. He wanted desperately to see her and was trying to think of a way or an excuse to do so.

"Oh Tilly's alright now. I think she's asleep. She's getting used to having babies, and will soon get over it" came the insensitive reply. Oswald felt empty as he collapsed in a chair. He remembered what Gustav had said about Ernest and now it was not what had just been said that angered him, but the manner in which Ernest had said it. He suddenly realised for the first time how much he himself disliked this man.

Although there was plenty of opportunity during the next few days for Oswald to talk to Otilia in the way that he had intended, his courage had left him and he wondered whether he ought to leave and find new lodgings. However, the thought of possibly never seeing her again was too painful for him to contemplate. The words that Ernest had spoken to him when he had walked into the house haunted him. It was the reference to 'OUR new baby' that he couldn't get out of his mind. It was impossible for him now, he thought, to speak to Otilia about his love. At the same time, he knew that he must remain there to be near her, even if she never declared her love for him.

Ernest was now spending more time at home and Oswald wondered why. He couldn't bear to be in his company and decided to stay in his bedroom more often or join Gustav amd Bertha to see the sights of London when they were free to do so. When Oswald joined the Biedermanns for a meal he was now unusually quiet, and only once when Ernest was not there, did Otilia question his silence.

"You are not your usual jovial self lately, Oswald," she commented. "Are you not well?"

Oswald moved the salt pot on the table a few inches to the right, put the pepper-pot in the empty space as if playing a solo game of chess, closed his eyes tightly and opened them again quickly which he always did when feeling nervous, before he answered. He would have liked to have said, "It's because I can't stop thinking of you," but replied instead, "I'm alright. I just feel a little tired lately."

Otilia didn't pursue it any more, but gave him a smile as she looked at him inquisitively. She often appeared to be trying to read his thoughts and when he returned her gaze, she would give him that same little smile until he chose to look away, in the belief that the situation was hopeless.

Some months later, Oswald overheard Otilia tell Ernest that his sister-in-law, Eva, was going to have another baby later in the year.

"She wrote to me to say how pleased she and your brother were. She also said that the new baby would be company for little Kate. Shall we go to see her?"

Ernest ignored her question. "I'll go over to see them at Greenwich as soon as I can and have a beer or two with Leo to celebrate the event," was his only comment.

"Can't I come with you?" Otilia asked with surprise.

"No, Tilly. You can go later and take the children when I'm working."

After Oswald had retired to his room later that night he heard them arguing, resulting in an uneasy atmosphere in the house next morning. He noticed that Otilia looked hurt and that her eyes were red from crying. The tension between Ernest and his wife increased further over the next few weeks and it appeared to Oswald that the man he now disliked intensely was using visits to his brother in Greenwich as an excuse to come home late, or even to stay out all night.

Oswald became increasingly concerned for Otilia's apparent unhappiness, but was unable to pluck up the courage to ask her about it. When he and Otilia were together he was always willing to help her in any way that he could, even with some of the household chores, often cooking his own breakfast of sausages and bacon. When on the occasions he brought a piece of fish home for his supper, Otilia would dip it into beaten egg and fry it for him in the way that he liked it. She would take great care to lay a place for him at the table. W hen Ernest was not there, she always served the fish with fresh tomatoes and crusty bread which she knew that Oswald favoured. After he had eaten he would chatter to her constantly, telling her amusing but exaggerated stories about the day's happenings, while continually moving the condiments around the table as usual.

It amused her to watch his small twinkling blue eyes, twitching nervously as he related his tales, and it was moments like this when Oswald was tempted to declare his love for her, but he never found the courage to do so.

A couple of months passed by before Otilia was able to visit Eva, as she had wanted to do earlier with Ernest.

She arranged for her mother to have the children, and then took a horse-drawn omnibus from City Road to Greenwich, arriving at her sister-in-law's house later that morning. It was not long before Otilia opened her heart to Eva to tell her how unhappy she was, and to tell her that she missed Ernest when he worked late, and sometimes not coming home until the early hours of the next day. Then she often found him to be bad tempered. "Perhaps, though I'm worrying too much about that as I expect your Leopold often works late too." she said.

Eva wondered whether she should tell her sister-in-law that Ernest spent very little time with his brother after work and that it was extremely rare for Leopold to come home late.

"But I can't understand why he doesn't spend more time with you, Tilly. You have three lovely and healthy children, that should make him very happy."

"Oh no, he loves the children, but seems to have little time for me," Otilia confessed, and tears filled in her eyes. "If only he was as nice as Oswald is to me," she sobbed, "then perhaps we'd be happier."

Eva frowned, as she looked hard at her sister-in-law. "What do you mean, as Oswald is to you!? "

Otilia knew that she had to tell someone about her life and Eva was the only one she could confide in. She told her how happy she was when Oswald was there, how he appeared to enjoy the children and how relaxed she felt with him, especially during the times when Ernest didn't come home.

Eva noticed that she was shaking a little as she spoke. "I think that there's a danger that you might be falling in love with this Oswald, Tilly. Are you?" she asked.

Otilia got up from her chair and went over to the window. She spoke quietly.

"I know, Eva," she said, bursting into tears, "and I don't know what to do. I think about him all the time, wishing that I was married to him and not Ernest."

Eva didn't speak for a while. She was thinking what advice she could give her sister-in-law. "Why don't you ask him to find somewhere else, before you regret it?" Eva suggested. "Out of sight, out of mind, is the best way."

Otilia was shaking her head, "If he left, I wouldn't be able to bear that. You see, Eva, I love him." and she began to cry even more.

Eva was shocked. "And does he love you?"

"I don't know, but he looks at me in such a loving way sometimes, and often there is a sadness in his eyes."

"I think that you are imagining things, girl. Go home and just remember that you are married to Ernest and that you have three of his children and forget all about Oswald."

"Oh Eva, I wish it was as easy as that. I'm so much in love with him and I'm sure Ernest doesn't love me any more." She began to cry again. "I'm so unhappy, Eva."

"You've got to do something to stop this nonsense, Tilly, for the sake of the children.

When Oswald came home that same evening, he noticed immediately that Otilia had been crying. She was sitting with her hands on her lap, tightly clenching a damp handkerchief, which she occasionally used to dab her red eyes. He wanted desperately to ask what, or who, had caused her to cry, and he felt angry that it might have been her Ernest who had upset her. It wasn't the first time that he'd seen her like this, but now she appeared to be more distressed than usual.

He sat down at the table where she had laid his supper and, picking up his courage, asked her quite firmly, "Has Ernest caused you to be like this, Otilia?" He began moving the cruet to different positions on the table and twitched his eyes.

Otilia didn't answer immediately and he wondered whether perhaps he shouldn't have asked the question. After all, it wasn't his business whether she and Ernest had had an argument. He didn't notice that Otilia was looking at him, waiting for him to speak again.

She had never seen him look so concerned before about her relationship with her husband, but had often noticed that he looked disapprovingly on the occasions when Ernest had spoken to her sharply. She was also aware that her heart had missed a beat when Oswald had spoken her name so endearingly. It was also an opportunity for her to tell him how she felt about her husband.

"I'm sorry, Oswald. I didn't mean for you to see me crying. No, it's not because of Ernest," she answered quietly, and then added, "but he told me that he wouldn't be coming home tonight again."

Oswald was aware that it hadn't seemed to bother her unduly when he stayed out before, so why was she so distressed this time? But she had said that it wasn't because of her husband. He was now curious to know why she was so upset. He cut himself a piece of cheese and buttered a crust of bread. "I don't like to see you like this, Tilly, so tell me why have you been crying?" he asked sympathetically, and then added in his typical joking manner trying to make light of the situation, "Was it because I was late coming home tonight?"

He heard her give a little laugh, then turned his head in her direction and noticed that she was smiling.

"You're so good for me, Oswald. You would make a very good husband for someone."

Oswald contemplated whether to say that say that he would like to be a good husband to her, but reminded himself that she was a married woman.

"My chance has gone!" he said softly.

"What do you mean, Oswald? 'your chance has gone?'"

Oswald turned back to his supper and wondered whether he ought to continue with this conversation. He knew what he would like to say next, but could not decide whether to or not. However, as this might be his only opportunity, he got up from the table went over to where she was sitting, fell to his knees and took her hands into his.

"I mean that if I had married you, Otilia, I wouldn't want to stay out all night as Ernest does."

Otilia waited a second or two, expecting him to joke about it, but he was looking at her very seriously.

"I can't stand to see you unhappy or hurt. I love you, Tilly."

Her eyes immediately filled with tears. Oswald took out his handkerchief from his top pocket and it to her. "Now don't start crying again. Dry your eyes and tell me what's wrong. I'd like to help."

She dropped her head, not bearing to look at him as she spoke. "It's you really," she said almost in a whisper.

Oswald stooped down to try and look into her face. "Me!" he said quietly but with incredulity. "What have I done?"

"You're here," she said, her eyes still looking into her lap.

Oswald put his finger under her chin and lifted up her face to read what he could see in her eyes. Her skin felt soft as his hand lightly touched her cheek. She gave a slight gasp as he did so, her lips parted in anticipation that he would place his lips against her own. Tears were trickling down her face.

"Do you mean that you can't stand the sight of me, or do you love me as much as I love you?"

Her head fell forward on to his shoulder, "Oh, Oswald," she said, sobbing, "I do love you so. What are we to do?"

"I love you too, Tilly." He said it again and this time with more feeling than before so that there would be no misunderstanding of how he felt. He slowly lifted her head with both hands and wiped away her tears with his fingers. "I've been wanting to tell you that for such a long time."

" And I have been wanting you to for ages and ages. Hold me, Oswald. I only want you to love me."

He kissed her gently on her mouth and as he did so he could feel her body trembling. The salty taste from her tears mingled with the warm sweetness of her saliva. She felt the tip of his tongue against her lips and thought that her heart would burst. He moved his lips to her cheeks kissing away her tears.

"Did you really wonder whether I loved you? Is this why you've been crying?"

Otilia nodded, "I thought this moment would never happen. I've loved you for a long time, my darling. Please don't leave me." She closed her eyes as Oswald kissed her on the forehead, and again on each damp cheek. She was in the dream world that she had dreamt about many times, but one, which she didn't ever believe, would really come true.

"Of course I won't leave you, whatever made you thing I would?"

"It was Eva. She said that I must turn you out."

111

"Why did she tell you that? Does Eva know that you love me?

I had to tell someone as I was going out of my mind and I trusted Eva. She was worried in case you fell in love with me and what unhappiness it would bring. Otilia's face suddenly lit up, her dark watery eyes twinkled as she smiled for the first time. "But now I don't care and I want to tell the world."

He put his arms around her holding her close to him. They stayed close together for some time, neither of them speaking. Occasionally she touched his face gently, and, as he removed a large pin from her hair, he ran his fingers though the long dark tresses. He could feel her heart beating as his body pressed close to her. There was no need for conversation, each one with their own thoughts of how this relationship couldn't possibly exist, but knowing that that it must never end.

Oswald broke the silence. "Are you certain that Ernest will not walk in?" he asked sounding concerned.

"I know that he won't be coming home because he told me before he left this morning. It's his way of making an excuse to stay out all night. Why do you want to know?" She asked the question, trying to sound innocent, but then gave herself away as she felt the blood rushing to her cheeks. She put both hands to her face as if to hide her blushes although she knew that they were caused more by excitement than by embarrassment. She of course knew why he was asking the question and to anticipate the inevitable was almost too much for her to contemplate. She had dreamt of this moment and even longed for the time when she might feel his hands touching the skin of her naked body. Whatever Oswald intended to do she had no intention of objecting or resisting his advances.

"Darling Tilly. I want to make love to you as I've never loved anyone." He kissed her again on the mouth, which opened slightly as their tongues met. He pulled at the buttons down the back of her dress, his fingers digging into small areas of her flesh. Otilia thought about the time when Ernest had wanted to touch her and make love to her before they were married, and how she had no desire for him to do so, but now she wanted Oswald to carry her away in his arms, take off all her clothes and make love to her as if nothing else in the world mattered. The frustration had gone: the passion in her was uncontrollable.

Oswald didn't want to pursue the subject of Ernest further, so he asked the next question very quietly, close to Otilia's ear, "Where are the children?"

"They've been asleep for some time," she replied equally quietly.

"We must be very quiet so as not to wake the household," he said quietly, then whispered in her ear, "I think I'll take you to your room."

Otilia got to her feet, and now trying to control her emotions said haltingly, "Shall I go first or will you?"

"Neither, I'll carry you," he replied boldly. Otilia giggled in disbelief.

Oswald was not a strong man, but lifting her up in his arms he found her, thankfully, lighter than he had imagined. One hand was holding the top part her bare thigh beyond her stocking top and she could feel the stiffness inside his trousers against the other. She held him tightly around his neck, giving him kisses as he climbed the stairs.

"I'll drop you, Tilly, if you keep doing that."

"Shh, you'll wake the children," she teased.

Once inside her room, he placed her gently on the bed resting her head on the pillow, and then drew back the curtains allowing the gaslight from the street lamps to give the room a soft warm glow. He hesitated for a moment as he suddenly remembered that this was the bed that Ernest also slept in, but the thought quickly went away as Otilia held out her arms invitingly towards him. They kissed again, long passionate kisses as he held her body close to his own.

"I do love you, Oswald, I can't believe that this is really happening. Please stay with me tonight."

Oswald pulled away, his face in shadow so that she could not see his expression.

"Try and keep me away," he said.

She kissed him again and then pushed him playfully off the bed in order to get undressed.

Oswald hurried to his room and returned dressed only in a loose nightshirt. Otilia was standing by the window facing him. Her naked body silhouetted against the soft light from outside. He moved slowly towards her allowing himself to enjoy this moment that he would remember for ever, and longing to hold her lovely pale skinned body in his arms. She had now let down her hair completely and her long dark tresses fell gracefully over her bare shoulders. He thought how beautiful she looked. "You'll get cold there my darling, come to bed."

She turned towards him and put her arms around his neck and gazed into his face, "I want these moments to last forever. I still can't believe that this is happening to me. Are you sure I'm not dreaming?" His nightshirt fell to the floor as she slowly pulled it off his shoulders.

"If you're dreaming," Oswald told her tenderly, "then I must be too." He lifted her up, carried her the few paces to the bed and laid her gently down. Her heart was drumming and she was hardly breathing with the passion of it all. She wanted him as she had never wanted Ernest, and could barely keep her body from trembling. His hands ran over every inch of her flesh feeling every contour. Her firm round breasts were rising and falling with every breath, his soft loving hands caressed them as he entered her body. He was so gentle at first and then with more passion, his actions became quicker and rhythmically as she arched her body to meet him.

Otilia experienced for the first time the thrill and excitement of making love, and not the way Ernest used her just for his own sexual satisfaction. She felt weak in Oswald's arms, yet strong in her desire to give herself to him, over and over again, not wanting it to end.

CHAPTER TEN

1896-1898.

Eva Biedermann's baby was another girl born in October. Leopold was overjoyed, but secretly would have liked his second child to have been a boy. Otilia visited her three days later, but Eva was more interested to know what had happened in her sister-in-law's life, than her own.

"What are you going to call her?" Otilia asked, picking up the baby to nurse in her arms. "She is beautiful, Eva."

"Leopold chose Isabel as her first name because it was your maternal grandma's name, he said. He thinks a lot about you, Tilly, but come on, tell me your news. Is Oswald still with you?"

Otilia felt the blood rush to her cheeks. "Probably the cold air has given me a fresh complexion," she said, ignoring Eva's question, and began to rock the baby gently while singing a German lullaby that her mama used to sing to her.

Eva eyed her sister-in-law with suspicion. "Come on, Tilly, tell me," she said again, only this time a little impatiently.

"If you mean what song I'm singing, it's Brahms....."

Eva interrupted her. "I don't mean the song and you know it. Don't be infuriating. Your eyes have a sparkle that I have not seen there for a long time. What has happened between you and Oswald since we talked last?"

Otilia replaced the baby in the crib and sat down on the bed close to Eva.

"If you really must know," Otilia began, then hesitated for a moment, uncertain on whether she should tell her what had taken place, especially considering that her husband was Ernest's brother. At the same time, she was longing to tell someone how much she and Oswald were in love, and Eva was the only person she knew that she could trust with her secret.

"Promise me first that you won't mention a word to Leo about what I'm going to tell you," Otilia asked.

"I'm beginning to think that it is the opposite to what I was expecting to hear, but don't worry, Tilly," Eva assured her, squeezing her arm, "whatever you tell me it will be safe with me."

115

"As I told you the last time we talked," Otilia began, "Ernest and I are not enjoying the best married life we could wish for and he has been staying out all night, more this summer than ever before. He tells me that he has to cook 'Midnight suppers' and sometimes I think he might be telling the truth, but not all the time. He loves the children, but never says any word of endearment to me. I thought I loved him when I married him, but I am not so sure now that I've found out what true love really is. Eva, he loves me and I love him and we don't know what to do!"

"I presume you are talking about that man Oswald now," Eva queried.

"Of course I mean Oswald. It was you who told me that I had fallen in love with him if you remember!"

"Perhaps I did, but I also said that you can't carry on like that and told you to get rid of him if you remember. It looks as if you ignored my advice. What about Oswald?" Eva asked. "Does he love you as much as you love him? Are you sure that you are not both victims of the problems that appear to have arisen in your marriage? I can guess what has happened. He is taking advantage of the situation. Have you thought that perhaps he is just feeling sorry for you, Tilly?"

Otilia ignored her questions as she realised that Eva did not understand what she was trying to tell her. Burying her face in her hands she began to sob. "I'm so much in love with him and he loves me and I have three children and I don't know what to do. Help me, Eva, what shall I do?"

"Do you mean that you and this man are lovers?"

Otilia kept her face hidden and just nodded.

"Doesn't Ernest suspect anything?"

"No I don't think so," she mumbled. "If he did find out, I think he would go mad and throw Oswald out."

Otilia now took her hands away from her face and wiped her eyes with her handkerchief. "I couldn't bear that to happen" and then added as if she had not really considered it previously, "If he did, then I would go with him." She began to cry again.

"Dry your eyes, Tilly, tears don't help." Eva felt a little annoyed with her sister-in-law being unfaithful to Ernest, even if he wasn't giving her all the attention she was seeking. At the same time she felt unable to help, convinced that their love was nothing more than an infatuation. There was also every reason that Oswald was probably feeling sorry for Otilia, and resenting the way that Ernest was behaving. "Tilly, I think that this is something that will pass. Give it time and I believe that everything will work itself out. Don't worry about it, but I think that you would be wise to stop this affair. Think of your lovely children and..."

Otilia had stopped crying and was looking at Eva in disbelief. "You don't understand, Eva, neither of us has ever felt like this before. I love him so much that I would even give up my children for him. It would break my heart, but if it meant losing Oswald...., I would sacrifice everything."

Eva could not believe what Otilia was saying and felt a little cross with her sister-in-law. "Don't do anything that you may be sorry for later on. I would not like to see you hurt, Tilly. I don't want to discuss it any further. Now I will go and make us both a cup of tea, and then we will talk about something else."

If Ernest Biedermann had noticed that his wife was being over-attentive to Oswald Siebenhüner, he said nothing, and throughout the following year Otilia and Oswald became devoted lovers. Gustav knew of course but made it quite clear to Oswald that his wife wanted nothing to do with her sister especially as Bertha was expecting their first child. She threatened at one time to tell Ernest what was going on but Gutav was able to persuade her to wait and see what happens. Oswald and Otilia, however, were under constant threat of being found out by Ernest and they knew that if they were, their deep love for each other would be interpreted as nothing more than just a sordid affair. Otilia was also concerned that her mother suspected something was wrong with her marriage and she worried in case she discovered the truth about Oswald and her.

"You look very serious lately, Tilly," her mother told her one day when she brought her three grandchildren to visit her. "Is there anything wrong?"

Otilia's heart missed a beat and then she felt the blood rush to her cheeks and went a bright red. She felt scared for a moment in case her face gave her away.

"No, of course not, mama. I have probably been overdoing it. I am just a little tired with three children to look after."

"Is everything alright between you and Ernest?"

Otilia knew that her mother was aware that Ernest had paid little attention to her for some time and her probing question made Otilia feel uncomfortable. How could she possibly answer that question truthfully? she thought.

Amelia did not wait for a reply before she asked her another which caused her daughter to blush even more. "Is Oswald still with you?"

Otilia now realised why she was being questioned. She guessed that her mother suspected something or perhaps had listened to what someone had said. Furthermore, she was perfectly aware that Oswald was still living with them. "Can we change the subject, mama, and leave me to live my own life?"

Amelia glared at her daughter in disbelief, then spoke sharply to her. "I only hope you know what you are doing, Tilly."

*

One evening a few months later, Oswald came home to find Otilia sitting alone, staring into the fire, her hands tightly clenched on her lap. "What's wrong,Tilly? Does Ernest know? Has he found out about us?" He suddenly felt relieved. At last the truth could be told and he would confront Ernest and take her and the children away with him.

Otilia shook her head and started to cry. "No Oswald. I'm pregnant."

It was something that they had feared but hoped that it would not happen. Now suddenly the situation was different and Oswald could see that people would misinterpret the situation. He was certain that when it became generally known, everyone would think that he had taken advantage of a young married woman with three children, and that Otilia would be branded as being unfaithful to her husband and be in disgrace. Even if Ernest's infidelity and wild life-style also became known at the same time, most men would sympathise with him when his wife's adultery was found out.

Oswald tried to think what should be done. "Are you certain, Tilly?"

"I have been for at least two months. What are we going to do?" she said, drying her eyes on the handkerchief Oswald had given her. "Ernest will be bound to know that the baby isn't his."

As Otilia was talking, Oswald was trying to think out the best way of doing the right thing.

"We'll wait until your brothers are married in a couple of weeks' time and then we will tell Ernest, and then do as we have often planned: go away with the children and live our lives together." He held her in his arms, not wishing to let her go.

"Can we wait that long, darling Oswald?"

"We'll have to for both your brothers' sakes. We'll not spoil their day. Time will soon pass."

But the two weeks to Easter were the longest two weeks of their lives. Otilia's brothers, John and Charles, were married in a double ceremony, while Otilia and Oswald kept themselves apart throughout the proceedings. Otilia sat with her husband, Ernest, and the children, while

Oswald stayed with Gustav and his wife, Augusta. No one appeared to suspect anything, although Oswald noticed Amelia looking closely at her daughter on a number of occasions as if trying to read her thoughts. Only once did she look at him and he wondered why she had not spoken to him. Surely she could not have known anything.

Everyone else appeared to be relaxed, but the tension that Oswald felt was almost unbearable. He was fearful of what might happen when Ernest would find out that his wife was pregnant with his child, and especially when she she would brake the news that she was leaving him!

A few days later, Amelia called in to see her daughter and finding her alone with the three children asked her bluntly, "Are you pregnant again, Tilly?" Before her daughter could answer she added acidly, "Whose is it?"

Otilia took in a deep breath, and she looked hard into her mother's face, ready to deny that the baby was anyone's other than Ernest's. But Amelia was waiting for an answer with tight lips and Otilia could see that she had guessed the truth. The delay in answering confirmed her mother's suspicions.

"I thought so," Amelia said sternly, "and what are you going to do about it?" Her mother did not give her time to answer before adding, " We suspected what might happen because of your relationship with this Oswald, and when I told your papa what I thought had happened, he was disgusted with you both. It is only through my intervention that has stopped him from disowning you altogether. Whatever were you thinking of, girl?"

Otilia was crying. "Crying will not help. Is there any way that Ernest could suspect that it was not his?"

Otilia suddenly felt angry, firstly because it was not really any business of her mama's anyway, and secondly because her parents had condemned her without their knowing or asking her about the circumstances. She stood up and glared at her mother.

"Yes, there is. There is, because my so-called dear husband, has not loved me properly since the day he made me pregnant with Maria! I don't love him! I'm in love with Oswald and he loves me, and I am going to leave Ernest and go away with him." She burst into tears again, and sat down heavily on the chair. "So now you know and I don't care."

Amelia's heart softened as she now saw Otilia as her little girl in desperate trouble. She put her arm around her shoulders. "Stop crying, Tilly," she said softly. "We will sort this out together. I have suspected for a long time that something was wrong between you and Ernest, but I never thought that it was as bad as what you just told me. I could not help noticing how much attention Oswald was paying to you, and how he looked at you when Ernest was not there. My sympathy has been going out to Ernest all the time and now I can see how wrong I might have been."

Otilia thought that this was the time to tell her mother about the rumours that were circulating about Ernest's lifestyle.

"My husband's not really loved me all the time we have been married, mama, and no doubt he's been getting all he needs from those women in Whitechapel and Bishopsgate that I've heard about, and I expect that is why he doesn't bother with me anymore," Otilia said with a bitter tone in her voice.

Amelia too had heard tales about Ernest and had dismissed them as gossip, but now to hear Otilia now talking about him in that way gave her quite a shock, and she looked at her with incredulity.

Otilia saw the look her mother had given her, so went on to explain. "He often comes home very late, and sometimes he stays out all night on the pretence that he is working. Oswald has been nicer to me than Ernest has ever been. I'm worried about Oswald, mama. I am frightened of what might happen when Ernest finds out."

"You ought to be more worried about yourself," her mother said sternly. "When is the baby due?"

Otilia stopped crying now that her mama appeared to be talking to her in an understanding way. "At the end of October. Why? What difference does it make?"

"I am thinking that it might be best not to tell Ernest until you have to. Leave it to him to find out for himself. It's far too early to tell him yet and, in any case, anything might happen between now and then."

Otilia was horrified when she suddenly realised what her mama had meant. She could not bear to think that she might lose Oswald's baby, but she was right; it would be best to leave it until Ernest discovered that she was pregnant. What he would do then though made her shudder, as he would know that it couldn't possibly be his baby.

"I dread to think what your father will say when I tell him. He's suspected that you and Oswald were a lot closer to each other than you should have been, and I think he knew a lot more about Ernest that he told me, but when I have to tell him that it is Oswald's child you are carrying, he will blame you for what you have done, in spite of what he might think about Ernest."

Amelia returned home and waited for Henry to arrive. He took the news calmly at first, probably realising that because he had thought that his daughter's close relationship with Oswald would inevitably lead to disaster. Then he felt angry with both of them and it took Amelia all her time to persuade him not to go round to his daughter's house to try and sort everything out. Finally, he had to be content to announce that his daughter was a disgrace to the family and that she had made her bed and must lie in it and take the consequences that would ensue.

"She needn't think that she can come round here when Ernest throws her out," he told Amelia. "I want nothing to do with her or that baby when it's born, and that's final."

It was the sort of stance that Amelia had expected that her husband would take and, when he had calmed down, she eventually persuaded him not to say anything about it to anyone until after they heard what would eventually happen.

"I won't even mention again it then," Henry retorted.

Even though it was obvious to everyone else, it was the end of July before Ernest suspected that his wife was pregnant. At first he said nothing because he could see no reason for her being so. He could not remember when he had last made love to her, but it was true that he woke up sometimes in the morning after an evening of drinking, and was unable to remember what had happened the night before. He wondered if perhaps....he had to ask. "Are you expecting Otilia?"

"Yes. Have you only just realised!" she replied casually, as she put his meal down in front of him. She began to fear that this was going to be the confrontation she had dreaded, but surprised herself by remaining so cool. She was glad after all that Oswald wasn't there.

"But..." Ernest began.

"Never mind about but," she interrupted, "just get on with your meal. I am going to see to the children," and Otilia left Ernest to ponder over what she had said.

How on earth could it be his? he thought, but then, who else could be the father? Otilia was not that sort of woman...... or was she? There was Oswald of course, but no, not him - not in his own house! Anyway he was too much of a gentleman and never talked about being interested in women. He wondered whether Otilia had found out what he himself got up to when he didn't come home, and was playing him at his own game - but surely she wouldn't, not Otilia! He looked down at his empty plate. He could not remember what he had eaten. What was he to do? How could he ask if the baby was his? That would make him look foolish. He considered that it would be best to say nothing, but was confused and needed time to think about it: some place away from the house.

"I'm just going out for an hour," he shouted.

Otilia knew what that meant: he would be at the nearest alehouse for two or three hours at least.

Oswald came home soon after Ernest had left. "How are you, Tilly? Is he home?"

"Yes, but he has gone to the tavern and won't be back for ages," and then she started to laugh.

Oswald kissed her and asked, "What's so funny?"

"Ernest asked me tonight if I was having a baby and looked puzzled, but he didn't pursue it. I wonder what he is thinking?"

Oswald looked serious. "He's getting close, Tilly. Perhaps we ought to tell him before he discovers the truth from someone else. If he decides to ask Eva whether she knows, we can't expect her to lie for us. If we don't tell him, we must be prepared to do what we have planned as soon as he finds out. Eva's arrangement for you to have the baby in Brighton while she looks after the children will give me time to get those rooms in Twickenham ready for when you return. I cannot fix anything up for certain until I know when you want to leave." Oswald held her in his arms. "I do love you, Tilly, I can't wait until we are together. I don't thing we can wait any longer. You had better go off first thing tomorrow to see Eva, after taking the children to your mother's. I will wait here until you return and then we'll face Ernest together."

Otilia agreed. "Alright. I'll pack the things we need in our bags tonight then, to be ready to leave in a hurry,"

That night Otilia found it difficult to get to sleep, and when Ernest eventually came into the bedroom in the early hours of the morning, it was obvious that he had had too much to drink. As he began taking off his clothes and dropping them all over the floor, he blurted out something to the effect that the baby could not possibly be his.

Otilia began by telling him that he didn't know what he was doing sometimes when he came home in the state he was in now, but Ernest interrupted her.

"We'll sort this out in the morning," he just managed to say before staggering towards the bed and falling heavily on to it. He was asleep almost immediately and began to snore loudly.

Otilia lay awake for hours worrying about what was going to happen next day. She knew that Ernest would not be awake for some time as he would be sleeping off the effects of the drink, so she got up early and took her children to her mama's before going to see Eva at Greenwich.

"Has he found out yet, Tilly?" Eva asked.

"I think that he knows, but last night he couldn't believe that it could have been anyone else's other than his own at first, but now I think he strongly suspects that it isn't his."

"How do you know? Has he told you that.?"

"He was too drunk last night to talk to me about it, but I left before he woke up. Oswald is waiting at home, so when I get back without the children, we will tell Ernest what we are going to do. If he goes to work before Oswald has chance to talk to him, we will just leave him a note and then go and pick up the children from mama's."

"But you've got to face him, Tilly. You must explain why you are leaving him. Surely you can see that. Oswald should leave as soon as you get back, while you tell Ernest why you are leaving him. I could pick up the children for you from your mama's, then later, we will meet somewhere, and then you can all go off to my cousin in Brighton to have your baby."

Otilia shook her head. "I don't think I can do that and Oswald would not leave me to tell him on my own and I don't want you to get involved. You must stay here, and you can come and see me in Brighton."

When Otilia returned home in the late afternoon, she was completely unprepared for what was about to happen. She felt that she and Oswald had done everything theycould but was taken by surprise to see Ernest still in the house and looking very stern. She was also surprised to see her three children huddled together on the floor and knew immediately that everything had gone wrong.

"I've been waiting for you to return you hussy," he said in a loud voice. "Your lover boy has gone. I've thrown him out. I know that the baby you are carrying is his and now I want you to leave and not come back until it is born. Do you understand?" Ernest spoke firmly, stressing every word, but now raised his voice even further to almost a shout. "Everyone but me seems to have known that you are carrying that swine's baby!" He pointed to the children without taking his eyes off her. "You can see I have been to your mother's and I'm keeping them here until you return, and then we'll talk again. I don't care where you go, but I want you to leave NOW, and don't bring that child back here. Do you understand?"

Otilia began to shake almost uncontrollably, her calmness gone. Her eyes filled with tears but she was too scared to cry. If only Oswald was here, she thought, he would know what to do, but he wasn't and she had not even seen him outside. Where was he? She was confused and in a panic. She couldn't find her voice to say anything back. Her whole world was falling apart.

"I discovered these two bags already packed with your things, so it was obvious that you were planning to go, so you can go now," he said, and he picked up the bags and put them outside the door. Before she could speak, he took her firmly by the arm and put her outside with them. In a state of complete shock, and feeling completely helpless, she heard the door shut with a loud bang behind her and the bolts go across. Even through the closed door she could hear the heart-rending cries of "Mama, mama," from her children inside. She collapsed on the step over her things, sobbing uncontrollably.

Oswald had remained close by the house most of the day ever since Ernest had forced him to leave. It must have been while he had been taking his own bag and case to Victoria railway station that he had missed Otilia's return. At the very moment he was hurrying back to the house, he saw Ernest put Otilia's things outside the door, bundling his wife out with them. Oswald ran up to her and picked her up to hold her tightly in his arms.

"Come on, Tilly," he said quietly and reassuringly, "let's get away from here; we have no choice."

"But my babies, my children," she cried, reaching out towards the closed door.

"You will see them again when we come for them after our baby is born, then we'll all go away, far away from all this unhappiness."

Oswald picked up her bags, and they hurried down towards Liverpool Street railway station to catch a horse omnibus which would take them close to Victoria station, where they could board a train to Brighton.

CHAPTER ELEVEN

1898-1908.

Amelia had been pleased to look after the children on that morning when Otilia went to visit her sister-in-law.

Leaving them with her was not something that Otilia often did, but this time Amelia had no idea that it was for a particular reason. All her daughter had said was that she would call for them later in the day. When Ernest had called to pick them up soon afterwards she immediately suspected that something was wrong. He was very angry when he arrived and she was shocked when he told her that her daughter was a whore and that he had thrown Oswald out of the house. He said that Oswald had told him that it was his baby that Otilia was carrying but was unaware that Amelia had known that for some time. He left with the children before Amelia could question him as to what he was going to do. She sat for a long time in her chair not knowing what, if anything, she should do and wishing that Henry had been there to take control of the situation. She worried terribly about what would happen when Otilia returned home after visiting Eva and, bearing it no longer, went to the house to see if she could help. When Henry arrived back from his calls later that afternoon, he found his wife in tears and between sobs she told him what had taken place.

She explained that she had called round to the house after worrying about what might happen, but had been too late. Ernest had thrown Otilia out and told her not to come back until after the baby was born. No one had any idea where she had gone, or indeed, whether she had even gone off with Oswald, but Amelia could not understand why her daughter had not come to her first before going off somewhere. Nevertheless, she had a great deal of sympathy for Otilia and was angry with Ernest for what he had done. Perhaps it was because she had already known that Otilia's baby was Oswald's and had felt so sorry for her knowing the plight she was in, and that she would eventually have to face Ernest's wrath.

"Where can she have gone, Henry? Do you think she might have gone to Eva's?"

"Wherever she's gone doesn't matter as far as I'm concerned. I have no

125

feelings one way or another for her and it's a good job she's gone away to have that child," Henry announced sternly and without any feeling of remorse for his daughter.

"You mustn't be so hard on her, Henry," his wife pleaded. "After all, she is your daughter."

"No daughter of mine would do what she has done," Henry said coldly, "and as for that er..." he began to splutter trying to find the right words, "that brazen...jumped up Saxon hairdresser..." Henry began to walk away in disgust at his own thoughts.

Amelia followed him into the other room. "I think that everyone is judging Tilly too severely. I think that Ernest was wrong to throw her out the way he did - it was an unkind act, especially in her state."

"But that's why he did throw her out, don't you understand? If you were having a child by another man... I'd have thrown YOU out!" Henry yelled.

Amelia reflected on what he had said, leaving Henry to have the final word, as she could find no answer to his last remark.

Henry sat down, but having lost his appetite he just picked at the food his wife had prepared for him. He turned towards Amelia and spoke quietly but very positively. "And wherever she's gone, I don't want her to come back here with it: is that clear?"

Amelia thought that he could not have made it clearer, but thought it unkind that he had referred to the forthcoming baby as 'it'. "If Oswald and Tilly are together, then they are most unlikely to come back here anyway," she said half to herself and then added, "but I wish I knew where she had gone."

"Well, she couldn't have gone far," Henry observed, trying to give his wife a morsel of comfort, "as she would not want to leave her children for too long."

"But Ernest told me that he had told her not to come back until after the baby was born, and then not to bring the baby back with her." She started to cry again as she realised that whoever baby it was it would still be their grandchild.

Henry made some sort of grunting sound, which sounded neither like an approval or disapproval. "I don't want to talk about it any more," he said, "and stop crying. It is not our problem."

*

It was at the beginning of September when Amelia was told the awful news. At first she couldn't believe it, and hurried to the house to see for herself: The rooms where her son-in-law and Otilia's three small children had lived were empty. She stood looking at the scattered papers, the wide-open and empty drawers and the children's toys that had been left behind. It took her some time to come to terms with the truth that they had gone without saying a word. She hurried back in a daze to her home in Earl Street.

She burst into the room where her husband sat quietly sewing. ""Henry, Henry, they've gone! All of them, gone! He's taken them to Germany," and she collapsed into a chair sobbing loudly.

Henry stopped what he was doing and turned to face his wife. "Now tell me what you are talking about? Who's gone to Germany?" Then suddenly realising what she might have meant, asked quickly, "You don't mean Ernest?" Henry wanted to be reassured that she had not meant that it had been their son-in-law and the children.

Amelia nodded slowly, her eyes full of tears, "We'll never see our lovely grandchildren again." She began to cry even more loudly.

"Are you sure?" Henry asked, trying to sound calm and at the same time, desperately hoping that it was not true.

"The lady at the corner shop told me that she had seen them leave yesterday afternoon. Ernest had already told her husband that they were going to Germany to be with his wife who was already there. I've just been to their home and it's true. They've gone, Henry."

"Then he's a liar," Henry spluttered angrily. "What did he mean, 'his wife was in Germany.' Tilly's in Brighton according to Eva!"

"But nobody knows where she is but us, so he's got away with it. I expect he's told people Tilly had gone there, if they were wondering why they hadn't seen her. But what about our grandchildren, Henry? He didn't even bring them to say goodbye to us, and what will Tilly do when she finds out?"

Henry had recently learned the truth about Ernest and the sort of life he'd been living. He had wondered previously whether it all might have been partly his daughter's fault, but now that Ernest had taken his grandchildren away, any respect he had for his son-in-law had gone. Henry pondered for a moment or two. "Perhaps it's best that she doesn't find out until after her baby's been born. She has a new life to live now." He turned away biting hard on his bottom lip.

*

On arriving in Brighton, Oswald had to make a number of inquiries before he found Guildford Street where Eva's cousin lived. Number 36 was in the middle of a long row of terraced houses and was much smaller than Otilia had imagined. Eva had said nothing about her

127

cousin's family, only that she would give her shelter and somewhere for her to have the baby. For a moment they wondered whether they had done the right thing by coming to the house of a complete stranger.

Oswald knocked on the door and a woman in her mid thirties opened it. She was small, rotund, and her fair hair framed an attractive healthy looking face noticeable by the rosy cheeks. She gave them a broad smile when she the two of them standing outside.

"I suppose you're Otilia. I'm Ellen Wenham." She reached out, her hands resting on Otilia's as she kissed her on both cheeks. "You must be tired after your journey. Come straight in and meet my family." As they both entered the house she turned to greet Oswald. "And you must be the happy father to be."

Oswald put down the bags he had been carrying and took Mrs Wenham warmly by the hand. "Can I thank you kindly for letting Otilia stay with you until the baby is born. I do hope we are not putting you to too much trouble."

Eva's cousin gave him a reassuring smile. "Don't worry. I'll look after her."

Oswald made his excuses saying that he had to get back to London immediately. Thanking Mrs Wenham again for her kindness, he now knew that he would be leaving her in safe hands. He kissed Otilia on her cheek and squeezed he hand. "I'll come and see you whenever I can, meanwhile don't worry." He leant forward to whisper in her ear, "I love you."

Oswald stood outside looking at the closed door for a minute or two with a feeling of guilt and loneliness. He knew that he must start planning for the future and was anxious to get back to London where he hoped that he could find somewhere for them to live in Twickenham.

Otilia was surprised to see six children in the room. Ellen explained that the eldest was eleven and that the latest addition to the family was her little baby girl who appeared to be only a few weeks old lying in a cot in the corner. Otilia's eyes filled with tears as the baby reminded her of her own little ones she had left behind in London. She hoped that the time would pass quickly so that she could get back home to her three lovely little children. But she knew that the three months she was to spend in Brighton waiting for her baby to be born was going to be the longest three months of her life.

*

Eva was shocked when she learnt that Ernest had gone back to Germany with the children and wondered how her sister-in-law would react when she found out. Ernest had confided in his brother asking him to promise not to tell Eva until after he had gone. She wondered how on earth she would be able to keep the news from Otilia when she visited her in Brighton. Otilia was bound to ask her about the children. She decided that she would make the excuse that she had not seen them, which was true of course. The last thing Eva wanted to do was to upset Otilia while she was waiting for her baby to be born.

Oswald came down to Brighton as often as he could, but his presence did little to comfort Otilia. She was missing her children terribly: their laughter, even their tears, but most of all the time during the evening when she had put them to bed. In her dreams she saw Henry, Marie and little Emily calling to her. She often asked Oswald if he ever saw them, but he was now living and working in Richmond and she understood that he would have no reason to go back to the house where she still believed that Ernest and the children were living. Oswald also thought it best not to visit Otilia's parents, as he did not know how they had taken the news that he had run away with their daughter or the fact that Otilia was expecting his child.

Nor did he see his friend Gustav very often, but one day towards the end of September Gustav came to see him, and told him the news about Otilia's children. Oswald was distraught and blamed himself for what had happened. "It's all my fault. This wouldn't have happened if..."

Gustav interrupted him, "If you hadn't taken advantage of her. It's a bit late for that, my friend!"

Oswald glared at him, and Gustav immediately regretted making light of what was a serious problem when he saw the look on Oswald's face.

"How on earth can I tell Tilly?" Oswald said, not wishing to comment on what Gustav had said to him.

"Perhaps it's best that you don't tell her until she's had the baby," Gustav suggested.

"But I can't pretend that I don't know. Perhaps I will write and tell her that I'm unable to visit her for a while. The baby isn't due for about a month. She'll understand."

Gustav looked closely at his friend. He wasn't sure that Oswald was making the right decision. "I don't think that will be a very wise thing to do, Henry. Tilly will want to see you. If you don't visit her she'll wonder why you are staying away and worry in case anything is wrong. She needs you, Oswald. You'll have to keep it to yourself until the baby is born. After all, there's no reason why you should have found out what has happened to the children. Tilly's parents could not have contacted you to tell her because they don't know where you are. So just keep on seeing her and pretend that you know nothing. Just remember, she'll need your full support when she does find out."

Oswald knew that his friend was right, but he worried about what Otilia would think of him when she discovered later that he had withheld the truth from her. He made regular visits to see her, pretending that he knew nothing, before finally arriving the day after her baby had been born.

Ellen met him at the door. "Eva is with her now and has been here for a few days and she has told her all about what her husband has done. She thought that it was best if she told her before you arrived. Otilia's devastated over the loss of her children, but in between her tears, she keeps looking at the baby and saying how pleased you will be to see your little girl. She's so confused."

Eva's cousin went on to explain that she was convinced that it was only because Eva was here to help Otilia with the birth of her baby, and to comfort her afterwards, that had kept Tilly from breaking down altogether. "I'll go and see if it's alright for you to go up."

As she left the room to go to the bedroom, Oswald felt relieved that Otilia now knew the truth. He resolved that when she was strong enough to return to London he would do everything in his power to try and make her happy.

Otilia clung tightly to Oswald when he reached her bedside and for a while they said nothing. It was some time before she was able to speak. "This is our baby, my darling," Otilia told him. "What do you think of your first daughter?" then only after a brief pause, "but what am I to do without my little ones? Oh! Oswald, help me?"

He put his arm around her and held her tightly as she began to sob uncontrollably. Her eyes were red and tears ran down her cheeks. Oswald wiped them away with his handkerchief. He looked down at his newly born child and parted the shawl that was wrapped round the baby to reveal a tiny screwed up face. She looked no different to Otilia's baby girl, Marie, who he had seen soon after she was born at his lodgings in London, but wouldn't say so. "She's beautiful," he said and then his hand gently stroked Otilia's face as he told her, "I want you to make a quick recovery and then we'll start our new life together. I love you, Tilly."

"And I love you, Oswald. I want to be your wife but I don't know what I'm going to do without my children." Tears continued to run down her face as Oswald prepared to leave her noticing how tired she looked.

"I'll help you, Tilly, in every way I can." He kissed her again and bent down to kiss the forehead of his newly born daughter. "I'll leave you now, Tilly. Try and get some sleep and I'll be back to se you later. Oh, I nearly forgot, what name have you chosen?"

"I've always like the name Rosa," Otilia answered.

Oswald squeezed her hand. "Then I would like her second name to be Otilia, after you." He kissed her again.

Downstairs, Eva explained to Oswald how difficult it had been to explain about Ernest returning to Germany, especially when Otilia realised that she would almost certainly never see her children again. "At first she couldn't come to terms with it, and thought that Ernest would write to her mother and father to tell them that he would come back, but I had to tell her that her parents had already received a letter from him telling them that they would never ever come back to England. It nearly broke her heart, but the birth of the baby was her salvation. She is still very low and I believe it will be some time before she recovers completely, so you will have to have patience, Oswald, and not try to rush things."

Oswald listened carefully to what Eva was saying and promised that he would give Tilly all the support he could. When Gustav had told him about Ernest's departure with the children, he had had no doubts that they would never return, but had under-estimated the effect it would have on Otilia. They were Ernest's children, but they were hers too, and he had not realised until that moment when he has seen his own child, the love that a mother has for her children.

"What can I do?" he asked, now realising that he was completely at a loss as to how to handle the situation.

"Just let things take a natural course until she's come to terms with it, and then she'll need all the support that you can give her."

Ellen arranged for Oswald to stay for a couple more days but he wanted to get back to London to continue to earn some money as a journeyman hairdresser. Even in that short time, he had noticed that Otilia was making a good recovery and beginning to come to terms with her difficult situation. However, it was to be another six weeks before Otilia eventually felt able to walk into Brighton to register the birth of her baby, giving the Brighton address to the Registrar. After thanking Eva's cousin for all she had done, Otilia left Brighton with her baby to join Oswald in their new rooms in Twickenham.

"Aren't we going back to where I lived to collect the rest of my things?" she asked.

Oswald tried to sound as casual as possible in explaining that other

131

tenants now occupied the rooms and that her mother had collected everything that she thought Otilia would need to take to their new home. Amelia had given them to Eva who in turn had passed them on to Bertha and Gustav. Her mother had been careful not to select anything that would have reminded her daughter of her three children, especially avoiding any of their clothes, which Ernest had left behind. She had thought it best not to tell Henry about whet she had done, or that she had been to see her daughter on a number of occasions since Otilia had returned from Brighton. Amelia was certain, however, that Henry was missing his daughter dreadfully, but even if he suspected that his wife was meeting Otilia, he never asked about her.

On one occasion, Otilia asked her mother if she had heard anything about her three children.

Amelia thought that there would be no harm after all this time in telling her what she had heard. She believed that there was very little chance that they would ever see the children again and any news about them could possibly be a comfort to her daughter. "Gustav said that he was almost certain that Ernest had taken the children to Neustrelitz - but he's not sure. You probably don't know that Leopold has also taken his family back to Germany, not many months after you left Brighton. Eva hinted to Bertha that they may be going to Neustrelitz and when she told Gustav, he said that was probably where Ernest was. It's really no more than that."

Otilia had wondered why she had seen nothing of Eva Biedermann since Rosa had been born in Brighton. It was not until now that she discovered why. She had felt hurt that Eva had gone without saying goodbye, but would always be grateful to her for the kindness and help she had given when little Rosa was born. At the time, she had been told the sad news that Eva had lost her own little girl, Isabel, when she had been only two years old, and perhaps it had been that which caused her to leave so suddenly. Otilia was sorry that she would probably never see her sister-in-law again.

Oswald and Otilia soon settled in their new way of life, living happily together. Oswald was earning an adequate wage as a journeyman, while Otilia took in some sewing for local tailors' shops. Time was becoming an important healer and her new baby, Rosa, was a great comfort to her. Two years later, their second child, Edith Florence, was born. Oswald was now working in and around Twickenham as he went from one hairdresser's shop to another, and Otilia and the children went with him, always managing to find somewhere else to live. These moves caused some hardship to Otilia, but she loved him dearly as would go with him anywhere, but no one ever knew that they were not married.

During the next four years they had two more children, George Edward was born in 1902 and, after moving to Richmond, Mabel Violette in 1904. By the following year, Otilia had now been separated from Ernest for seven years and was free to marry again, so immediately they made arrangements to be married at Shoreditch Registry Office. They thought they would ask Gustav and Bertha to be witnesses now that Bertha had forgiven her sister and become friends again. Otilia now felt confident enough to go to visit her mother and tell her the news. Leaving her children with a neighbour, she went by train and bus to Shoreditch. It was a long and tedious journey to the East End of London and the nearer she got the more apprehensive she felt about how her father would greet her. Henry opened the door of her parents' home and they both stood staring at each other for a while like strangers. They had not seen or said a word to each other for over seven years and she thought he looked a lot older. Otilia began to feel scared, wondering what his reaction was going to be. He was the first to speak.

"How are you, Tilly?" he said it in a kindly way as he held out his hands to greet her as if it only been a month or two since they had last met.

Otilia fell into his arms as he gave her a hug. "Oh, papa, I've missed you so," was all that she managed to say before bursting into tears.

When Amelia heard Henry speak his daughter's name she ran to the door to see them in each other's arms, and knew that all was well between them at last. She put her arms around them both, kissing Otilia on the cheek. "This is the happiest day of my life," she said joyfully.

While Otilia was taking off her hat and coat everyone began to speak at once as if trying to fill in all those lost years. Otilia told them that she was now able to marry Oswald at last, but Henry wanted to know more about the children and how long it would be before he saw them.

"They are my grandchildren after all," he said proudly, without the slightest sign of his previous displeasure as to what his daughter had done, "and while you two are talking, I'll go and make a pot of tea."

As he left the room, Amelia pulled a face behind his back and smiled at her daughter. "It doesn't seem long," she said quietly, "since the time your papa didn't want to know about your first baby, Rosa, but when I told him that you had your third and that it was a boy, I believe that he even looked disappointed that he hadn't seen any of them. The only thing he ever said to me was that he wondered how many more I thought that you were going to have."

Otilia noticed that her mama's last remark sounded more like a question than a repeat of what her father had said and that she appeared to be waiting for an answer.

"Well, mama, you can tell papa that after Rosa and Edith were born, Oswald said that we'd go on until we had a boy, then after George came he said, 'Oh let's go on for the half-dozen!'" and she burst out laughing.

"That's a typical remark of my Oswald, he always jokes about everything."

"I'm certainly not telling your papa that you are still going to have another two, that will be nine altogether!...." Amelia stopped suddenly, and put her hand to her mouth as if to silence herself, regretting that she had included her daughter's first three children in the total.

Otilia's colour went from her cheeks as she remembered their smiling faces. "Have you ever heard anything about them, mama?" she said softly, her eyes looking down into her lap.

"No, I'm afraid not, Tilly. We've heard nothing more since that time when Gustav thought that they'd gone to Northern Germany."

Henry came into the room carrying the tea. "Now, you two, you've had long enough." He turned to his daughter, "When am I going to see my four grandchildren?" Henry didn't wait for Otilia to reply and continued, "I've been thinking while I've been making the tea - why don't you get married from here, and then we can look after the children when you go to the Registry Office?"

"He seems to have it all worked out, Tilly," Amelia said, smiling.

Later, when Otilia was leaving to go home, she told her, "I've not seen your papa as happy as this for a long time."

On the way home, Otilia felt elated, thrilled at her father's suggestion and the way he had welcomed her back. She hoped that Oswald would be just as pleased. She had not told him that she was going to visit her parents that morning, thinking that he might not have approved, but now could hardly wait to tell him what her papa had said and of the plans they had made.

Oswald listened carefully and was pleased for Otilia that her father had welcomed her back after all this time. He had always thought it unfair that her father had taken the attitude he had, even though he understood that the circumstances had been difficult for him to come to terms with.

"I told them that I'd ask you first, but I hope you'll agree that it'll be alright," Otilia said. She went on to tell him about how her father wanted to see the children, but as Oswald had not once heard his own name mentioned, he knew that he would probably never be really accepted as a true son-in-law. "I'll agree to everything you want to do, Tilly, and if you want us to get married from your home, then it's alright with me. I'd better tell Gustav to arrange to be there with Bertha."

Otilia felt very happy but again her first three children came into her mind. Henry would now be thirteen, Marie eleven, and little Emily, nine. She often wondered what their father had told them to explain her sudden absence. Had they now forgotten her? She thought that if only they were here then life would have been perfect.

Oswald noticed how sad she looked and guessed what she was dreaming about. He decided that he must get her away from London. "I've been thinking a lot about our future, Tilly. I don't want us to stay here for the rest of our lives, especially with all that happened before Rosa was born. I've heard that I would have a better opportunity of getting a more permanent job if we moved out of London, perhaps to the Midlands or the North. Someone told me that Leeds would be a good place to try, so if we could find somewhere to live there, maybe I could set up on my own eventually. What do you think?"

After seven years Otilia had just made friends with her father again and now Oswald wanted to take her away from him. She thought about it long and hard before answering. They had often talked about going away and at first it had seemed the best thing to help to erase the memories of Ernest and the three children. To start a new life away from London had always seemed to be an exciting adventure to embark upon, but this was the first time that Oswald had talked about it seriously. He appeared to have given it a lot of thought, but why today of all days? "Perhaps we can decide after we are married," she suggested, wishing to put off her decision. "I think I've got to get used to the idea first. Is that alright?"

Arrangements were made for the following week and they all set off but said nothing to the children of what they were going to do. They did, however, tell them that they were going to meet their grandparents and the three eldest were very excited and couldn't wait to get there. Mabel, who was just a year old, cried most of the way and did not enjoy the bumpy journey one little bit.

Henry made a great fuss of the children and took them around the house to introduce them to everyone. "These are my grandchildren," he told them all proudly, "and this fine fellow is my son-in-law," he added, pointing to Oswald.

At Amelia's suggestion, they agreed to give two different numbers of houses in Earl Street to the registrar as their places of residence. "It'll stop the Registrar from knowing that you are already living together," Otilia's mother said.

"But what about our four children?" Oswald quipped. "Who's claiming to be their parents? I had planned for them to witness the ceremony."

Henry chuckled at Oswald's joking and thought how different he was from Ernest. He was beginning to see why Otilia was so taken with him. "We're claiming those four as ours while you go off and get married," Henry replied, as he too joined in the fun. "It's good too that you've agreed that Bertha and Gustav are to be the witnesses."

"Don't forget we want our children back!" Oswald shouted as they left.

Oswald thought it best to say nothing more about leaving London and they spent the next two years happily as a family.

In the summer, on a particularly fine day, Oswald took them all to spend the day in Richmond Park. Their fifth baby, Clare, had been born the previous October and he and Otilia sat on the grass with their children playing happily around them.

"Oswald, you're unusually quiet this morning; is there anything worrying you?"

He smiled and looked at his wife. He knew that he could never keep any secrets from her and always said that she was able to read his thoughts.

"It's not really worrying me, but I think that I would like to go back home to see my parents. They're now both in their eighties and I would like to see them for the last time. We've got a little money, and if you wouldn't mind....."

Otilia interrupted him. "Then you must go, Oswald, and why don't you visit your sister, Helga and her family in Berlin, at the same time?"

"You wouldn't mind then, Tilly?"

"Of course not," she said without a moment's hesitation. "We'll make plans as soon as we return home today."

However, it was not until the following Spring that Oswald left for Germany on the long journey across the mainland of Europe, travelling through France and Germany to his village of Riestedt where his parents lived. They greeted him warmly and were so pleased to hear that he had settled down so well in England. He told them nothing about Otilia's first marriage and of all the ensuing unhappiness she had endured. They were thrilled to hear about their five grandchildren and the sixth on the way. Oswald visited his old friends and looked in to the barber's shop in Sangerhausen where he had worked with his friend Gustav. A lot had happened since they had had that conversation with Johannes Weinerlein in the shop some fourteen years earlier. There was so much to talk about during his stay, but he soon began to miss his family, and longed to see them again. Soon he was making arrangements to return to London. He embraced his parents for the last time, both knowing that they would not see each other again.

"Write to us Oswald," his mother said, "and let us know how you get on when you move north."

Back in London, the children saw the postman come to the house. "We've had a postcard! We've had a postcard!" Rosa shouted excitedly, waving it in the air.

Otilia bent down to meet her daughter who stopped suddenly to avoid running into the wide brim of her mother's new hat.

"It's from dada and it's in colour."

Otilia took the card from between Rosa's fingers. "Let me see."

"It's from my dada and he's coming home soon," Rosa told her mama before she had chance to read it.

The colour picture on the front was a view of the small village of Riestedt taken from across green fields, showing the white painted houses beyond contrasting with the red roofs of most of the buildings. There was a place below the picture for writing and Otilia read aloud what had been written.

"Dear Rosa, Edie and George,
This lovely green village is your dada's birthplace in Germany. This is also the place where your German grandmother and grandfather live. Please, dear Rosa, Edie and George, show this picture postcard to my darling Mabel and baby and tell them I am coming back very soon."

Otilia had gathered her children around her with one hand holding the postcard and the other resting on her tummy as if trying to convey the message to her unborn, sixth and final child, Lily, who would complete the family.

CHAPTER TWELVE

1910-1915.

Some ten years had passed since Rosa was born in Brighton. Otilia was pleased that Gustav had persuaded her sister Bertha to forgive her and become friends again soon after they moved to Twickenham. Now they had moved back to Shoreditch to be close to Otilia's parents and this meant that the two sisters could see a lot more of each other. Oswald and Gustav were both working as journeymen hairdressers and they often met to talk about old times. The subject often arose about what was happening in Europe and what appeared to be serious political conflicts affecting their homeland. From what they read in the newspapers and, in particular, the news they received from their relations still in Germany, caused them considerable anxiety.

"I think we got out of Germany at the right time, Oswald," Gustav suggested to his friend. "It appears that the German empire is being built up into a military colossus under William II, which seems to be dominating the centre of Europe."

"He certainly appears to have transformed the country as we knew it, into a thriving industrial empire," observed Oswald, "and he's apparently able to feed the huge increase in population better than when we were there."

"Maybe," Gustav agreed, "but what about all that business which has been reported in newspapers, about the German Navy and the British Navy? Germany's big fleet expansion is for what purpose? Can you tell me what that's all for?" he continued. "And then there's all this tension building up in the Balkans. I tell you, Oswald, I'm glad we left Germany when we did, but I'm worried about what all this will lead to."

Oswald grinned at his friend. "Your problem, Gustav, is that you worry too much. Why don't you count your blessings and stop thinking about wars, and remember that as long as hair keeps growing, you've got a job for life!" Oswald gave one of his infectious chuckles, which stopped Gustav from looking so serious.

"The trouble with you, Oswald my friend," Gustav retorted, "is that you don't take life seriously enough." Gustav looked very solemn for a moment before adding; "I'm going to miss you a great deal, Oswald, when you leave London. We've been friends for such a long time."

"Oh, we'll keep in touch, and I'm sure we will see each other again. You look after Bertha and I'll look after Otilia." He then leaned forward and added quietly so that their wives couldn't hear, "and when we get tired of them, we'll all meet again and swap over!"

Gustav knew that he didn't mean a word of it and the two men burst out laughing causing their wives to turn around.

"What on earth are you two talking about?" asked Bertha. "A moment ago you both looked as if you were trying to solve the world's problems and now you're giggling like a couple of schoolboys."

Otilia shook her head. "They're incorrigible those two and I don't know how we put up with them, but I expect we will have to for a long time yet," and then both added in unison, "we hope." It was now their turn to laugh at the men.

During that summer, after Oswald had again suggested to Otilia that they move to a town in the North, he spent a couple of weekends in Leeds looking for both a job and somewhere to live. On the second visit he was successful in both, and so they planned to move in the autumn when the house he had found became vacant.

Bertha's daughter, Millie, was now fourteen years old and frequently helped Otilia with the children. She was distressed to learn that her aunt was moving out of London to go to Yorkshire.

"We had often talked about it over the years, Millie, and your uncle thinks that it would be a good time to move," Otilia explained. "Lily is almost two years old now and, as we've decided not to have any more children, we want to start a new life away from London."

Otilia told her how they had both laughed when after George had been born Oswald had said that they might as well go for the half-a-dozen.

Millie thought that her uncle's way of treating everything as a joke didn't seem quite as funny now. She was not looking forward to losing her six cousins. "When will you be leaving, Auntie?"

"Your uncle has already been to Leeds and found a house, and we have to be ready to move in about two months time. He's also got a job with a barber in the city."

"But there's so little time left!" Millie said, sounding very upset and knowing that she would miss them all.

The next eight weeks seemed to go far too quickly for everyone. Henry and Amelia wanted their daughter to bring the children to their house in Earl Street every day to enable them to see their grandchildren as much as possible before they left, while Bertha and Gustav gave Millie as much time as they could to spend with her cousins. Millie was only two years older than Rosa and they were great friends and she was going to miss her more than the others.

Oswald and Otilia saw that it would be impossible for them to take all their possessions with them, so they packed what they could of their personal belongings, together with some furniture and kitchen utensils, into three crates which had been supplied by The Great Northern Railway Company. They had arranged for them to be transported to their new home close to the centre of Leeds, at a cost of four pounds, one shilling and a penny.

Their house was the third from the end of a very long terrace block. The back yard led into a narrow cobbled street with a similar row of terraced house on the opposite side. At first, Otilia was very disappointed. The houses were built of black bricks and smoke from the coal fires in the houses spiralled into a darkened sky from thousands of chimney pots. Otilia opened a wooden gate, which led into a small yard containing a tiny toilet building which she noticed was reached by descending three or four steps. As she passed by she mentioned to Oswald how dangerous they were, suggesting that perhaps he could whiten them in order to make them easier to see which would prevent any of the children from falling down to the bottom, especially when it was dark. A few strides across the yard took her to the door, which led straight into the living room. Oswald had previously arranged for the next-door neighbour to light a fire, creating a warm and cosy atmosphere as they entered their new home. In spite of Otilia's immediate misgivings, it was their first home in England, which they could call their own. The house had a cellar as well as an attic with a bath on the third floor. It was going to be like living in a palace compared to what they had been used to before.

Later in the day the furniture arrived and Otilia soon managed to arrange the two rooms downstairs, but as the living room was so small, it left only a narrow gap between the table and sideboard. On the opposite side of the room was a black range where she would do most of her cooking and, in the corner recess, there was a double gas ring as well as a small washbasin. She arranged the remaining furniture into the room at the front of the house. This room was much lighter and looked out to a wide street with more houses some distance away. From the front door, four steps led down to a little iron gate, which opened on to the pavement. "I think I'll whiten these steps too," Otilia said quietly to herself.

Oswald hung a mirror on the wall next to the back door, which later became in great demand first thing in the mornings. Otilia would take it down and prop it up on the table to comb her dark hair, tying the long black tresses into a bun. When the children came down after Oswald had lit the fire to warm the room, she would brush and comb the girls' hair in turn, but, unlike her own, letting it hang loosely down their backs. During the next three-and-a-half years the mornings became busy times in the Siebenhüner household.

Oswald's joking and friendly manner soon endeared him to the customers who came into the shop in The Headrow in Leeds City centre, and he quickly became well known in the neighbourhood. Each morning he would walk from his house dressed smartly in a suit with a cornflower in his buttonhole - whenever he could get one - to catch the tram into the City. Otilia was also very meticulous about the children's appearance, and took great pride in keeping them immaculately dressed before sending them to school.

Oswald often missed the companionship of Gustav, his old friend and brother-in-law, as he walked alone to catch his tram, especially as the news from Europe became graver. He wondered what he would have said about the Balkan States attacking the Ottoman Empire, and of a war, which appeared to be threatening as a result of this confrontation between Austria and Russia. Most of the papers also believed that the situation could easily escalate into a European conflict. When it became known, following the murder of Archduke Franz Ferdinand, who was the heir to the Austrian throne, that Germany was involved; the general view was that if Germany supported Austria, a European war would be inevitable. The assassination of the Austrian royals had taken place in Sarajevo in June 1914, causing that country to declare war on Serbia at the end of July.

Events now began to move quickly and when Germany declared war on France and Russia, and then invaded Belgium in order to quickly defeat the French army, it came as no surprise to Oswald when England declared war against Germany almost immediately afterwards.

The European conflict was the main topic of conversation by the customers in the barber's shop in the Headrow the following day, some expressing their views that Germany would be defeated very quickly. However, some anti-German opinions were becoming more frequent and one or two expressed their objection to Oswald still being allowed in the shop because he was a German. Previously on most mornings, Oswald had greeted the lady who owned the greengrocer's shop on the corner with a cheery, "Good morning," as he bought his usual cornflower for his buttonhole.

But now she replied "Morning, Mr Siebenhüner," in a more subdued manner. Although she had no personal grievance, she hoped that he would not come now for fear of offending her other customers. Next day, Oswald thought it best not to call into the shop and he noticed as he passed by, that there were no cornflowers on display either in their usual place outside the shop or even in the window.

As soon as it appeared that war would be inevitable, the newspapers began to express strong feelings about the amount of Germans in the country. Only three days after war had been declared, it was announced that all Germans who had never applied for naturalisation were ordered by the Government to immediately register themselves at the nearest police station.

Oswald began to worry about all this for the sake of his family having the German name of Siebenhüner, and set off first thing next morning, as instructed, to the City Police Station to register. There were many more people there than he had thought there would be, and he had to wait his turn before giving all the details about himself to the police sergeant at the desk. The sergeant noted his date of birth and called over his inspector. Oswald was surprised that the inspector showed him no sign of recognition. He had been a regular customer at the barber's shop and Oswald had often cut his hair. However, this time he only gave Oswald a cursory glance, pretending not to know him. After examining the entry showing Oswald's age to be 41, he told the officer in a quiet voice, "Okay, miss him out."

As Oswald made his way home, he contemplated what the Inspector had meant, but all was revealed next day when he heard that fifty Germans who were between the ages of eighteen and forty had been arrested and taken to Leeds Town Hall to await their fate. He read in the "Yorkshire Post" that the following day they had been taken to York to be interned. He wondered how long it would be before his turn would come.

"What happened, Oswald?" Otilia asked when he returned.

"I thought it best not to ask questions, and the police didn't appear as if they were prepared to answer them if I had, but there's no need to worry. They're not going to lock me up, Tilly," he chuckled. "Not me! I'm too well known." Seemingly unconcerned about what had happened, he unwrapped the German meats and cheeses he had bought from the Market Hall laying them out carefully on the table in front of him. Whatever the future held it certainly was not going to interrupt his supper.

He opened his newspaper and noticed a piece about Belgian refugees coming to London because the Germans had marched into Flanders. The report stated that they had brought with them tales of atrocities being inflicted on their countrymen. He read that the sight of these refugees incited some Londoners to react against Germans living in the area, causing considerable trouble to those who were living in the East End around the parts where Oswald and his family had lived.

A few days later, Otilia received a letter from her sister Bertha and, as she read on, she not only became very disturbed and worried for her sister and her husband, Gustav, but also for her mama and papa.

When Oswald came home that evening Otilia sat quietly as her husband enjoyed his meal, watching him move the items on the table around all the while he was eating in his usual nervous way. She thought that he appeared to be quieter than usual, hardly speaking throughout his meal. Only when he had cleared his plate did she tell him about the letter she had received from her sister that morning.

She picked up the letter. "I received this today from my sister and I'm worried about them."

"Why? What does she say?" he remarked with consternation.

"Bertha has written about some awful things that are happening in London and I don't know what to do about it." She told him what was in the letter and that Bertha was becoming frightened because people were starting a hate campaign against all Germans. Gustav had lost his job and no one was employing Germans any more. She read out loud one of the lines that her sister had written, "We are sometimes afraid to go out of our homes in case we get attacked."

"I am also worried about mama and papa," Oswald. Do you think we can have them here? It seems so much quieter in Leeds."

Oswald did not answer for a while. He had known about the trouble in London of course which he had read in the "Yorkshire Post". Furthermore, he had noticed in the headlines and editorials of some of the national newspapers that they appeared to be instrumental in inciting those anti-German feelings. He had kept all this news from Otilia so as not to worry her, but now she knew about it from the letter she had received, he knew he had to try to convince her not to worry. He was also aware that the restrictions being placed on German aliens prevented any alien from travelling over five miles without a permit so that there would be no chance of Otilia's parents being able to come.

"Oh they will be alright, Tilly. These things are only isolated incidents and will soon die down as people get used to war. After all, we have been living in this country now for many years. Your mother and father

143

have been here for over forty years! I'm sure that there's no need to worry."

Otilia thought about her children. Rosa was now sixteen and had been working as a domestic servant for over three years. Edith, who was two years younger, had a job in a factory packing ladies' and gents' hats into boxes, while the four youngest were still at school.

"What about our children, Oswald? Will they be alright?"

Oswald laughed. "Of course they will, they're English aren't they?"

"Rosa keeps complaining about her name being Siebenhüner and says we ought to change it."

Oswald appeared thoughtful. "Has anyone said anything to her in the house where she works?" he said quietly.

"No, I don't think so. I was only talking to Mrs Butterfield this morning at the shop, and she said that she was satisfied with her work, but she did tell me that she thought she had an eye for the boys."

"Ah, now we know the truth". Oswald fiddled nervously with his moustache. "She thinks that her name will stop her from making it with the lads."

Otilia looked hard at her husband. She didn't think that he should be treating so lightly the knowledge that their daughter was possibly flirting with boys at her age. "Hm! Like father, like daughter," she said under her breath.

She decided that she would have a quiet word with her when she arrived home.

Oswald had little to do. His employer had told him that it would be unsafe for him to return to the shop and, in any case, no one was being encouraged to employ any Germans except those who had been naturalized. He had heard that it was extremely doubtful if even they would be able to find work of any importance.

Oswald was lucky to have kept his German customers on a private basis and cut their hair in their own homes, so he managed to earn a little money in that way. During the next few months he tried to carry on normally but in a quiet way. Their next-door neighbours treated them quite normally but the youngest children who were still at school, received some verbal abuse from the other children. This happened regularly whenever the casualty lists included men from Leeds, and no doubt encouraged to do so by their families. However an event caused the situation to change dramatically in May the following year.

Rumours spread quickly that a German submarine had sunk a ship and there had been a great loss of life. Oswald saw the headlines portrayed on a board advertising the Yorkshire Post. "Lusitania, Sunk" "Over 1,000 lives lost" All of the newspapers in the shop were full of reports about the sinking of this passenger liner by a German submarine. He read that over one thousand-two-hundred passengers were reported to be either drowned or missing and, further down the page, the newspaper reported that anti-German riots had broken out in parts of London and other towns and cities in the country. There had been attacks on German property with homes and shops ransacked by angry mobs, and all their furniture and personal belongings stolen or burnt. Germans living in Liverpool, too, had suffered badly as many of the crew of the Lusitania who had lost their lives had their homes there and the relatives and friends attacked anyone or anything German. He hurried home in case any danger threatened his family and found Otilia sitting quietly in contemplation by the fire.

She knew about what had happened from her next-door neighbour who had not wished to discuss it further and had gone back into her home and closed the door.

"I think she doesn't wish to get involved if we have any trouble," Otilia said with a slight quiver in her voice. "I'm worried about Edie. I hope she is alright in the factory."

Otilia had no need to be concerned because she knew that Edith had no interest in boys and had many friends. Although much prettier than her elder sister, Rosa, she always dressed very plainly and was a very innocent and shy young lady. Otilia did not have the same concerns over her sixteen-year-old eldest daughter. She knew that she could look after herself and had long ago given up worrying about her. She had heard many stories about her exploits with young men but when she suspected that she was meeting them, Rosa always denied it. Edith was an antipathy of her sister. Two years her junior, she was not at all interested in boys, but no-one knew that she had had a secret admirer for some time.

He was a young commercial traveller who called at J.H.Cronk's factory of on a regular basis. He began to take a devious route walking through the packing department on his way to call at the office to collect samples of suit material. It wasn't necessary for him to go that way but he had noticed Edith on previous visits and wanted to see her each time he called.

Bertie Nelson lived with his parents in a small terraced house in Burley. His elder brother, William, had a job as rates clerk in the offices of the North Eastern Region of the L.M.S. Railway Company which gave him security and a good future to look forward to with excellent prospects. He was engaged to be married in September. Bertie, however, was content to find work in the clothing and tailoring trades around the Bradford Leeds area. He was only just over five feet tall with a slightly uneven way of walking, having been born with spina bifida. He was unable to walk properly until he was seven years old, missing some schooling as a result. He left at 13 years of age to work in a tailor's shop in Bradford and learnt very quickly about the different qualities in cloth for men's suits. He had not been called to serve his country due to the slight deformity of his spine.

Hidden from the girls behind some boxes, he stood looking at the one girl he had seen and admired on numerous occasions during his visits. He knew that one day he would approach her but she always dropped her eyes when he came near and a faint pink colour came to her cheeks as he passed by. He noticed that she always seemed to wearing the same plain blue dress, which did nothing to enhance her slim figure, but it was not this that attracted him to her. It was the soft unblemished skin of her very pretty face, which was devoid of any artificial embellishment. He loved the way her dark wavy hair framed her young innocent beautiful face, and the way in which she held herself, with poise and maturity, as if she was trying to prove something to herself and others. Yet he had learnt that she was not yet fifteen and so was too young for him to ask her out.

Bertie was an attractive man with dark wavy hair parted neatly and precisely down the middle. The shirts he wore were white with a high stiff collar and mainly a conservative plain tie. He was a 'good living' man and at twelve years of age, was the smallest choirboy at St Columbia's Church in the village of Burley. Leaving school at thirteen, he worked as an apprentice in a tailor's shop learning the trade and dealing with customers. He visited many of the clothing factories in Leeds and surrounding area, collecting suit cloth as well gentlemen's trilby hats, bowlers and other items, as required by his customers. Always dressed in a smart single-breasted suit, he looked a dashing figure as he travelled around the Yorkshire towns. He worked long hours and was always too busy to have any serious female distractions. However, this young lady, packing hats in Cronks factory in Leeds was different from any other girl he had known and he thought that he had fallen in love with her. She was never out of his thoughts but so far he had been too scared to approach her in case she turned him down. Did her blushes give her away by indicating that perhaps she felt the same way as he did or was she just very shy? He could wait no longer to find out, so throwing caution aside, he began to walk towards her smiling as he did so. All the girls saw him coming and looked towards Edith. Instinctively she stepped back a few paces from her colleagues. Bertie stopped and spoke quietly to her. "Do you mind if I talk to you?" he asked, almost whispering the question so that no one else could hear. She nodded her head, and then heard the other girls starting to giggle. She felt her face beginning to burn with the warm blood that had rushed to her cheeks.

"Then I would like to ask you to come out with me sometime. Perhaps we could go for a walk on 'The Ridge' on a Sunday afternoon?"

Edith had seen many a couple walking hand in hand and sometimes a girl with the man's hand around her waist, walking on the footpaths between the flower gardens on the popular place known as 'The Ridge'. She had envied the girls who had looked so happy and full of life.

She looked up into his face and saw his eyes, unblinking, and looking deeply into hers waiting for her answer. She had never looked closely into a man's face before except her father's and she felt her heart beating faster than it had ever done before. It was almost a pleading look he gave her and she desperately wanted to say 'Yes' but thought of her Mama and whether she would approve. That gave her the answer she was searching for.

"I will have to see if Mama says it's alright." She then suddenly thought of her German name and that of her father who had lost his job due to his nationality. It would be unfair not to tell him these things before agreeing to meet him, but how?

He could see the worried look that had come over her as she took a sharp intake of breath as if about to speak but said nothing.

"What's wrong?" he said with all the compassion he could muster. "If it is about your father, then I know all about what has happened to him and that you were born in London and your name is........". He stopped, not certain how to pronounce it.

"Siebenhüner," she said quietly. Now she had suddenly regained her composure and her face almost returned to its normal colour. She smiled as he gave a little chuckle.

"I suppose I'll get used to that. I am Bertie Nelson by the way. Then is it yes ?"

"You will have to wait until I have asked my Mama," she repeated shyly.

"I'll be here again this time next week and I hope that your answer will

147

be, 'yes.' " He gave her a smile as he said, "Goodbye."

Bertie had a spring in his step as he walked away quite briskly, but aware of the commotion going on behind him.

"Who is he?" " What did he say?" "Does he want to go out with you?" The questions from the other girls were coming fast.

Edith felt the blood rushing to her cheeks again." I'm not telling, but he is going to see me again next week, so you will have to wait until then."

"But isn't he too old for you?" the girls chorused. "How old is he?" one of her colleagues asked. "You are only fourteen!"

Edith had not considered their age difference. He had been charming and she hadn't thought about how old he was.

Now she began to wonder. "I suppose he could be a few years older than me, but what does that matter? - anyway, you're all just jealous," she added indignantly, and carried on packing the hats into boxes.

Edith couldn't sleep that night. She thought about Bertie: said his name to herself over and over again and when she did finally close her eyes he was in her dreams. Next morning she decided that she would tell her parents about him when she came home in the evening.

However the sinking of the Lusitania changed her plans as all the talk that evening was about the tragedy at sea, and whether it would stir up hatred for her father and those others who had not yet been interned.

CHAPTER THIRTEEN

1915.

Next day, Oswald caught a tram to the City. He bought a copy of "The Yorkshire Post," and sat reading the latest news about the Lusitania. There was also further disturbing reports of the rioting against Germans in towns all over the country, especially in Liverpool where most of the crew of the ship came from.

All the time he was aware of another male passenger who kept glancing in his direction. He was roughly about his own age, dressed fairly smartly in a dark suit and wore a black Derby trilby hat. Each time Oswald looked towards him, the man stared back at him over the top of his thick-lens spectacles perched on the end of his nose. Oswald felt a little uncomfortable being scrutinised in this way, but at the same time not particularly threatened being in the presence of his fellow travellers.

When they reached the top of The Headrow, Oswald got off and began to walk briskly along the pavement. He could hear footsteps quicken behind him and, without turning around, knew instinctively that the man he had seen on the tram was following him. When the stranger was almost level he heard his name spoken quietly.

"Mr. Siebenhüner, Mr. Siebenhüner," the man repeated, "please listen to me. I need to talk to someone about our fellow countrymen."

Oswald stopped abruptly at the realisation that it was a friendly face that confronted him. He shook the man's out-stretched hand warily as he introduced himself as Miritz Heuer.

"I live close to Erwin Haussmann whom I believe you know. He's often spoken to me about you."

"He used to come into the shop where I worked to have his hair cut," Oswald said impassively.

The stranger looked around quickly to see if anyone was close by, and then whispered something that Oswald had been dreading to hear. "The police came last night to take him away."

Oswald felt a sudden dryness in his mouth. "Do you know where to?" he asked, his voice quivering a little. "You make it sound as though he's gone for good. Are you sure that he has not just been taken away for questioning?"

"The police told his wife that he was going to be interned, and all he could take with him was one case which he had to pack in a hurry."

"Do you think they are coming for all of us?" Oswald remarked. "Have you registered?"

"Yes, of course, but did you know that Mrs Haussmann was also born in Germany? She told me that the police said that all Germans with German wives were going away: some of the wives are being deported. I'm thankful that I married an English girl. What about you, Mr. Siebenhüner?"

Oswald was stunned by the news. "Yes, yes, my wife is a Londoner, but do you think that will make a difference? I think I'm still regarded as German because I have never become naturalized."

"Neither have I, so I think we had better be prepared. I hope that you did not mind me telling you this, but I thought that you would not have heard as the arrest only took place last night around midnight. That was three hours after the time we have all to be home since we registered as aliens!"

Oswald thanked his new acquaintance as the two men shook hands. "I must admit, Mr. Heuer, that when I saw you on the tram I began to worry a little who you were."

"Forgive me for that, but please, call me Miritz. I'm sure that we'll meet again."

Oswald looked back after taking a few paces along the road, but the man had disappeared. He wondered whether he had been right to assume that they would see each other again and under what circumstances.

He passed the shop where he used to work, not daring to go in, knowing that he would not have been welcome. He recalled a conversation that had taken place on a day in the previous July. While he had been cutting a customer's hair he had been daydreaming, wondering what might happen if England declared war on Germany. He had been suddenly aware that his customer had spoken to him.

"Are you listening to me, Oswald? Does tha' know what, I don't believe tha's heard a word I've said to thee."

"Oh yes I have, Mr. Appleyard," Oswald lied, after coming to his senses, "you've been telling me that you are having your hair cut by the best hairdresser in Leeds."

Mr Appleyard looked at Oswald through the mirror, and grinned. "Tha's a ree'ht clever lad, Oswald. All'us got answer. I suppose that's why I keep comin'. Don't ever go away, will thee lad?"

"Not if I can help it, Mr Appleyard," Oswald had said with more feeling than usual.

Oswald now began to be concerned about what his new acquaintance had told him. When he returned home he did not tell Otilia in case she too would worry. He decided to go into the city next morning to see if he could find Miritz Heuer again. He watched three trams go by, looking for him without success. Catching the fourth, he alighted at his usual stop and walked round the city streets not even daring to go into the Market Hall should anyone recognise him, and wondering how they would react if they did. He spent the evening in the cinema arriving home just before his curfew time of 9 o'clock, where he found Otilia in tears.

"Tilly, what's wrong?"

"They've been, Oswald. The police have been and they're coming back for you tonight."

"Tonight?" Oswald said in disbelief. "Surely not, you must have misheard."

"No I didn't. They told me to pack a suitcase for you and they are taking you away tonight. Oh, Oswald, what will become of us? - and what of the children?"

"Where are the children, Tilly?"

"The little ones are in bed and Rosa and Edith are keeping them calm. It frightened them when the police came."

"I'll go up and see them in a minute, but first I'm going to have my supper, and then I'll be able to think better."

Otilia lifted up a plate which covered all the things that her husband usually enjoyed for his supper: smoked sausages, cold meats, tomatoes, mahogany-brown bread and some stollen which she had kept in an air-tight tin since Christmas. She opened a bottle of light ale and gave it him. She knew that he always preferred to pour it out himself. 'Women don't know how to pour beer,' he always maintained.

"I've already packed a suitcase for you with what I think you might require, including all your shaving things, your scissors and haircutters just in case they keep you overnight." Otilia was trying her best to keep calm, but her eyes were full of tears.

"I don't think I'll be away that long, Tilly my love. They won't keep me." He pushed the saltcellar away from him and changed its place with the mustard pot.

"Don't joke, Oswald, and get on with your supper in case they come back soon." He was only half way through it when they heard the gate open outside. They sat motionless, listening in an eerie silence at the sound of footsteps crossing the yard, and then a loud knocking on the door, the noise reverberating across the room. Oswald had a sudden sickening feeling inside.

"Oh, Oswald, they're here!"

"Well let them in, Tilly. Let's see what they have to say," Oswald said calmly. Two uniformed policemen entered looking extremely serious. "Richard Oswald Siebenhüner," said one of the officers, reading from a paper he held in his hand, "you're to come with us to be interned, by order of the Home Office."

Oswald could see that there was no point in arguing with these officers. He decided that he would ask to see the Inspector when they reached the Station. "Won't you sit down while he finishes his supper?" Otilia asked the men politely. "He's only just come home after a long day in the city."

"We've no time for that," the other officer said sternly. "You're not the only one we're dealing with tonight. You're to come with us right now and we can't wait." They both moved threateningly towards Oswald.

Oswald rose quickly from his chair. "I'll just go upstairs and say goodbye to the children."

"Oh no you don't. You can't leave the room and you heard what we said - RIGHT NOW," the first one told him sounding impatient. "You should have said your goodbyes before we returned. Your wife must have told you we were coming. We've got no time to hang about as we've others to collect so you'd better come with us straight away."

Oswald could see that they meant what they said and picked up his suitcase and mackintosh. Otilia began to cry and, hearing what was happening downstairs, the children also began to cry for their papa.

As Oswald kissed his wife, he felt a firm hand on his shoulder and the two officers hurried him out of the door. Otilia, who was now crying hysterically, collapsed to the ground in the yard as the two policemen left with her husband between them. Quite a crowd had gathered, mainly women, quietly watching the proceedings with their arms tightly folded across their chests. There were one or two mumbled cries of 'shame', but one older man whose son had already been killed in France, shouted out loudly, "That's ree'ht lads, take 'em all away!"

Gertrude Smith, who lived next door and shared the yard helped Otilia to her feet, took her inside the house, sat her down, and made her a cup of tea. "He'll soon be back, you'll see," Gertrude told her. "Sit there and drink your tea luv, while I go upstairs to comfort the children."

None of them could have envisaged at the time that it would be over four years before he would be allowed to return home.

Oswald was ushered into the back of a vehicle parked at the corner of the street and out of sight of the onlookers. As one of the policemen helped him into the back he noticed that there were three other occupants in the vehicle. He recognised Miritz Heuer immediately.

"This is it then, Mr. Siebenhüner. I thought that it wouldn't be long before our turn came," he said solemnly.

Oswald was surprised seeing others being taken away at the same time. He thought that he would have been the only one. "I think we'd better be resigned to the fact that we'll probably all be away for some time," he said. "We'll all just have to make the best of it."

"Where do you think we're going?" asked one of the others sitting at the front of the vehicle.

Oswald didn't recognise them and they looked very young. "Who are you both?" he asked.

"I'm Otto and this is my brother Karl. They told us that we'd be interned until the end of the war. Do you think that's true?"

As the vehicle began to move, one of the young men remarked nervously, "I wonder where they're taking us."

No one bothered to answer as any of them could have asked the same question. Twice more the vehicle stopped to pick up more passengers before it reached the Town Hall. Here they were all told to get out and joined others who had been brought in from different parts of the city. Shepherded into the Victoria Hall they were told to settle down on the camp beds, which the army had supplied for their purpose. Soldiers of the Territorial Army guarded them during the night and, next morning, the men were unceremoniously directed into buses, which took them to an internment camp some miles away.

They first saw the barbed wire surrounding what looked like a park. As they approached the tall iron gates they noticed that armed soldiers guarded the entrance.

"I think I recognise this place," Miritz remarked. "I've been here with my family. This is Lofthouse Park near Wakefield. Perhaps it won't be too bad after all."

Once inside, they gave their names to an army corporal who looked far too old to be an active soldier. He ticked them off from a list he was holding and gave each one the number of a hut they had to go to. After collecting a couple of dark brown blankets and a pillow they proceeded to their hut which they had been allocated. The long wooden buildings contained little else but steel beds placed closely together on either side of the huts. Each had a thin mattress rolled up on top of the springs.

Fearful of what sort of future for them lay ahead, the men had only slept fitfully at the Town Hall the previous night, but after a meal of soup, stale bread and a mug of tea, they lay on their straw mattresses in a state of exhaustion. Later that morning they were bundled out of their huts into an open area where they were told to lay their bags and cases on the ground in front of them. A burly Sergeant addressed them. Oswald noticed his weather-beaten features and guessed that he had seen service in many theatres of war, but now appeared to resent the fact that he was given the less important job of dealing with alien civilians. Oswald was beginning to feel like a prisoner of war.

"You are 'ere as prisoners in a place wot used to be known as Lofthouse Amusement Park, but you won't be amused 'ere," he observed. "Some of you will be leaving to go to the Isle of Man and some will remain 'ere. All of you will be be'ind barbed wire until the end of the war," he yelled, and then added with a sneer, "unless we can ship you all back to Germany before then."

Someone close to Oswald protested at this last remark by trying to explain that they all had homes in Leeds, but the sergeant would have none of it.

"You're all Germans and yer the enemy and this is yer NEW 'ome. So now you can all open yer cases so we can search 'em for things yer not suppose to 'ave."

The sergeant walked slowly down the line of the new intake as the men unfastened their cases and bags.

"Now tip 'em up and then STAND STILL," he shouted.

The contents spilled out on to the dirty ground and the men watched in despair as the soldiers rummaged through their possessions, confiscating all scissors, pocket-knives, razors, and any tools that the men had brought with them which they thought might have been useful.

Oswald explained to the soldier who was rummaging through his things, that he was a hairdresser, and asked if it would be possible to keep the tools of his trade. "I could be useful by cutting the men's hair while they're here," he suggested.

The sergeant heard what he was asking and came briskly over to stand immediately in front of Oswald putting his face close to his.

"You're not an 'airdresser now," he said menacingly, leaning forward almost on tip-toe, and then added slowly and deliberately, the whites of the knuckles showing on his tightly clenched fists, "you're a German prisoner of war!"

Later, Oswald sat next to Miritz Heuer at a long wooden table where they completed a form they had all been given. It was headed, 'Prisoner of War'. Oswald wrote down his name and address in the space at the top of the paper. "What do we put here where it states, 'When captured'?"

"I suppose we put the date when taken away from our homes," Miritz suggested.

"It ought to have said, "When rescued from our wives," said another.

This comment caused some amusement, especially when they saw the man grinning. "But now I don't know which is going to be worse," he added, much to the others amusement.

"Obviously he hasn't left the same sort of wife that we have been separated from," Oswald said quietly to Miritz. After handing in the forms they were all given numbers on slips of paper. Some of the slips, including those given to Oswald and Miritz, had the words 'Knockaloe Alien Camp' written alongside. So that was to be their destination they concluded. However, it would be some weeks before they were to arrive in the Isle of Man where that camp was situated.

When they had been at the Lofthouse Camp for about a week they were told that they could write to their wives and families, and could have a brief visit from their closest relative. Oswald wrote immediately to Otilia on a postcard they had been given, telling her where he was, and inviting her to come to the camp the following Saturday. This was to be the only day of the week when visiting would be allowed There wasn't much room on the card for a long message and he was anxious to ensure that she brought extra clothing, including his overcoat. He was now certain that they would be interned during the forthcoming winter at least and, if the sergeant was to be believed, for the duration of the war.

Otilia's spirits rose when she received the letter from Oswald telling her to come and visit him. She packed a bag with the things that Oswald had requested her to bring, and, with his overcoat over her arm, she hurried to catch first, the tram to City Square from the top of Blackman Lane, and then the tram to Wakefield. The tram was packed with other women obviously doing the same as Otilia and they all got off together when they reached the camp after a long and tiring journey. No one spoke as they all clutched tightly the large cloth bags containing the things that their loved ones had asked for. After they were checked in by the guards they were taken to a hut where they were seated on benches down one side of long wooden tables. Soon afterwards the men entered from a door at the far end and sat down opposite their visitors. Armed soldiers, their rifles slung over their shoulders, paraded around inside, while two officers stood at both ends of the hut. A couple of interpreters strolled up and down behind the visitors, presumably there, Oswald concluded, should anyone speak together in any other language but English. He saw Otilia immediately, sitting there patiently waiting for him, and hurried to her. As they had been put deliberately on opposite sides of the table, he had to lean across in order to give her a kiss.

"Oh my dear Oswald. Are they treating you well?" Oswald saw that one of the guards was standing behind Otilia, staring at him. He recalled the early morning parades they had had each day since their arrival, where no-one dared speak for fear of being put into a cell, and that any disturbance or protests against the conditions was severely dealt with. He knew he had to be careful how he answered.

"Yes, Tilly dear, we're being well looked after. It's just like a holiday camp."

"And the food, are you getting plenty to eat?"

Oswald screwed his eyes tight to try and forget about the daily stew. Stew, Monday to Saturday, and then stew again on Sunday! Sometimes so high that it was barely fit to eat and the bread was always stale and hard.

"Just like eating in the restaurants in The Headrow," he replied with a broad grin on his face, mainly for the benefit of the guard, who then turned his attention towards someone else. Taking advantage of the situation, Oswald reached across the table to take his wife's hands in his. "How are the children?" he asked, his small blue eyes filling with tears.

"Oh they're alright and send their love to you."

"What are you doing for money?" It was a subject that he was reluctant to bring up, as whatever her reply would have been, there was very little he could do about it. Nevertheless, he needed to ask her that question because when they asked their guards what was happening to the families they had left behind, they always got the same reply. 'It was nothing to do with us,' and the soldiers would shrug their shoulders then walk away.

"You're not to worry about that, Oswald. We've been told that we're going to get some money from the government, so we'll manage until you come home.

"Have you brought all the things I asked for, Tilly?"

"Of course, but why do you want your overcoat? Are you expected to be here during the winter?"

He could not bring himself to tell her about his impending internment in the Isle of Man, and had promised himself that he would not do so until he knew for certain when he would be going. He considered that it was not necessary for her to worry prematurely about something which might never happen.

"Where's the bag?"

"Like the others, I had to leave it outside the hut. I put your overcoat on top so that you'd be able to recognise which was yours after I had gone."

Oswald said nothing as he envisaged what probably would be happening to it at this very moment. There was no doubt that the contents were being examined very carefully as they talked.

"OK! visits are over," the sergeant's voice boomed across the room.

"But we've hardly had any time together," Otilia said quietly, squeezing her husband's hands and not wanting to let go. They leaned across the table towards each other to kiss briefly.

"Alright, alright, come on then." The sergeant attempted to speak in a kindly way, but the words still came out like an order as he shepherded the visitors out of the door. Oswald stood for a moment watching Otilia walking towards the exit. He caught her brief and final glance in his direction before she left the building and returned to his hut with a heavy heart. He was desperately missing his wife and children and particularly the happy life they had had during the last fifteen years they had been together.

The sergeant had told them that they would remain prisoners until the end of the war, but what length of time was that, he wondered? If he were to be moved to the Isle of Man, how long would it be before he saw his lovely children again? He knew that he would have to bear this isolation, but what of his family? How would they be able to cope? He suddenly felt very angry. Why in God's name did there have to be a war between his old country and the country he had adopted as his own?

Behind the barbed wire fences the men found that they had little or nothing to do between visits from their loved ones, and it was clear to Oswald that a moral decline was in evidence, especially with the internees who had been in the camp for some considerable time. He learnt that they were at least three separate camps in the park and that there was a certain amount of freedom of movement allowed between them. However, this free movement appeared to be a privilege given to a large number of German professors and university students only, who had found themselves in Oxford or Cambridge when war was declared and were unable to return to their own country. He learned that they had formed a sort of college and attended lectures given by the German professors on a manner of subjects as if they were still in their universities. It appeared to be an exclusive group and very intellectual.

"We too must all find something to do," Mr. Heuer suggested to Oswald, "something to occupy our minds. I'm surprised that nothing has been organised by the military. Everyone appears to be depressed. Quite a number are either walking aimlessly about or sitting idle."

"I agree that we must have a purpose, Miritz, but how can we talk to the authorities. We don't appear to have any way of explaining our needs to them."

Miritz said that he had seen a civilian looking around the camp with an officer a few days ago and heard someone remark that the stranger was a Quaker. He apparently had asked the authorities if he could come into the camp to see what could be done to improve the morale of the prisoners.

"I knew about the Quakers in Leeds," Miritz said. "They used to meet in a hall in Woodhouse Lane and, just after war was declared, I heard that they had set up an Emergency Committee concerned with the care of interned civilian enemy aliens and their wives and children. I never dreamt that I or my family would be needing their help."

"Perhaps they are going to do something here for us," Miritz said, hopefully.

"Well let's hope so, but I wouldn't be surprised if nothing happens."

A few days later, books and magazines arrived at the camp and the men took it upon themselves to appoint a librarian. The men also learned that the Committee of the Society of Friends were also arranging to have wood and tools delivered which would enable the men to occupy their time more purposefully by making handicrafts. They also supplied a quantity of leather and the necessary tools for shoe mending, and lengths of cloth and sewing materials for the tailors in the camp to repair and make items of clothing. The men's spirits seemed to be uplifted now they had something to do and many ideas began to form in their minds as to how they could improve their humdrum lives.

The weeks seemed an eternity to Oswald as he waited for Otilia's visit each Saturday, but sadly the visits only lasted for the short period of ten minutes each time. It gave them so little time together and all the time Oswald had to be very careful what he said to Otilia in the presence of the guards. He had always been extremely fussy about keeping his shoes highly polished, but Otilia noticed how dull and dirty they were now.

She chastised him. "You must take more pride in your appearance, Oswald, and your hair looks as if it could do with a wash. I've also brought you some shoe polish and a brush. I think you need me here to look after you."

Oswald was disinclined to tell his wife that soap was as valuable as gold and, due also to a shortage of water, both were used sparingly. He also decided not to tell her that his razor had been confiscated. "I've been on a working party cleaning the camp, and haven't had time to clean myself up before you came," he lied. "Oh, and this," he pointed to his chin, "I've decided to grow a beard. Don't you like it?"

"I think you look scruffy, Oswald. I'd like you to shave it off before I come again, or at least, trim it to make it look neat."

'If only I could get hold of a pair of scissors,' Oswald thought, and then suddenly had an idea. "You haven't got a small pair of scissors in your handbag by any chance, Tilly? I've lost mine."

Otilia looked aghast, "Fancy losing them. I'll bring you another pair when I come again but I have brought you another shirt and tie this time."

"Where are they, Tilly?" Oswald looked concerned as he thought that if she had left them outside it would be doubtful if he would ever see them.

"I've got them here in this bag. The guard wanted me to leave the bag with him, but I opened it and showed him what was inside and insisted that I gave the things to you personally."

"And he let you? Just like that!" Oswald looked amazed.

"He started to say something, but I smiled at the officer standing next to him who waved me on into the hut."

Oswald was surprised at his wife's bravado and wanted at that moment to hold her in his arms and tell her how much he loved her, but his dreams came to an abrupt end at the guard's loud bellowing of, "Time's up!"

On one of her visits Otilia said that she'd heard from Bertha and that Gustav had been taken away to a camp at Alexandra Palace. Oswald was distressed at the news and wondered how long it would be before they would be moved to the Isle of Man. The following evening one of the new arrivals at Lofthouse talked to a group of them about the Knockaloe camp near the town of Peel.

"I was one of the first to go there, and I helped to erect some of the huts," he told them. "The camp was being further enlarged when I left, but the conditions here are a treat compared to that camp, so I don't envy any of you that are going there."

It had not been one of the best of recommendations that they had ever received, but the men tried to convince themselves that things may have changed in the Isle of Man camp since the time when the first internees had arrived. The fellow was interested to know what the men did before being interned. When he learned that Oswald had been a hairdresser he took him to one side.

"They were building a hospital of sorts in Camp 3 before I left, and they'll want some attendants. Being a barber, you'll stand a good chance of being recruited to work there and you'll be able to live a lot better than the others," he explained.

Oswald was mystified at the man's reasoning. "Why should I have a better chance because I am a barber?" Oswald asked.

"The red and white pole!" the man said, as if trying to make Oswald understand. "Blood and bandages! They took on a barber to be a hospital orderly while I was there," but then he said as an afterthought, "although in his case he had previously dealt with the wounded during the Franco-Prussian war in Germany." and then added enthusiastically, "but before that he had just been a friseur!"

Oswald had heard that barbers in the previous centuries had not only cut hair but did teeth extractions, minor operations and blood letting, and that this was believed to be the origin of the red and white pole. He wondered whether there was any truth in what the man was saying about taking on barbers as hospital orderlies, but hoped that it was true.

"Mark my words," the man continued, "if you can, take the opportunity of volunteering for the job when you get there, you won't regret it."

Oswald smiled and shook his head to the preposterous conclusions the man had reached in regard to the necessary qualifications to be a hospital orderly. However, he had accidentally drawn drops of blood on occasions when he had been shaving his clients with his cut-throat razor. This had not worried him, but surely operations and illnesses were a different matter. Nevertheless, he thought it might be worth trying to do as the man had suggested if and when he was moved to that camp.

Very early the following Friday morning, and with little warning, Oswald and Miritz, together with about fifty others, were told to pack their suitcases and leave everything else except their mugs as they were to leave Lofthouse immediately to go to Knockaloe Camp in the Isle of Man. There was no way that they could tell their relatives about when they were leaving as all moves of prisoners were subject to security. They were told that they could write home when they arrived.

The journey in the train to Liverpool took hours and hours, made unpleasant by a bitterly cold wind that penetrated into the carriages.

Their discomfiture was all the more pronounced due to no heating on the train. They concluded that this had been done deliberately. In addition, they were heavily guarded by armed soldiers all the time. The prisoners were also the focus of attention whenever the train passed through stations on the route. They wondered how the people waiting on the platform for other trains knew who they were, as when the train stopped, derogatory remarks were shouted at them. At one station where the train stopped for a few minutes, one woman spat at the window of the carriage where Oswald and Miritz were sitting, calling out, "Dirty Huns."

The two men passed the time by telling each other about their experiences, where they had come from in Germany and the reasons which had brought them to come and live in England. They told each other about their private lives and Oswald suddenly found himself telling Miritz about how he had married Otilia, and also of the guilt he felt of being responsible for her losing the three children of her first marriage. Talking to a comparative stranger about how it had all happened seemed to help him come to terms with his conscience.

"I loved them, although they were Ernest Biedermann's children," Oswald admitted, recalling their names. He talked about Marie and Emily, and how he was living at the house when they were both born. He went on to try and explain what sort of man their father was and how he had taken them away to Germany while Otilia was having their own baby in Brighton.

"Those children must be grown up by now," he said almost to himself, and then realising how old they must be, suddenly exclaimed, "Good gracious, Miritz. Henry, the eldest must be twenty-four. He could even be fighting for Germany in the war."

The two men could hardly believe how things had changed so dramatically in such a short time, and they cursed the Kaiser for ruining their lives by causing a World War.

Arriving in Liverpool they queued for sandwiches of corned beef and a mug of soup and then were marched to the docks where they joined a huge crowd of men waiting to board the ship which would take them to the Isle of Man. Oswald calculated that there must have been four or five hundred civilian aliens assembled on the docks who had come together from different camps around the country. There were also a few of them in sailor's uniform whom he took to be German merchant seaman.

He also heard that there was a group from the camp at Alexandra Palace in London and wondered whether Gustav, his brother-in-law, might be among them. It was a chance in a million if he could find him. Nevertheless, he searched for some time without success asking a lot of people if anyone knew Gustav Matzke. He realised, of course, that there must have been other times when men had been moved from one camp to another, but as he had not heard anything from his brother-in-law for some time he wondered whether he might find him going to this camp.

The ship taking them across the Irish Sea took longer than Oswald had envisaged. Many of the men were seasick during the voyage but eventually they arrived at Douglas. Here they were crowded into the ancient carriages of the trains, which took them across to the other side of the island to the tiny fishing port of Peel.

The prisoners were formed into squads to march along a country road to the camp at Knockaloe two miles away. It was during this time at the point of assembly that he lost all contact with Miritz.

The men were weary after their long day travelling. As they approached their destination, Oswald was astounded when he saw the enormity of the place. The camp almost filled a large wide valley of the countryside. There were many separate areas, surrounded by high barbed wire entanglements, all very heavily guarded by soldiers wearing heavy warm overcoats and armed with rifles. He noticed that some of those men had their rifles sloped over their shoulders as they slowly walked around the perimeter fence, while others stood at ease at the gates, their rifle butts resting on the ground. Rows and rows of long wooden huts were uniformly spaced out in lines inside these camps, which he thought must be housing thousands of prisoners. There was a lot of activity going on too. Many men were erecting more huts, others laying down sleepers and working on a railway line. He looked up into the darkening sky and noticed formations of seagulls flying high, wending their way towards the sea where they would roost for the night. He envied them their freedom. The sight was in stark contrast to what he would have to endure in this huge miserable-looking place for the next four years.

Once inside the camp he learned that there were many prisoners who had originated from other countries as well as Germany. They were separated into groups of their own nationalities and allocated huts in different parts of this huge complex of buildings.

Oswald was taken to one of the compounds in Camp 3, where it appeared that they were all Germans. He thought it fortuitous that he was allocated a hut in this camp, the very place where the stranger he had met at Lofthouse had told him that a hospital was located. He was unaware at that time that there was one of these hospital huts in all of the four camps.

The new inmates were given three blankets each to take to their huts and then had to queue to receive a plate of salt herring, some vegetables and a slice of bread. They ate hungrily having had little to eat all day. At nine o'clock they were called to stand outside their huts to be counted. This ritual, Oswald was soon to learn, would take place every evening and again at a very early hour most mornings.

Although the person he had met at Lofthouse had warned him about the conditions inside the camp, they were worse than he had imagined they would be. The latrines were in a disgusting state and completely inadequate for the number of men requiring to use them: wooden posts were in place instead of seats, and the excrement collected in open buckets underneath. The washing facilities were also dreadful with only a few taps for the many hundreds of men in this camp. Someone explained to him that only a small number of buckets and tubs were available and these had to be used for both personal hygiene and for washing their clothes in. What drinking water there was appeared to be almost undrinkable and very dirty. The hut to which he had been allocated was very dilapidated, but he was thankful that he had not been sent to the tented accommodation he could see on the hillside around the central area.

Next morning, Oswald asked if he could search his compound in the hope of finding a better hut than his own, unaware that he would not be allowed to move, but he discovered that all the accommodation appeared to be about the same. Most of the huts were in a rough state, and it was obvious even to his untrained eye that they had been badly erected. The sections did not fit together properly which allowed the wind and rain to penetrate from every corner. He learned that many of the prisoners had complained in vain about the dampness of the huts and of the mould, which often formed on their bedding after days of heavy rain.

"And it does rain here; you'll soon find out," one of them told him, "but no one seems to take any notice of our complaints".

It was now the end of October, and over in that part of the island where the camp was situated, the westerly winds blew icy gusts and storms across the Irish Sea reaching their valley. Oswald was thankful that he had his overcoat to keep out the cold.

"Is there no heating in any of the huts during the winter months?" he asked, noticing that there wasn't even a stove in the one which he had been allocated.

"Earlier this year we were promised them but they never came. Now they tell us that we will have them for this winter. Two to a hut if we're lucky," one of his new companions informed him.

"But we will believe it when we see them," another remarked cynically.

Oswald looked around, trying to calculate the measurements of the hut. The others saw what was going through his mind.

"If you want to know the size, they are about 180 feet long and 15 feet wide, and you'll no doubt be thinking that two stoves won't be enough for each hut - well, you're probably right, but if we complain we'll be regarded as trouble-makers and taken away."

Oswald did not question what happened to those the army disapproved of. He recalled that at Lofthouse Park, he had seen men who questioned the authorities put into cells for a while, and, if he believed the stories he had been told about Knockaloe, then the conditions and discipline here were probably worse than that previous detention camp he had been in. Returning to his hut, he lay down on his hard and uninviting bed with a heavy heart. He was so far away from the family that he loved and began to wonder whether he would ever see them again. His thoughts turned to Miritz and he asked the Hut Leader whether it would be possible to trace his friend in another part of the camp.

"You've got a hope," he told him. "I can ask the other hut leaders in this compound, but it's not possible for you to visit him even if we could find that he is in one of the other compounds in our own Camp 3 without a special permit, let alone the other camps. You will have to stay here where you've been put, and that will go for your friend as well - wherever he is."

"It is best to stay here anyway," another told him, "as we've heard that some of those in another part of the camp started to cause trouble over the conditions and appeared to be threatening the guards. We don't know what really happened, but we heard shots being fired and word got around that someone might have been killed."

Oswald decided not to pursue the matter further as he didn't want to be branded as a troublemaker.

It was not very long before he discovered that the same problems prevailed at Knockaloe as in the camp at Lofthouse Park, and that the deterioration of the men's moral standards and physical well being was even worse here in the Isle of Man. He was told that there was no-one in authority who took very much notice of the men's requests, but occasionally there had been a couple of visits by representatives from the American Embassy who listened to their complaints.

He could see and hear more huts being erected over a very large area to enlarge the camp and, apart from the guards who told them nothing; they could only assume that more and more aliens were being brought in to the camp to be interned.

The Commandant of Camp 3 was a Major Quayle-Dickson, who never spoke to any of the internees and was virtually unapproachable. He was easily recognisable strutting around Camp 3 in his three-quarter length army coat and expensive-looking mushroom-coloured khaki breeches pulled in tightly at the calves by brown shiny leather leggings. Being an ex-cavalry officer, he always wore a pair of highly polished riding boots but without the spurs. His peaked cap sat squarely on his head, leaving only a minimum of short cut grey hair visible at the sides. The jowled jaw and white walrus moustache gave him his true appearance of a very long serving army officer, well past retirement age.

On the third day after he had arrived, Oswald made his way over to a small complex of wooden buildings with a red cross painted on the doors. As he entered, a young man, wearing a blue coat, asked him what he wanted.

"Have you come to visit someone?"

Oswald explained that he had just arrived at Knockaloe from another camp and that someone there had told him to report to this hospital, as he was a barber. He suddenly realised how silly it had sounded and began to laugh. The young man looked tired and had a haunted look. He didn't even smile when Oswald laughed, but told him to wait by the desk until he could find doctor Strom. Oswald looked down the ward and was surprised at what he saw. It did not appear at all how he had imagined a hospital ward should look. It was larger than one of the other huts, but little had been done to change its appearance to try to make it resemble a place where sick people were being treated. At least all the beds were spaced further apart than in his own hut but the place gave him an unpleasant feeling. Looking down the ward at the men lying in their beds there was a peculiar atmosphere of hopelessness. There was no one attending the men who lay there in silence. They did not give him the impression that they appeared contented to be there, but all looked too ill to do anything themselves to aid their own recovery.

His analysis of the situation was interrupted by the appearance of a man wearing a white, lightweight coat who stopped in front of Oswald. He was of about fifty years of age, shorter than himself, about five feet six inches tall, with a neatly trimmed white beard and well manicured moustache. He looked up at his visitor through a pair of rimless spectacles.

After introducing himself he told Oswald, "I am in charge of this hospital of Camp 3 and I understand you wish to help. Is that not so?"

He had a very abrupt manner and Oswald began to wonder whether he had made the right decision to offer his services to this man. He had expected to see a German doctor but this man was an Austrian.

Oswald told him about himself and gave the implausible explanation as to why he had come. The doctor was somewhat amused by the suggestion that his profession appeared to qualify him for a role in a hospital. His reasons caused the doctor to give a short outburst of muffled laughter. He looked over the top of his spectacles.

"There is no doubt your informant was having you on, but I could do with an extra attendant, who is both reliable and capable of being trained in the rudiments of camp hygiene."

Oswald opened his mouth to ask a question, but the doctor hadn't noticed as he continued, "There are few people, in my experience, able to fit into a hospital and carry out the duties of attendants unless, firstly, they are used to people, secondly, are meticulous about their appearance - in particular their hands - and thirdly, they do not suddenly pass out at the sight of a drop of blood. I hadn't thought of it previously, but perhaps barbers fit into this category perfectly." He chuckled at his own ridiculous diagnosis of the qualifications for barbers becoming hospital attendants.

Oswald began to warm a little to this man with his unusual sense of humour and had already decided to agree to help if he was accepted.

"So alright then," the doctor said confidently, as if indicating that Oswald had passed all the tests satisfactorily, "in addition to you helping, you could also do any shaving that was necessary as well as cutting the patients' hair."

Oswald smiled to himself at the thought that he might have to also repair the damage he might inflict on the men whilst shaving, and he twitched his eyes, trying to control himself from bursting out laughing. He looked at the doctor who was in turn looking at him with raised eyebrows, waiting for him to answer.

"Well if you can use me, I'd be very willing to help in any way that I can."

The doctor looked pleased. "Good, that's settled then. You can start here tomorrow. I'll take you to our isolation hospital here in Camp 3."

CHAPTER FOURTEEN

1915-1916.

Otilia walked up the long drive to the gates of Lofthouse internment camp, her pace quickening with each step. Inside the large bag she was carrying were all the things that Oswald had asked her to bring during her last visit. In her other hand she held a small bunch of his favourite cornflowers one of which he had always liked to wear in his buttonhole. She so looked forward to seeing her husband each Saturday even though they were only allowed a short time together. The cost of the journey prevented her from visiting him more than once a week and Saturday was the best day for her to come. All the time she was away, she worried about the children even though Edith was quite capable of looking after the youngest ones.

The day had begun dismally overcast but as she approached the gates the sun broke through to uplift her spirits. A stern looking soldier stood on guard, the sunlight reflecting on the bayonet of his rifle. She gave him a smile and waited for the sergeant to emerge from the guardhouse with the usual list of the prisoners on a clipboard. She identified herself and waited for him to find Oswald's name before telling her to proceed to the hut where the visitors met their loved ones.

He appeared to take an interminable length of time to find her husband's name but then he placed the list flat to his chest, looked at Otilia over the top of his steel-rimmed spectacles and spoke in an unusually quiet voice. "Your husband has been transferred to the prison camp in the Isle of Man, madam."

Her eyes opened wide not believing what he had just said. "In the Isle of Man? For how long?" she asked, her voice not quite sounding her own. She knew that she would not get an answer to that question so she added quickly, "How can I visit him there?"

The sergeant still eyed her over his glasses. "I don't know the answers to your questions, madam. The only thing I would suggest is that you write to 'im at the camp at Knockaloe, quoting 'is number. But as the camp there is so large, it might be better until you wait to 'ear from 'im, and let 'im tell you what part of the camp 'e's staying in."

She turned and walked slowly away from the camp feeling utterly dejected. Her eyes filled with tears but she was too shocked to cry.

As Otilia returned home, she began to realise for the first time that Oswald would probably not now be released until the war was over and that she might not see him again for a very long time. Travelling in the tram back to Leeds, she looked sadly at the bag she had carried all the way to the camp containing bars of soap, a couple of her husband's small shaving towels and a number of other small items he had requested. She had also included a small bag of his favourite sweets. With a heavy heart, she looked sadly at the small bunch of cornflowers she was still holding, their heads beginning to droop in the heat of the day as if in sympathy with the way she was feeling. As the tram trundled through the suburbs of Leeds, she looked out of the window at the long straight rows of dark grey houses wondering how many men were absent from those homes due to the war: young men, fathers of the children she saw playing in the streets, perhaps at this moment in the blood-stained muddy trenches fighting a war against her husband's countrymen. She had seen the lengthy casualty lists in the newspapers following a battle near Ypres, and knew that many of these men would never come back to the people they loved.

She could see why people should think it unfair that her husband, who was German, would return to his family after the war unscathed while all these Leeds lads would probably be badly wounded or killed. Oswald had always been a peace loving man and hated war. Otilia had never ever seen him lose his temper let alone fight anyone. Hearing stories from different parts of the country that Germans were being sought out and in some cases attacked, she was grateful that Oswald was out of all that, but nevertheless, worried about his safe return from the comparative safety of the internment camp.

As the weeks went by, she began to wonder how she would be able to manage without any money from her husband, especially with four children under the age of twelve to care for. Rosa was not yet seventeen and earning very little money as a daily-maid, while Edith was bringing home only a few shillings a week packing hats at a local factory. Over the next few months, Otilia tried her best to keep out of debt ensuring that she had enough money to pay the rent and other essentials. By using her ingenuity and inventiveness she made satisfying meals out of what little meat she could afford in order to keep her children reasonably well fed. Fortunately too, her tailoring skills enabled her to alter clothes which had been handed down from one child to another.

When Otilia called at the corner shop near her home, the owner, Mrs

Hulbert, often asked about her husband and said that she missed his cheerful smile on his way to work in the mornings. The shopkeeper was aware of Otilia's plight and asked only a few coppers for her purchases of vegetables, knowing that if she gave them to her, Otilia would be too proud to accept charity. She knew that it would be a benevolence, which could be resented rather than welcomed.

Otilia looked forward to receiving the occasional letter from Oswald and there was not a morning that went by without her looking for the postman to arrive. His letters always told her not to worry, how he had made lots of new friends and that life was not too bad in the camp. She suspected that what he was telling her was far from the truth, but when she read that part of his letters to the children, it was a comfort to them to know that their father was alright. In one of the letters he told her how they had received a visit from a small party from The Society of Friends who had taken their names and home addresses. He explained that they had been told by one of these Quakers that it was possible that someone might call to see the families they had left behind.

She wondered who these Quakers were and why they had taken an interest in the men in the camp but she gave it no more thought as the months went slowly by. The answer to her question came during the following January. Otilia was sitting quietly sewing a badly worn skirt of nine year old Lily which had been handed down from her older sister, Clare, when she heard the click of the latch on the back gate, followed by a gentle tapping on her door. She was very cautious as usual, first going to the small window and moving the net curtains to see who had entered the yard. She had experienced little trouble from neighbours, although some people further up the road crossed over to the other pavement when they saw her coming. She could just see the faces of a man and woman in the yard. They were strangers, but Otilia thought that they looked friendly.

Still being cautious of people calling at the door that she didn't know, she called out asking what they wanted. The lady who spoke in a loud whisper answered her question. "We're from the Society of Friends, Mrs Siebenhüner. We've come to offer comfort and help."

Otilia was wondering whom these "Friends" were when she heard the man's voice.

"May we come in and talk? We have heard from our people in the Isle of Man that your husband is well and working in a camp hospital as an attendant."

This information was new to Otilia. Oswald had not mentioned this in his letters, but she was thrilled and excited that she was talking to someone who had news of him. She opened the door cautiously and asked them in. "How is he? Is he happy there? Are they well fed and being well looked after?" She wanted to ask so many questions.

"We can't answer your questions, because we don't know," the woman answered, "but we are more concerned about YOUR welfare. Perhaps we should explain why we are here."

"Would you like a cup of tea? Please sit down." Otilia was so excited that they had brought news about Oswald that she wanted to do everything she could for this wonderful couple. She listened quietly as they told her about the organisation they represented, popularly known as Quakers. They told her about the special committee which the Society had formed soon after war had been declared. "This committee," the man said, "has been formed with the sole purpose of assisting with the care of interned civilians, their wives and their children."

After enquiring about what children she had, the lady asked her if the older children were having trouble where they worked and if the younger ones were finding difficulties at school.

"Apart from Dad, we were all born in London," Otilia explained, "but I know that the youngest three have experienced some verbal abuse at school which gives me constant worry, but with a name like Siebenhüner, I suppose it is only to be expected."

But then remembering what they had said about assisting the families of the internees, she asked somewhat bewildered, "I cannot understand why should you want to help us. Germany is at war with Britain, and my husband is interned because he is regarded as an enemy alien and German!" Otilia sounded puzzled.

"The Society formed this Emergency Committee precisely to help Germans, Austrians, Hungarians and all others who have been interned in this country. You see, we are pacifists and reject all wars as evil, consequently we want to do everything we can to help the families who are suffering through no fault of their own. Incidentally, we are doing similar work in Germany for those in prison camps over there. We have few funds, but having received a generous donation from a kind benefactor, we decided at our meeting the other evening to give some small grants to families whose husbands have been interned. You are on our list and we would like to give you this to help to bring a little brightness into your lives with our blessing."

They handed Otilia an envelope with a few pounds inside, which she

170

accepted humbly but gratefully.

"You are so kind to do this. It's not just the money I want to thank you for, but knowing that someone cares about is happening to us." It had been almost a year now since Oswald had been taken away, and they were the first people she could talk to about her concerns.

"Do let us know if there is anything we can help you with and we will call again to see how you are getting on if you don't mind." Before they left they asked Otilia to join them in a prayer in which she found tranquillity.

They visited her again in February to invite her to their Sunday evening meeting. They explained that they had now visited as many families as they could in and around the City of Leeds, and the committee had decided to try and bring the families together to talk about their problems and experiences. In addition, the Society wished to distribute some gifts of food and clothing where it was needed.

"Please come and have a cup of tea with us in our meeting rooms on Sunday evening and bring the children. I will be a nice outing for them." She gave Otilia an understanding smile. "You will also meet others who are in the same circumstances as yourself. I think that you will find it rewarding."

"Where do you meet?" Otilia asked.

"In the building next to the Baptist Chapel known as the Carlton Hill Meeting Rooms. You must have passed it lots of times on the way to town and not noticed it."

"I have seen the sign outside - 'Friends Meeting House', "Otilia said, "but I didn't realise what it meant until now."

Otilia was pleased that it would be getting dark when they were to make the short journey to the Meeting House. She was very always very concerned at going out during the day as perhaps someone might scorn them because she had married a German. She brushed and combed the three youngest children's long black hair and dressed them in warm clothing to protect them from the icy winds of that cold late February night. George did not want to go and Edith said that she would look after him. Rosa said that she didn't want to go to mix with Germans but slipped out of the house soon after they had gone to meet one of her latest boyfriends.

The younger children were excited to be going out together with their Mama and clung closely together as they walked the half-mile or so to the Friends' Meeting House.

As soon as they entered the hall, a middle-aged lady with a kindly smile

171

immediately befriended her. She and talked to her for while about Oswald and the children, and about her present situation. Otilia thought how understanding and sympathetic she was to her plight and particularly concerned for the children's welfare as well as her own. The lady asked how she was managing and Otilia explained how difficult it was without Oswald's money. She told her that the government allowed her a basic amount of eight shillings a week and one shilling and sixpence for each of her youngest children. "With the little money that Edith and George brought home together with what the government allowed, we do just have enough to live and I am grateful for that. I am worried about the children though," she said, "but I do have some more furniture I can sell if I need to and a kind Officer from the Salvation Army brought Edith a nice winter coat last December which kept her warm as she walked to work during the cold winter mornings. I do wish I knew how long this war was going to last."

"We all wish it to end now," the lady replied sympathetically "All this waste of human life is sad and causing untold misery to many families."

Before she left the centre, Otilia was given a few groceries and also offered two pounds in money, which she felt she could not accept.

"Please take it, Mrs. Siebenhüner," the lady insisted, thrusting the two pound notes into her hand.

Otilia gratefully put the money into her purse. It would help, she thought, to pay the rent for some time.

Upon her return, Edith helped to wash her three younger sisters and put them to bed. George was in his bedroom but Rosa was still out. Her mother did not even ask where she was because she knew that either Edith would not know or would not tell even if she knew. Edith was not a telltale.

He mother looked tired as the two of them sat by the fire trying to keep warm. Edith knew that this was the time to tell her mother about Bertie.

It had been eight months since she had told Bertie Nelson that she would speak to her parents about him but with all the events that had happened since she had not done so. Bertie had understood and waited patiently for this. He always spoke to her when he came to the factory and she told him about all of the events as they happened. She looked forward to his visits and once he told her that he loved her which made her blush, the colour remained in her cheeks long after he had gone.

All her friends were aware of what had happened to her father and felt a great sympathy for her, often telling her not to worry. No one made fun of her again or asked any questions about her associations with her young admirer. They felt that it was the best thing to have happened to her with all the worrying times that she must have been going through. She had never experienced the sort of feelings that she now felt for Bertie and thought that she must have fallen in love with him. Knowing that he would be coming on certain days seemed like an eternity as she waited for him to turn up. On the last occasion, he told her that he had been called up to serve in the army and they had spoken for a long time about it. A number of times she thought that she would tell her mother about him but something always prevented her from doing so or her courage deserted her at the crucial moment, but now seemed the right time, especially that he would soon be leaving for France. She thought that she could make it sound wonderful and that her mama would be delighted that she had found love.

She reached out to take her mama's hands in hers. Otilia looked up at her and saw that her daughter had tears in her eyes yet her face had a strange angelic appearance.

"Mama," she began, "I have met someone at work who wants to meet you. He also wanted to meet papa before he was taken away and has waited all this time until things had settled down. He will be going in the army very soon and I will want to write to him when he does and I know that he will want to write to me." A tear rolled down her cheek as she spoke and she felt her mama give her hands a slight squeeze. Edith dropped her eyes from her mother's gaze not bearing to look in case her mother would not approve. She felt herself begin to shake and almost burst into tears.

"Do you love him? her mother asked quietly. She could see immediately that she if she refused to see him, her lovely daughter would be distraught. Knowing how shy Edith was, she was aware that it must have taken an enormous amount of courage on her part to tell her about him. Otilia recalled the time when Oswald fell to his knees to hold her hands in his when he first told her that he loved her. They had been so happy throughout their life together. Now he had been taken away for how long she didn't know, and they were all so unhappy. If she could bring some happiness to at least one of her daughters then she must try to do that.

Edith looked down into the fire. "I don't know, mama. I don't know, but I can't stop thinking about him and wanting to see him all the time."

Otilia squeezed her daughter's hands "Look at me. If you feel like that then bring him here and let me meet him. Has he kissed you?"

Edith shook her head and looked shocked that her mother should have asked that question. Some of the girls at work had said that if a man kissed you in a certain way, you could have a baby, but there was no one she could ask if that was true or not.

"We have only talked together at work and I look forward to our meeting twice a week, and then added to show her mother that it wasn't something that had just happened, "We've known each other for almost a year now."

Otilia put her arms around her daughter and gave her a hug. "I'm so pleased that you have told me and not gone out to meet him secretly like Rosa does with her boy friends. Remember, you are not sixteen until July, but I do understand that you can feel like you do about someone. I think that I almost know him already. When will you see him again?"

"Tuesday morning, I hope."

"Then bring him here in the evening if he can make it."

That night, Edith had very little sleep. She knelt by her bed in prayer to thank God for her happiness but cried on her pillow when she thought of her papa and how he was unable to see how happy she was. She knew that he would have loved to meet someone who loved, what he had always said, was his favourite daughter.

Rosa didn't return home until almost 11 o'clock. Otilia waited for her before going to bed. She noticed how ruffled her clothes were but dare not ask what she had been doing or where she had been.

Otilia spoke to her sternly. "Get to bed, and make sure that you get up early enough to go to work."

The following evening, after supper, there was a knock on the door and Rosa jumped up quickly before Edith could move. "I'll go," she said in her usual loud voice. I bet it's your man."

Amelia took to the young man almost straight away but was a little concerned that he was so much older than Edith with a difference of twelve years in their ages. He appeared to be very much younger and Rosa made eyes at him during most of the time he was there. Bertie was relieved when George came into the room to shake his hand warmly. He had been listening secretly at the bottom of the stairs for most of the time, but when he heard Bertie tell that he had been called to serve in the army he desperately wanted to talk to him about it.

George would not be fourteen until the end of June but had also left school to work in a factory. He wished that he had been a few years older so that he could have gone into the army and fight. He also thought that if he had been old enough to join up, it might have somehow made amends for his father being interned as an enemy alien

174

and then perhaps the authorities might have released him. Now he thought that this was a good opportunity to ask this man who had come into their lives at what age he could join up.

"You'll have to wait another four years, George, before you volunteer, but I do know of some that get in before their 18th birthday."

Otilia interjected. "You can take that silly idea out of your head, Georgie. If I had my way you would not go. Have you not seen the casualty lists in the paper." Her attention was drawn to Edie who had put her hand to her mouth to stifle a gasp.

Otilia quickly realised that she had made a tactless remark. "Oh! I'm sorry, Mr Nelson, I said that without thinking about you going into the army."

"There's no need to worry about me," Bert reassured her, "You see, because of my back problems, they've not passed me fit to serve as a fighting soldier. I didn't volunteer. I was called up under the Lord Derby's scheme and put in the Lincolnshire regiment to be a stretcher bearer and all that that entails." He had not told Edith this previously and she now put both hands to her face as she felt the blood drain from her cheeks. She was aware that as a stretcher-bearer, he still could be right at the Front. Bert saw this and added quickly. "But I believe that I'll be involved with horses at first because they've said that I'd be a shoe-smith - whatever that means!"

Edith's colour returned to her cheeks. "Will I be able to write to you, if you don't mind," she said shyly.

"Mind? Of course I won't mind and I can tell you all what I get up to."

After he had left, Rosa tried to question her sister about her relationship with her Bertie, some of them being very personal, but Otilia stepped quickly in to tell her eldest daughter to mind her own business and not to worry her younger sister with stupid questions.

The Quakers called again at the house on a number of occasions, Otilia being very pleased with the help she received from them. In her letters to Oswald she told him how kind these people had been to her and how she valued their visits. She also explained that some of the people who called and brought gifts of clothing and food were not all Quakers, but just supporters of their organisation. "Their prayers, too, are a great comfort to me," she wrote. "We are so grateful for the generosity and concern of this Society. They are all so kind and understanding".

Otilia hoped that by telling Oswald all this would stop him from worrying about them in his absence.

CHAPTER FIFTEEN

1916

Oswald was not finding his own life very easy at Knockaloe and the first five or six months had seemed like an eternity to him. He missed his wife and the comforts of home, but most of all he missed the children. Previously he had always been a jovial fellow but now he rarely smiled. His job at the two hospitals kept him very busy but, as with the other attendants, they found the work far from rewarding. The twenty-five or so patients in their own camp hospital were easy to deal with, but more problems arose when looking after the fifty or more men who were in the isolation hospital. Most of them he discovered, were suffering with acute tuberculosis or the advanced stages of venereal diseases. Although they were mainly his fellow countrymen, Oswald had little sympathy for the ones who were suffering from illnesses brought on by their own foolishness in their previously permissive lifestyle, but he also knew that the men suffering with consumption were not being helped in their recovery by the poor conditions they had to endure. Some of those who had the most serious complaints were transferred to the Hospital in Douglas but Oswald did not know what happened to them afterwards.

The Isolation Hospital was situated on the hillside within the Camp 3 perimeter and both hospitals huts were badly designed: neither windproof nor rainproof. They were also ill equipped. Neither had urinals or baths. In addition, Oswald discovered that the ordinary hospital had no tap that could be used for washing pans or bottles. This converted hut was not only badly situated, but had coal stocks alongside the whole length of the building. There was the inevitable danger of coal dust getting inside the hut if the windows were left open during windy or stormy weather. He noticed that when it rained hard, patients occupying beds along the outside walls were obliged to place blankets strategically between themselves and the walls. The dampness resulted in many patients suffering from neuralgia and rheumatic pains in addition to their other complaints.

During the middle of December, they received a visit from two members from the American Embassy who came to inspect the camp. Oswald supported the resident doctor when he took advantage of the visit to complain about the conditions. The result was that some improvements were made and, soon afterwards, the inside of the buildings housing the sick patients were whitewashed and made to look more like hospitals. For the first time too, the men received pillowcases. However, the situation for many of the other internees did not improve. The incessant drizzle in these first months had turned the paths between the huts into a sea of mud, and some of the wooden buildings had deteriorated so badly that many of the internees were taken ill during the winter. Separated from their families, many had a feeling of hopelessness and Oswald noticed that there was an air of despondency throughout their compound. For a number of the prisoners there was a feeling of isolation, in spite of being with others in the same circumstances. The meagre supply of stoves that the camp authorities had provided did hardly anything to improve the cold and damp conditions of their living quarters. Some suffered from many chest complaints and severe cases of rheumatism and pulmonary illnesses became quite common among the internees. Oswald was kept very busy in the hospital helping to look after the sick and making them comfortable, especially during the hours of darkness when the long nights became particularly stressful for those in pain.

It was during one of these all-night vigils when he thought he recognised a voice calling from one of the beds occupied by the chronically ill. He went over to where the sound had come from and looked into the man's face from the light of the candle he was holding. He stared with incredulity at the person in the sick bed.

"Gustav, is that you?"

The man opened his eyes slowly when he recognised the voice of the attendant.

"Oswald," he whispered, "I thought you were at a camp in the north."

Oswald looked closely at the man who had been his closest friend, and with whom he had travelled from Germany over twenty years previously hoping to find peace and happiness in England. But he was not the same Gustav that he had known then: his face was drawn and thin, his moustache hung limp and his eyes were sunken into deep, dark sockets. The high colour of the sparse flesh covering his cheekbones told Oswald that his brother-in-law was very ill indeed.

"What do you want, my friend? What can I get you?"

"Can I have some water, Oswald?" His voice was but a whisper.

177

Oswald hurried to find some fresh cool water wishing that he could bring a magic cure in the glass he carried back to the bedside. As he did so, he heard the telltale cough which indicated that Gustav was in the chronic stages of consumption. He knew that he could not possibly recover from the illness by remaining in this place. Oswald promised himself that he would see both the doctor and Commandant of the camp first thing next the morning. He would ask them to get him moved to the hospital at Douglas where he would stand a far better chance of recovery.

He stayed by his bedside throughout the night, and tried to remain awake as his friend snatched a few moments of sleep. By the early hours of the morning, Gustav appeared to be sleeping quite peacefully. Oswald, who had had a long and tiring day, found his eyelids growing heavy and had difficulty in keeping his eyes open. Soon, he too fell asleep.

As the early morning sunlight shone brightly through the hospital window into Oswald's face, waking him, he looked down at the white-faced, motionless, cold and breathless body of his friend, and wept.

Later that same morning, after learning that there would be an inquest into the death of his brother-in-law, Oswald put in a request to the officer of the day through his hut captain, asking to be able to attend. Two days later, together with Lieutenant Cubben from Compound IV, Doctor Marshall, who had attended Gustav in the isolation hospital and two of Gustav's friends, he sat in the court at Douglas listening to the depositions of the witnesses. His thoughts throughout the proceedings were with his sister-in-law, Bertha, and her daughter, Millie. He heard how a telegram had been sent to Gustav's home address but no reply had been received by the previous evening. Upon hearing this, Oswald feared for their safety as he had heard nothing from them since May of the previous year when rioting had taken place in the East End of London.

Oswald returned to the camp with a heavy heart. Away from his family the loneliness and deprivations were bad enough, but the death of his brother-in-law played on his mind. He would hopefully return to his loved ones when peace came, but Bertha would never see her husband again. He sat on his bed contemplating what action he could take. If he wrote to Bertha, would she ever receive the letter? He knew her address and the court had confirmed that that was where they had sent the telegram. If the authorities had received no reply to the message they had sent, then why should his letter be able to find her? He would include all this in the next letter to Otilia and perhaps she would find out where they were, but first he would try to discover if there had been any further developments.

The next morning, the Captain of Oswald's hut, Ludwig Lemke, asked to see the officer of the day. He learned that the police had found Gustav's wife and that she had already been in contact with the camp requesting that her husband's body be sent to London to be buried by the family.

"But all the others who had died have been buried in the churchyard at Patrick! Why should they make an exception in Gustav's case?" Oswald asked in disbelief. His hut captain told him that to the officer's knowledge, this was the first time that the relatives of a deceased had made this sort of request, and that he, Lieutenant Cubbon, who had been at the inquest representing the camp authorities, could see no reason why they should not grant what Gustav's widow had asked for. Oswald learnt through Ludwig the following day, that Gustav's body was being sent to London, and he was given his sister-in-law's new address to enable him to write to her. Oswald received a reply from Bertha a week or two later to tell him that Gustav had been buried in Abney Park Cemetery and that her parents, Henry and Amelia Rolfs, were able to attend. Oswald had not previously learned what had happened to his father-in-law, but was comforted now to know that he had obviously not been interned.

During the summer, Oswald observed that all building work now appeared to have stopped, and he assumed that the camp must now have been completed. The doctor told him that there were now over 4,600 men in Camp 3 alone with something in the region of 900 men in his own compound. With little or no information reaching the men in Camp 3, Oswald found an opportunity when things were quiet to have a talk to the doctor about what was happening in the other camps.

Doctor Strom stroked his beard between his first finger and thumb as he looked at Oswald over his rimless spectacles. "Well, Oswald, I can tell you that there have been a lot of improvements made here at Knockaloe since I have been here. Life at first was difficult enough for the men living with very poor sanitary arrangements and with inadequate washing facilities but, as more supplies became available, the huts have been made a lot better. Certainly they have been made waterproof and the toilets are more hygienic and water more freely available. It has been a huge problem for the authorities to organise this camp with so many people interned here, but I'm pleased to say that things are getting better all the time. Part of this is due to the men coming to terms with their loss of freedom and they are forming themselves into groups. You must have heard music coming from Camps 2 and 4. Musicians in these camps have formed small orchestras and are practising hard to be able to organise concerts.

"You must have seen the inspectors from the American Embassy who visit each camp and compound at regular intervals, we doctors have talked with them and the Camp Commandant following complaints they received from the men about the inadequacy of the food diet."

Oswald thought that this was a good time to make a point about the lack of variety of the main meal of the day. "I think we certainly have too much salted herring and not enough fresh vegetables."

"That's true the doctor agreed, "but recently they have promised us more meat, even if only tinned bully beef. They said it would take time to organise. Let's hope it's soon."

"Perhaps we don't complain enough," Oswald suggested.

"Well, some do," the doctor said. "At the last visit by the American inspectors, a number of German prisoners in one of the other camps made out sworn statements stating that they were at present having to endure their worst conditions since they were interned here. These written statements were given to the inspectors and word soon spread that the authorities would have to take notice and make improvements in the areas complained about. For instance, the bread which was made in a central bake house for all the four camps now housing some 23,000 men was of poor quality."

"I couldn't agree more," Oswald interjected.

"Yes, but we didn't complain like they did, so after inspection, they found that it was mainly due to the quantity being baked with inadequate storage space. This meant that the bread cooled slowly causing the centres to be soggy and unfit to eat. So now, flour is going to be made available to the individual compound cookhouses to enable them to bake some themselves."

"And while we are on the subject of food, I had intended this to be a surprise, but I can tell you now that the visiting Medical Officer I met yesterday here at the hospital, told me that he had discovered that the daily calorie count for the men throughout the camps was below average. He had met the Commandant and suggested that breakfasts should include porridge and syrup every day to restore the balance and he agreed."

"Well, that's good news for the men who can't afford to pay for that bit of extra food from the canteen," Oswald observed.

"Yes, I'm pleased about that as well. I've always believed it to be unfair that if the men had the means, they could supplement their diet with the extras they could purchase two or three times a week," the doctor concluded as he got up to leave.

Quickly changing the subject, Oswald asked him if he had any news as to how the war was going and if anyone was winning, or whether a peace settlement was imminent.

"All I know," he said, his eyes searching the ground, "is that they are killing each other in the hundreds of thousands in each battle. It's madness and it could still go on for years." The doctor walked away with his hands thrust into his long white hospital coat pockets thankful that he didn't have to deal with those casualties who had been wounded in the battles in France and Belgium

In her letters to Oswald, Otilia never mentioned the hardships they were enduring, but she told him about the soldier that Edith was writing to and told him what a nice man he was. He smiled when Otilia had written that Edith had asked her if what she had put in her letters was alright. She also told him that Edith had begun her letters with "Dear Nelson" and when asked why she had written that, her daughter had said that she was too shy to call him by his Christian name. Oswald was pleased that life appeared to be going on quite normally at his house in Winfield Mount but prayed that this Bert Nelson would come home safely as soon as the war was over.

"But it looks as if it could be long time before we see our families again," he said partly to himself.

It was noticeable to the men that the men in Camp 4 appeared to be more organised and made better use of their time than in Camp 3. Oswald was informed by one of the men from that camp, who was in the isolation hospital, that in their workshops all sorts of activities took place from model making to theatricals. With this information, Oswald suggested to his hut captain that it could be beneficial if they did the same and was promised that it would be discussed with the other Hut Captains to see what could be done.

The weeks seemed interminably long to Oswald and his fellow companions. The monotony of each day caused the men to lose the sense of time and he and the other hospital attendants were on the constant lookout for the first signs of the men becoming depressed and lethargic. Learning from what was going on in Camp 4, a number of committees had been set up in the compounds of all the camps to try and find out the men's interests in an effort to keep the men occupied. Some of the suggestions included strenuous physical activities, but from the large numbers who were in the camps, few took part. The reason was due mainly to the fact that many were not strong enough to take part, or unable join the others because of their age or infirmity. Some of the prisoners, who had been teachers before being interned, gave talks on all kinds of subjects in an attempt to stimulate interest in those who had no desire to join in with any form of activity and preferred to study. Classes began for others who wanted to learn languages, but for some reason the authorities did not generally encourage this. Requests for books were granted and central libraries were set up in each camp with additional sub-libraries in the compounds. There were small string or brass orchestras in each camp now getting together to perform concerts in the evenings bringing some peace and tranquillity before 'lights out' at 10.30pm. At the end of the long days, Oswald would sometimes sit quietly with some of the patients listening to the music and thinking of home.

A number of the men were now working in the stores, offices and kitchens, while others were engaged in general work, including the unenviable task of cleaning the lavatories and washing areas. The work entailing the particularly unpleasant tasks was often shared out, not only to give as many men as possible something to do, but to enable more to benefit from the small payments given to them by the authorities for the work done. However, in spite of these few hours of work each day the long period of boredom still caused some men to wander aimlessly about on their own, sometimes parading the barbed-wire boundary for hours. Oswald was also paid a small amount each week for the work he was doing at the hospital, which enabled him to purchase pairs of scissors, combs, and razors to enable him to shave the men and cut their hair. The coppers he earned from those who could afford it, also helped him to buy the extra few things that he needed.

Returning from the hospital one evening, Oswald was told about a Mr Baily from the Quakers who had visited the compound that morning. He remembered that same man visiting the camp at Lofthouse. He now was told that he was resident at Knockaloe as Industrial Superintendent. His solution to the disconsolate attitude, which was prevalent in the compounds, was to give the men something to occupy their minds, and he arranged for tools and timber to be brought in to all of the four Camps. At first, few men took on the work, but gradually numbers increased until many began to repair their huts, build furniture and make equipment to be used by various trades. With other supplies being brought to the men, many reverted to the type of work they had done before being interned.

Due to the demands of the internees, there was ample work for tailors, carpenters, and other trades. Some preferred to use their own huts as workshops, where they lived and slept, but causing consternation to those who were elderly and those not in the best of health, who preferred peace and quiet during the day. As the men worked, the noises often sounded very loud and vibrated through the wooden buildings, but the work gave an impetus to the men to create new ideas of how to improve their lives. Some with the skills of basket making began a small industry, and others created a knitting department where three pairs of old socks were unwound and re-knitted into one new pair. Men with a particular talent for model making began collecting any scraps of wood and bits of metal that they could find to enable them to make various types of artefacts. Others collected the large meat bones from the kitchens to fashion into extremely attractive vases with cleverly carved patterns on the outsides.

In Camp 3, the hut captains agreed that the end of one of the huts, which was presently being used as a hall, should be set out as a workshop. They asked a Mr. Niemann to organise it. He had been a furniture maker before being interned and welcomed the task of teaching others the skills he possessed.

Oswald's duties at the hospital prevented him or the other orderlies from taking part in any other activities but following an inspector's visit they were given extra duties. He had recommended that the orderlies from the five compounds in Camp 3 should be given Red Cross armlets to wear to distinguish them from the others. In addition, he also had said that they should exercise supervision over the many areas requiring inspection, in order to make a safer and healthier camp. These duties would be under the direction of their medical officer and, hopefully, should be a way of preventing any serious outbreak of any illnesses or accidents that might have otherwise occurred.

Later that same summer, Camp 3 saw the arrival of more prisoners into number 3 compound, and from the outset began to cause some disturbance. A disagreement about some tunnelling, which had taken place under one of the huts, began at table 9 in Hut 3 between George Goller, who had been Third Officer on the Hamburg-America liner before he was interned, and another man from Stobs Camp in Scotland where they had all come from, called Cohen. When the authorities found out what the argument had been about, one of the hut captains was held to be responsible, and the others protested and all threatened to resign. Goller took it upon himself to call a meeting to enable the men to elect new hut captains. At that meeting he spoke about how he was dissatisfied with the way that the compound was being managed. The Head Captain informed the commandant with the result that Goller was moved to Compound 4. In the process, Oswald and some of the others heard Goller shout that some of the hut captains would 'feel it' that night and, much to Oswald's consternation, he understood that his own hut captain, Ludwig Lemke, who had helped him when Gustav had died, was included in the threat.

Later that evening, Oswald, and the other men of Hut 5a, stood helplessly by as they witnessed Ludwig Lemke being dragged out into the open by three men, and with the assistance of another fifteen who had also been transferred from Stobs, physically attack him. Immediately afterwards, those same three men also attacked two other hut captains, leaving two of the hut captains unconscious. Hearing the commotion, an officer with an armed guard rushed into the compound and saved the three hut captains from further injury. Oswald helped the men to get to the hospital for treatment. Goller, and the three other men from Stobs who had been the ringleaders, were arrested for inciting the men to mutiny and later, at a court in Douglas, to the delight of the rest of the prisoners in Compound 3, they were all found guilty. The two who had been the most violent were sentenced to twelve months and the third man to six months; all three sentences were with hard labour. Goller was sentenced to three years, which was later quashed - no one knew why.

It took a while for the situation to calm down, but helped by the support given to the hut captains by the men, everything eventually returned to normal.

CHAPTER SIXTEEN

1917-1919.

Oswald celebrated his second New Year's Day in the camp very quietly. His thoughts were with his family and he worried should he not be allowed to return home when the war was over.

Otilia did not write to tell him that during that winter the fuel stock in the cellar had diminished rapidly. She was forced to sell some of her furniture in order to purchase a further three-hundredweight of coal that was essential to keep the fire going in their living room. Not only did the heat from it keep the place cosy and warm, but also it was here where she did most of her cooking. Mabel, who was eleven years old, usually took it upon herself to black-lead the grate every Saturday morning and all the children helped in every way they could as they tried to live as normal a life as possible, but they missed their father dreadfully.

Otilia was aware how much the children were missing their papa and, in spite of the way that they were all coping, she knew that life was so empty for them without their father.

"When will dada be coming home?" the three youngest girls asked their mother incessantly, but Otilia could only answer in a way that would not give them false hopes.

"When this awful war is over," she would tell them and longing for it to be soon.

George had managed to get into the army as a cadet. There were a number of young boys who wanted to get to France and fight Germans, but George had volunteered for a different reason. Standing in his khaki uniform in the kitchen, his mother looked at him proudly but felt empty in the pit of her stomach at the thought of him being taught to fire a rifle in battle.

"I told them papa was only classed as an enemy alien because he was born in Germany but we were all against the Huns. I asked them couldn't they now release him? But they only said that it was nothing to do with them." George clenched his fists and sat down close to Otilia. "It seems that I will have to go over and fight Germans, Mama, before anyone will listen to me."

185

"You look fine in your uniform, Georgie, but are too young to do anything like that. You are only just fifteen. I pray that the war will be over before you will be old enough to go. You must put all those silly thoughts out of you head."

Edith had received a letter from Bertie that morning and she told George that he had said that it was awful over there. He was not near too near the trenches but he saw lots of wounded soldiers and helped to carry them to the dressing stations. She said that he thought that what they were doing was saving many lives. "Tell, George," he wrote, "not be in too much of a hurry."

George never told his mother that he had given his age as seventeen and that he had informed the army that he would be eighteen in three month's time. It was pretty obvious to the recruiting sergeant that he was not even near that age but he had been given unwritten instructions not be too concerned with detail when men volunteered. If a young man wanted to fight and looked strong enough and fit enough, so be it he was told. Because of the heavy loss of life that had taken place in many of the battles, the army was short of men and would welcome anyone who was keen enough to join.

So in October 1917, George was on a ship to Calais with a fresh Battalion of the Yorkshire Regiment of rifleman having had only three months training at Ripon. Otilia was distraught when she read in his letter than he was going over to France. Within three months, Otilia received a telegram to say he had been wounded and they were sending him home after finding out his true age.

"I was unlucky, mama. It was just a stray bullet." He didn't tell her that his friend was shot in the head by a sniper and the bullet had ricocheted into his arm. "I'm alright really but they found out my age and made me come home - but I want to go back."

"Well you're not going to," Otilia said firmly. I'm writing to the Commanding Officer at Ripon to tell them that you are too young."

Before she could get a reply, George had joined another group going over to France. Two months after that, he was sent home again, this time with a bullet wound in his thigh. He never said a word about how it happened. That night he dreamed he was back in the trenches, going over the top in no-man's-land, reliving the fear and horror that he had witnessed at the time. He saw brave men falling before they had gone more than ten yards, shells bursting around them, arms, legs, and parts of bodies flying through the air. He woke up with a start and recalled the pain in his thigh as the bullet entered his flesh just scrapping his femur before he fell into a crater unable to walk. He had lain there for hours, listening to the screams and groans of the wounded and dying, the night air scented with the smell of blood and death, before he crawled back to his own trenches under the cover of darkness to be once more found out and sent home.

"This time you will not go back, Georgie," his mother said with anger in her voice. "You will stay here and I'll make sure that the army does not take you in again. "You've made your point and next time you might not be so lucky, so I'm writing again to the Camp, and this time I will get my own way."

Next day, Edith received a letter to say that Bertie had been seriously wounded and would be returning home. She leaned soon afterwards that he was sent to St. Luke's Hospital, Bradford, to recuperate.

Edith cried bitterly when she heard the news having no idea how badly he was injured. What no one knew at that time that he was one of four men who were close to a shell when it exploded. Two were killed, one badly wounded and Bertie took the blast in his face which caused him to lose his sight.

As soon as she knew that he was in the hospital, she caught a tram and arrived there full of apprehension of what she might discover. Before going to see him she asked to see the Ward Sister who told her that he had no physical wounds but was blinded, hopefully only temporary.

"Blinded!" she exclaimed. How did it happen?"

"It's just the war," the nurse exclaimed disconsolately. "We have wards full of badly wounded soldiers. None of them ever want to talk about what happened to them, and we don't ask."

"But will he be ever to see again?" Edith asked with her eyes full of tears.

"I don't think there is any cause for serious concern. There doesn't appear to be any permanent damage to the eyes, but he can't see anything clearly at this early stage. The doctors believe that his eyesight will return but it will take time."

Edith was somewhat comforted by what the Sister had told her but had to wait until 2 o'clock for visiting hours to start before she could enter the ward. She sat patiently watching the hands of the clock go round slower and slower but with only fifteen minutes to go she saw an elegant lady with neatly groomed light brown wavy hair enter the waiting room. She immediate recognised her as Bertie's mother who came straight over to her. They had only met once before just before Bertie went into the army. Bertie's sister, Nellie, had written to Edith

187

several times to go and visit them at their home, but she was too shy to go and always made some excuse or other.

Edith didn't know what to say or do when the lady greeted her. She felt a mixture of shyness and embarrassment and felt that she should not have been there. She wondered whether his mother would be thinking that she was chasing after him, or that now he was partially blinded, he would not want to see her. She wondered whether she should she stay?

"Edie, how lovely to see you. I saw my son two days ago soon after he arrived and he's not too badly injured. The doctor's have said that he could recover his sight in a few weeks and that we would have to have patience."

Edith suddenly felt relieved and Mrs Nelson's warm smile made her relax and feel more comfortable. Bertie had told his mother how shy Edith was so she had come prepared to put her at ease as soon as she saw her.

"Bertie was asking about you when I came to see him two days ago, so I'm so glad that you are here."

They sat talking for while and then the bell sounded to indicate that the visiting had begun.

"Now you go in first, Edie and I will come in after a few minutes. I have something to do first." She had planned to say this before she arrived, knowing that Bertie would like to see Edith on her own.

As she entered the ward she saw him straight away sitting up in his bed. He recognised her voice immediately.

"You shouldn't have come all this way to se me, Edie. I'm going to be all right. Don't worry about me. I can now distinguish between light and dark so I am sure my sight will return. The doctors said that there is no permanent damage as far as they can tell."

Edith bent down and gave him a peck on his forehead. Her shyness suddenly having left her. Was it because he couldn't see her doing it? But looking at him she felt her heart beginning to beat a little faster as she realised how much she loved him.

"Hold my hand. I want to touch you. I love you, Edie. I've been thinking about you all the time. When I get out of the army, I will wait until you are eighteen and then I'll ask you to marry me."

Bertie couldn't see Edie blushing but could feel her hand shaking in his.

"Don't worry, my darling, I won't marry you yet. I promise to do so as soon as you are twenty-one."

Edith gave a little laugh. You will have plenty of time them to change your mind."

Bertie gave her hand a little squeeze and he looked very serious. "I will never change my mind," he said quietly.

*

As George approached his sixteenth birthday he became restless. His mother had succeeded in keeping him home for eight or nine weeks and his leg wound had made a full recovery. She had not heard anything from the army but it seemed to her that George had lost the urge to return to France.

Although Bertie's sight had only partly recovered, he was discharged from the hospital and soon went to visit Edie at home. George waited until they were alone and then started to question him about what had happened.

"Surely you have seen for yourself what is happening over there and have already been wounded twice. If you go back you might not be so lucky next time."

"Yes I know, but I want to get back because of my papa. Perhaps he wouldn't wish to know about me trying to kill Germans but I want to show people that we are loyally British." He asked Bertie if he could keep a secret.

"It depends what it is?"

"I'll be sixteen in July and I know that the army will let me go then, especially because I've had experience, but please don't tell mama."

"I wish that you hadn't told me, George, and I'm going to pretend that you hadn't."

When July came, they all learned that George had gone back to France. Bertie appeared to be as shocked as everyone else but felt that he ought to have tried to stop him.

Otilia, reacted in a completely different way to what the others had predicted. "I realise now that in no way can I stop him from what he wants to do, so I only hope and pray that he comes back safely when all this is over."

*

Towards the end of 1917, in Knockaloe, there was a lot of talk among the prisoners about repatriation, and some of the men were even requesting it. Not all the prisoners had families in the United Kingdom and there were some who had been arrested who had either been on holiday in Britain, or had been travelling from the United States back to Germany, when war was declared. In addition, there were also a number of sailors in the camp whose ships had been in an English port at that time that had not been allowed to return to their home country. They had

189

all been among the first aliens to be interned and most were naturally anxious to return to Germany as soon as they would be allowed to do so. To the relief of some of the men, the authorities were repatriating those who wished to go, providing they were over the military age of forty-two. There were others who were tempted to be included who had lived in England for many years before being interned and had married English girls. Some of these considered taking the opportunity of being released even if they had to return to Germany, but the thought of leaving their wives and families often deterred their desire for freedom.

In spite of this, however, some had decided to go, and when their wives came to the camp to say goodbye to them, the others witnessed many tearful partings.

The men who were to be repatriated were told that they would be going to Liverpool, and then to Boston on the Lincolnshire coast and across the North Sea to Holland in Red Cross ships.

No one knew how long the war would last or whether the men returning to Germany would be allowed back into the British Isles, but Oswald dismissed any thought of joining his fellow countrymen, not only because he had no desire to go back, but because there was also the fear of possibly never seeing his wife and family again. After all, he had left Saxony over twenty years ago chiefly to avoid doing military service, and by doing so had probably relinquished his German citizenship. If he did return, he wondered what might happen to him as a repatriated citizen returning to his old country in times of war.

During the past year, Oswald had seen men leave the camp, some being transferred to other camps for compassionate reasons or being sent back to Germany, while other men kept arriving. Rarely were there any empty beds in the huts. It took time, however, for new friendships to be forged and often the new inmates were distraught. This sometimes created despondency in the men who had been in the camp sometime and could see no sign of their release. It didn't help their morale either, when the guards deliberately passed on the information that there had been occasional Zeppelin raids on London, which caused some alarm among those who had families living there.

The last two years had seemed like an eternity to Oswald even though, apart from the weather, conditions had gradually improved. More parcels were received from Germany, Austria and other sources. Some were addressed to individuals and others containing items of food and flour distributed throughout the camps had been sent by the Red Cross organisation in German. However, some of the foodstuff, especially the sausages and fresh fruit, had deteriorated so badly during transit that it was unfit to eat.

During this third year in the camp, Oswald noticed that even more prisoners were leaving to be repatriated to Germany or Austria and he began to live in fear that he would he be forced to go. Fortunately the Red Cross armband gave him a certain amount of immunity as his work was regarded as essential to help to maintain the health of the camp and his invaluable help at the two hospitals would be missed.

Occasionally, things had happened which worried both him and the others and defied understanding. There were a number of boys in the same camp as Oswald whose average age was about seventeen. At the suggestion of the visiting inspectors, they were moved along with all the teenagers from the other camps to Compound 7 in Camp 1V. The idea was apparently based on humanistic principles and was thought necessary to separate the boys from the men. However it was an experiment, which didn't work out, and they returned after about a year.

The camp authorities were now beginning to relax some of the restrictions which had been placed on the prisoners in the early years. The men were able to go from compound to compound in their camps without a permit or a military escort that had previously been necessary, and this allowed more get-togethers for theatre productions and concert performances.

News spread quickly around the camp when it was learned that the armistice was signed and the war ended. There was now talk about everyone being released and Oswald's hopes were high that he would soon be returned to his family. But after a few days had passed, the men saw little change in the camp routine. Indeed, life went on as if the war had not ended.

In spite of numbers still being released for repatriation to Germany whether the men wanted to or not, more continually arrived to be housed in Oswald's Compound. He was dismayed to learn that some of these were alien criminals who had been transferred from Reading Jail. He also heard from the new intakes that other camps in the United Kingdom were closing down, but more men continued to come to Knockaloe to await their release.

Throughout the next winter the moral of the prisoners was low but the men tried to hide their disappointment by finding useful things to do. Oswald had always been intrigued by the ingenuity of some of the craftsmen in the camp who were making marquetry jewellery boxes and picture frames from scraps of wood. Using their skills, they used any bit of metal they could find to shape into hinges and fasteners. Many small items were also being made, including bookracks, pipe racks, trays, and ships in bottles. Skilled joiners had for some time been making toys and large pieces of furniture from the materials supplied by the Friends' Emergency Committee benevolent scheme, under the supervision of Mr Baily, the Industrial Superintendent at Knockaloe. Oswald learned that these items were sold in Great Britain and abroad and the money used to purchase supplies for the camp canteens. The men also were paid a small amount for everything they made.

Oswald thought that he would like to take home some artefacts for his children when he was eventually released, so hearing that a Mr. Wildmann had done some beautiful work carving boxes from hollywood, he sent word for him to come and see him at the hospital.

"Tell him that he can have a free haircut," he chuckled.

Mr. Wildmann came later that day and Oswald was surprised to see such a young man. He was tall, very fair with long hair but with an untidy beard and moustache.

"You wanted to see me, Mr.Siebenhüner? I understand that you want to cut my hair."

"Well, to be honest, that message I sent was to get you to come and see me. Whether or not you'll be able to do something for me, I'll still give you a haircut. If you don't mind me saying so, you look as though you could do with one." Oswald twitched his eyes nervously, hoping that he had not sounded too blunt.

"I can never find time to have a haircut because I'm too busy doing other things," the younger man replied.

"Well now you are here, let me smarten you up in case we are suddenly released without warning."

Mr Wildmann thought that to be a sensible suggestion. "You're right, and I'm not a man to turn a free offer down."

Oswald invited the young man inside the hut that was used by the hospital as a record office. A small area had been partitioned off which he used as an improvised barber's shop. There was a large mirror propped up against the wall resting on a small table. Oswald beckoned to his guest to sit down in the chair immediately in front of it.

"Someone told me how clever you are at making wonderful things out of wood. Is that not so? Was it your trade before you were interned?"

The man chuckled as he eyed his questioner through the mirror. "No, it wasn't as a matter of fact. Before I was interned I was a valet to a gentleman in Scotland, but I began to make things out of wood to occupy my time and it developed from there. Why do you want to know?"

Oswald explained about his children, telling him that he would like to take some presents for them when they all finally went home after being released.

"My materials are very limited," Mr. Wildmann explained, "but we do collect empty wooden cigar boxes and any other bits of wood we can get hold of to make things from. Fortunately, I have a good set of tools given to me by Mr. Baily a couple of years ago when he visited us at Handforth Camp. Before that I made my own tools out of old knife blades and nails."

"As you know, Mr. Baily is resident here now and he has done a lot for us, although I've heard it said that at first the army officers didn't take kindly to a Quaker pacifist coming into the camp. Apparently, they regarded him as anti-British because he appeared to be more on the side of the Germans. But it's not true. I understand that the Quakers are trying to give the same help to the British prisoners who are interned in the camps in Germany. We should all be very grateful for what he has done for us here in this terrible place."

Having got all that off his chest, he looked at Oswald through the mirror and smiled. "Now what would you like me to make for your daughters?"

"I wondered if you could perhaps make some jewellery boxes and something else for my boy, George?"

"Leave it to me to organise it for you, Mr.Siebenhüner. There are three of us working together, carving and cutting veneers, and Charlie Alun is very good at the in-laid work. I'll put him on to doing something straight away for you."

"I hope you won't charge me too much as I don't have very much money," Oswald said apologetically.

"Who has?" replied Mr.Wildmann, getting up from the chair and examining what had been done to his previously untidy hair. "I hope we can make as good a job with your boxes as you have done with my hair. How much do I owe you?"

"Oh, we'll call that a good-will haircut, my friend. You've given me something to look forward to in these dark and gloomy days."

For Oswald and everyone else, the next few months seemed to be interminably long. The weather on the island was not good and the cold and the wet were having a detrimental effect on all camp life in general, and the health of the internees in particular.

Oswald was also aware of large numbers of the men leaving, most of them appearing to be repatriated.

Eventually, Mr Wildmann came to the hospital with the items Oswald had asked for. "I didn't know whether I'd still find you here."

"I could not possibly go back to Germany after all this time, even though the war is over," Oswald remarked. "I want so much to go back to my home in Leeds to live a free and peaceful life once more with my family." He gave his guest a chair for him to sit down.

Mr. Wildmann opened the bag he had been carrying to show Oswald what he had brought.

"They are beautiful," Oswald remarked as he held first one jewellery box in his hands and then another. "Such wonderful work. They're so exquisitely made with these inlaid patterns of flowers and butterflies. Where did you manage to get these tiny hinges and clasps?"

"We get them from cigar boxes thrown away in the dustbins. If I told people to save them for me they would disappear. Then I'd have to pay for them as soon as people realised how important they were." He gave Oswald a broad grin. "Charlie had to make the boxes of different sizes, depending on what wood was available at the time, but he thought that you wouldn't mind as your daughters are all different ages. Will they be alright for you, Mr. Siebenhüner?"

"They are magnificent. Please tell Charlie how pleased and how grateful I am for what he has done. Now what else have you got there?"

Mr. Wildmann produced a pair of beautiful inlaid picture frames. "Thought you would like these for that wife of yours you told me about. Charlie made them last year and you'll see that they're inscribed on the back, 'Knockaloe 1918'." Oswald's eyes filled with tears as he thought of Otilia and the children. He could imagine the look of joy on their faces when the time came for him to be able to give them these lovely gifts.

"I've not quite finished yet," his friend remarked. "I couldn't think what you would like for your boy, so I got someone else to make this for him. He has made a number of them and he charged me two shillings for it." He handed Oswald a ship in a bottle.

Oswald gasped in amazement as he examined the delicate work of a three-masted sailing ship with full sails and Peel harbour in the background. "I've always wondered how they did that and now you are going to tell me," Oswald said hopefully.

Mr. Wildmann laughed. "I can't tell you, my friend, because he lets no one see him do it. So, like me, you will never know from him how he gets that ship inside the bottle!"

"How much do I owe you altogether, or can I give you free haircuts for life, my friend?"

"When I told him who they were for, Charlie said that he wants nothing for them and he hoped that your girls would like them."

"But I must give him something."

Both Charlie and me would like you to have them as a memento of our friendship and for the work you are doing in the hospitals. So, please, accept them with our thanks, but if you will give me the two shillings I paid for the ship in the bottle, will that be alright, Mr. Siebenhüner?"

Oswald was very grateful for all the gifts and thought about how long it must have taken for Charlie to make them and of the beautiful job he had done. He took two florins from the small amount of money he had in his purse. "Please take these," he said, "and give the extra to Charlie for doing such a magnificent job."

"I will tell him what you said, but as far as the haircuts are concerned, Mr. Siebenhüner, I hope you won't need to give me many more because I believe that we will be going home soon. I take it that you too, like me and the others, have applied to stay in England. We are all waiting to hear if our applications have been approved."

Oswald continued to cut Mr. Wildmann's hair until the following September when they were both finally released and allowed to go home. There had been still over 18,000 men in Knockaloe Camp when peace was declared, and the enormous task of either repatriating or releasing them had taken almost a year. The hospital was one of the last buildings to remain occupied, some of the sick having had to stay until they were well enough to leave or transferred to the hospital in Douglas.

As Oswald walked through the open gates he glanced back at the hospital on the hillside of Camp 3 which overlooked the many compounds where so much unhappiness and misery had taken place. He remembered the faces of the men who had died in that place, and where he had worked for four long years. He also recalled the last hours he had spent with his brother-in-law and lifelong friend, Gustav, before he had died, and how he had sat at his bedside throughout the night.

He had carefully packed the wooden boxes and picture frames into his bag, and wrapped the ship-in-the-bottle in newspaper to prevent it from getting broken. Then he made his way along the two miles of road to Peel carrying his bag in one hand and his small attache-case in the other. He remembered clearly the day when he had walked that same road in the opposite direction with Miritz Heuer and felt very sad that he had never seen or heard of him since. They had been separated when they arrived at the gates and Oswald presumed that he had gone to a different part of the camp. It had not been possible to enquire after him, even though he tried many times to do so. The guards had not been interested in arranging reunions and now, even as he left, no one would give him any information about where he might be, or whether he had left the camp earlier.

After he had walked for about half a mile with the others who had been released that morning, he took one last look at the camp. What had been his home for four and a half years, full of activity, crowded with thousands of internees was now practically deserted. Viewed from a distance, there was something rather sinister about the place.

There was also an unpleasant fusty damp smell coming from the direction of the camp which filled his nostrils and contrasted with the more pleasant fresh fishy smells in the light breeze drifting over the hill from Peel Harbour and the sea. He turned, quickened his pace anxious to get away. He knew that the memories of the camp would stay with him forever and he would never want to return to the island again.

CHAPTER SEVENTEEN

1919.

At about the same time that Oswald Siebenhüner was released from Knockaloe, the man who was in his thoughts was also travelling to Leeds back from Germany.

Miritz Heuer had been living with his brother in the northern German town of Neustrelitz for the previous eighteen months having been repatriated some six months before the war ended. This northern German town had been his home town before leaving almost thirty years earlier to go and live in England, but now, like thousands of others, he was making his way back to England to pick up his life that had been devastated by the war. He had neither seen nor heard from Oswald since they lost contact with each other in the Isle of Man on their way to Knockaloe. So much had happened since they travelled together from their first Alien Camp at Lofthouse. Now he was sitting in an old railway carriage passing through Germany on his way to Hamburg. From there he would get aboard a ship, any ship, which would to take him to a port in England so long as he would be able to get to a railway station. There he would hopefully get another train to take him back to Leeds.

He thought of the time when he first met Oswald Siebenhüner in The Headrow in their home city, and how concerned they were that they might be taken away from their love ones. He had often wondered what had happened to the friend he had made while lying in Leeds Town Hall on that first night after being arrested and unable to sleep. He wondered whether he too had managed to live through those awful months and years at Knockaloe.

He had written to his wife from Germany asking if she had any news of Oswald, but she had replied to say that she had never been able to find out exactly where his wife and children were living in Leeds. The truth was that she had thought it best not to get involved with other families of German aliens at the time, even though Oswald's family could not have been far away from Camp Hill where they had their shop.

"We were not exactly popular you know, married to Germans," she had written.

He had understood from that observation what his wife had meant, so he never asked her again. He could still see clearly the street where he waited in the back of that army truck with two young German lads and his surprise when the man he had introduced himself to some weeks earlier was brought to the vehicle. Deep in those thoughts, all that now seemed a long time ago and much had happened since.

Miritz was paying little attention to the journey as the train rumbled across Germany towards the port of Hamburg. He was idly staring out of the window wondering whether or not he should tell Oswald, if they ever met again, what he had learned while living at his brother's house in Neustrelitz. In any case, one of the first things he would do when he got back would be to try and find him: that is, if he was still alive.

*

When they had arrived at Knockaloe over four years previously, the men had been divided up so quickly into columns to give their names to soldiers at the desks that Miritz had suddenly found himself going in a different direction to Oswald and on his way to Camp 2. Having lost his friend, he felt frightened and isolated and at the first opportunity asked one of the guards whether he could discover where Oswald had been taken. Although the guard had promised to make enquiries, Miritz never saw that soldier again and, in spite of asking others, no one could give him any information about his companion.

"It's not unusual for promises to be made and not kept," one of his fellow prisoners told him, "It's a ploy on their part to keep us down and dampen our spirits."

Soon afterwards, a large contingent of men of different nationalities came from a camp at Stratford, who told their new fellow prisoners that the discipline in the London camp had been very strict. They had been housed in an old jute factory and had experienced some terrible conditions. The men, too, looked scared when they came, having heard such awful tales about the camp they were coming to. Miritz had considered himself fortunate to be at Knockaloe after listening to some of the experiences the men had had to endure at their previous camp and put their minds at rest in regard to their new camp.

"It is not idyllic here," he told them, "but it's better than your previous camp by the sound of it."

However, conditions in his own Compound in Camp 2 began to get even worse than when he had first arrived. In spite of the increase in numbers, there were no additional toilets or washing facilities provided, and the water supply had been totally inadequate for the thousand or more men now in their part of the camp. These deprivations occasionally caused men's patience to be exhausted, and quite often when their morale became low due to the lack of any form of work, fights would break out among them.

A year later, when the government was encouraging repatriation, Miritz, began looking for any excuse to get away from the camp. He wrote to the Home Office requesting to be considered for repatriation. In the following January, together with a number of others, he was transferred to Alexandra Palace in preparation to leave for Germany. However, shortly after his arrival, all repatriation stopped. They were informed that it was due to Germany intensifying submarine warfare in response to a successful Allied blockade, which, in turn, had reduced Germany's imports. Even though Dutch Red-Cross ships were used to carry the men back to Germany, it was now thought by the authorities to be too dangerous to cross the North Sea.

Miritz discovered that there were some three thousand Germans - divided into three battalions - interned at Alexandra Palace, with a third of them allocated to the main hall. As in his two previous camps, the place was very dirty: cleanliness and hygiene again seeming to be completely ignored to the detriment of the prisoners' health. He found to his horror that the same buckets that were used for washing up were also used for serving the soup. In addition, the food was often found to be pretty dreadful and, in some cases, almost inedible. At one particular meal, maggots were discovered in the salted fish and no potatoes at all were issued to the men throughout that summer, although broken biscuits were plentiful. Warm water was scarce, and the conditions inside the buildings were in stark contrast to the beautiful surroundings outside where areas of grass and trees gave a contrasting false impression of the place.

Although there was a skittle alley and a billiard table room where men could pass the time, Miritz usually preferred to idle away the long days walking around the pleasantly peaceful grounds. He would sit on the hill during the fine weather looking through the branches of the trees towards London, envying the inhabitants of the houses he could see in the distance where people were free to come and go as they pleased. It had seemed so long ago when he had sat with his wife in the evenings in his warm and cosy living room planning their future. Now there appeared to be no future. At the time, he wondered whether he would ever be able to return to the life he led before being arrested and interned. He recalled, how as a young man, he had arrived in Leeds from Germany to escape conscription, but now he was imprisoned which was probably worse.

He constantly thought of his wife, Eliza, and longed to be back with her, but from that day when he had arrived in the Isle of Man with Oswald Siebenhüner he had not seen her. They had fallen in love when they had first met and soon after they were married, he had bought a greengrocer shop not far from the centre of the city. She had told him in her letters that she was coping very well, but that some customers had not been into the shop since the day he had been arrested.

Eventually discovered that visits from close relatives were allowed at Alexandra Palace. Miritz lost no time in writing to Eliza and she came to London as quickly as she could. It was a long and tedious journey for her from Leeds City station to the small station at Alexandra Palace but she came s often as she could. They often talked about the life they had had together before the war and how long it would be before he came back home, but despaired of any possibility of his early release. They also discussed what would happen if he were repatriated.

"What would you do if you were told that you would be sent back to Germany?" she asked him.

"Anything would be better than being cooped up here: counted every morning and night, existing on poor rations and kept here as prisoners. I'd go, Eliza. I'd give anything to be free!"

Eliza told him that she could hardly bear to think of him returning to Germany without her, She knew, of course, that being British she would not be allowed to go with him while the war existed between their two countries. At the same time, she also realised that she must try to keep her husband's spirits high.

"If you were sent there, perhaps you could go and stay with your brother in Neustrelitz and then, when the war is over, come back to me in Leeds," she had suggested.

He told her about a letter he had received from his brother in Germany. "I told you that I had written to him but I didn't know whether my letter would ever get there. Hermann had said that his son, Paul, was in the army, and naturally was very worried about him. He had given no more details. I can hardly believe that his little boy was now a soldier. He had only just been born when I left Germany. If it was decided to repatriate me, I would write again to Hermann to tell him that I was coming."

As the weary months dragged on, some of the men were disappointed that they had heard no more about the repatriation arrangements and little or no news came through about the progress of the war. Then, early in the New Year, a notice was pinned up to say that repatriation would recommence. With relief and great excitement Miritz saw that his name was on the list as being among the first men to be selected. As this contingent would be going in about a week's time, they were told that they could write and ask their wives to come and see them before they departed.

Eliza caught the first train she could, dreading that she might be too late to say goodbye to her husband. She arrived the day before he was to leave Alexandra Palace. They had so little time together before their painful and tearful farewells, having no idea how long it would be before they would see each other again.

Only a few days after Eliza had returned to Leeds, Miritz had gone with the others to King's Cross station where the party of about 200, guarded by an armed military escort, boarded a special train which took them to a town in south Lincolnshire. Here they remained in locked rooms inside a large house for a period of four or five days, only being allowed outside for meals and exercise under a heavily armed guard. At the end of this time they were strip-searched, their luggage examined and anything of Government Issue confiscated. They were then taken to Boston harbour where they had to remain in the train until told to leave. Eventually they left their compartments, one at a time, giving their name and number to the port official before being allowed to board a steam tug. The boat made its river journey down The Haven until it reached the Wash. Out in the open sea, the Red Cross ships - painted all white with a red line around the outside to enable them to be easily identified - waited to take the men to Holland.

Leaving the soldiers behind, they scrambled aboard and had their first taste of freedom being heartily welcomed by the Dutch sailors. After being allocated their cabins the men sat down to a meal such as they had only dreamed about since leaving their homes. They remained anchored until each of the ships had received a full complement of men to be repatriated before setting off in rough weather to cross the North Sea. It was a perilous journey through minefields, but after two days they arrived in Rotterdam. Here Miritz and the other were closely questioned by the German Consul, and then given a free pass to enable them to get to their destinations.

Although having no idea when he would be able to return to his wife in England, Miritz felt wonderfully free as he viewed the open countryside through the window of the train as it began its long journey to Berlin. eventually, the train reached the Dutch German border after many stops and checks by officials, the train taking on more passengers. But now he was unable to rejoice fully in his freedom as he noticed the poor state and gaunt features of his fellow travelling companions. Most of them were emaciated and hungry-looking soldiers and had a far-away look in their eyes, their sad faces reflecting the torment they had obviously endured. In contrast, he looked remarkably healthy, and the others eyed him suspiciously. The journey proved to be horrendous finally arriving in Berlin the next day after a long, slow journey with many stops. On the platforms he saw many wounded soldiers, some with limbs missing and others blinded. It was a sad sight and not how he had imagined his return to Germany would be. He realised then that the war must have taken a heavy toll of human lives on both sides.

In the afternoon he caught a train to Neustrelitz and, as it approached the town, he felt immediately excited at being able to meet his brother again after so many years. Carrying his heavy bag he walked across the park to the yellowish brick-built Schlosskirke and sat for a while in the rear pews of the 19th century church in prayer, thanking God for his safe deliverance to his hometown.

It was late in the evening when he arrived at his brother's house to be greeted by Hermann and his wife, Heide. Miritz was surprised to see how thin their faces were, the dark rings round their eyes giving them both a look of desperation. They were pleased to see him, but his own story of deprivation was nothing in comparison to his brother's family's suffering at that time. Heide told Miritz that she often wondered where the next meal was coming from. Hermann explained that food was in short supply and many people in the town were starving. He also told his brother that there was a lot of unrest throughout Germany and asked if he had any information as to how the English were taking the war. As the casualty lists grew longer in the towns and cities throughout Germany, people were asking what the fighting was all for.

Trying to bring a happier note into the conversation, Miritz enquired about their son, Paul, but Hermann's face took on a very sad appearance. His shoulders drooped and he did not answer the question straight away. Miritz guessed what he was about to hear, fearing the worse.

"Paul was killed about a year ago at the Somme, together with his friend, Henry Biedermann," his brother said quietly. "They were fine handsome young men, full of life when they left here to go to the front. On his last leave Paul got engaged to Henry's sister, Marie. She still comes here often and only left to go back home a few minutes before you arrived."

Miritz was wondering where he had heard that name of Biedermann before and of the names of the two young people he had mentioned, Henry and Marie!

"She looks upon Heide as a mother," Hermann continued, "since her own mother left her three children when they were only small. At that time, in the late 1890s, they were living in London. Her father brought them back to Germany, followed by his brother Leopold and his wife Eva. They had only one daughter, but she and Marie are great friends."

All the while his brother was talking, Miritz was trying to remember where he had heard those names before, and then he remembered the conversation he had had in the train on the way from Lofthouse to Liverpool with his friend, Oswald Siebenhüner. It could not just be a coincidence, everything fitted: the number of the children, their names, and the circumstances. He also remembered that their father's name had been Ernst

Hermann was still talking. "We see a good deal of Marie's father, Ernst, and we try to console each other in our great loss. The war has taken an enormous toll on both of our families."

Miritz was now certain as to the identity of the family he was talking about. However, he knew a lot more about this man from what Oswald had told him, but it would not be right, he thought, to tell his brother what he had heard, especially as he didn't know for certain if it was true. In any case, Oswald had told him about his wife's past in strict confidence, so his secret would be safe with him. But both Paul and Henry, killed! He wondered whether Oswald's wife should know. After all, Henry was her son, but if he met Oswald again, it would be up to him to tell her.

Soon after the armistice in November of that year, Hermann visited Berlin, and told them about the people's unrest in the capital. He brought back a leaflet, which was being freely distributed, headed 'Down with the Kaiser!' "Germany will take a lot to recover from this defeat, meanwhile we starve," he said bitterly, his bony fingers pushing through his thinning grey hair.

Miritz had been reluctant to leave his brother and his family at this time, in the hope that he would see an improvement in their living conditions, but he had written to his wife in England, telling her that he would try to get a passage back home as soon as it was possible to do so.

That had been some months ago and now, as the train pulled into the station in Hamburg, Miritz experienced a great elation and excitement at

203

the thought that he now only had to cross the North Sea and then a train journey to be with his dear wife and family once more.

CHAPTER EIGHTEEN

1919

"COMING HOME"

All the family were thrilled and excited as they waited for Oswald to come home. The two youngest, Lily and Clare sat looking out of the window wanting to be the first to see him arrive. Edith busied herself making the house look tidy and welcoming, while Mabel helped her mama to prepare a meal that they knew he would like.

Only Rosa was a little apprehensive about his returning. Although she would welcome her father back, it would mean that she would have to curb her activities with the young men with whom she had become acquainted. She feared that her father would probably not fully approve of some of them, even though she had just celebrated her 21st birthday, albeit quietly.

As soon as their father turned the corner at the top of the street, Lily and Clare screamed with delight and ran outside to greet him.

Oswald's return was a moment of celebration for the family, and his daughters were delighted with the gifts he had brought for them. Oswald had imagined how thrilled his son would be to see the ship in the bottle, but George was now seventeen and was not at home to greet his father.

"Where's Georgie?" he asked, but Otilia just grunted in reply.

"And what does that mean? Don't you know where he is?"

"Yes, of course I do." Otilia thought she had better explain. "Our son is in the army and has been so for two years."

"Two years? He's only seventeen now! How could he have been in the army for two years?"

"I think you girls better go upstairs while I tell your father about your soldier brother."

"Whatever mama tells you about him," Edith said as she left the room, "we still love him because he's our brother."

"Well, what has he done?" Oswald demanded, waiting for his wife to answer.

"He went off when he was only fifteen without telling anyone where he was going. When he came back he told me that he had joined up and I naturally thought as a soldier cadet. I didn't worry because I knew that he was too young to be sent to war, but when he told me that he was going to France, I knew then that he had lied about his age. He said that he had told them about you and hoped that it would go in your favour and that you would be released. He is very headstrong and wouldn't listen to me. Then I had a telegram to say that he was wounded and I was frightened, but they sent him home. I wrote to his camp at Ripon and told them his true age, but they never even replied."

"So where is he now?" Oswald asked.

"Oh, that is only part of the story. He went back and was wounded again, but this time, I thought that he'd had enough and would tell them the truth about his age, but he didn't. He went back again and was wounded for the third time. He was lucky he wasn't killed. The last time I knew he was not taking any notice of me but spoke to that soldier friend of Edie's, but he couldn't do anything either, so I just let him get on with it!"

Oswald shook his head in despair. He didn't know what to say." Where is he now?"

"He said that he would stay in the army until you came home. I've written to tell him that you have been released so I expect that he will be coming back home soon."

Oswald took the newspaper wrapping carefully off the ship-in-the-bottle and placed it on its stand in the centre of the sideboard.

"As Georgie isn't here, it will stay there then for everyone to enjoy."

Otilia was delighted with the two picture frames, admiring the delicate patterns of roses inlaid with the different kinds of wood.

"These and the jewellery boxes for the girls must have taken someone hours and hours to make, and you say that the man charged you so little for them," she remarked.

"Whatever the men made, they took a long time doing it. It was something for them to do to pass away the hours of boredom."

Oswald talked about the long weary days at the camp and he tried to answer many of the questions his wife put to him without upsetting her. She was anxious to learn everything he had been doing since she last saw him over four years ago at Lofthouse, before he left for the Isle of Man.

She asked him about her brother-in-law, Gustav. "When you wrote and told me about Gustav you didn't say much about what had happened. Bertha wrote to me after she had had a letter from the Home Office to tell her that he had passed away, and that his body had been returned to her for burial in Abney Park Cemetery. I wondered whether you knew any details of how he died."

Oswald sighed as he remembered Gustav's face as he lay in the hospital bed and the last words he had said to him. "He came into the hospital where I was helping, and I was with him, Tilly, the night he died." Oswald's eyes filled with tears as he remembered Gustav's call for help on that evening when he recognised the dying voice of his brother-in-law. "Please don't ask me any more, Tilly, I don't want to talk about it. Whatever we say won't bring him back. All I can tell you is that he died peacefully in his sleep."

Otilia could see that he was getting very upset so she decided not to pursue it any more.

Oswald wanted to change the subject quickly. "What happened to your father? Was he interned?"

"Mama wrote to me to say that he had to register, but although the police came to see him, they left him alone after that. He did, have to report to them at regular intervals throughout the war. I know that he hasn't been well now for some time and I was hoping that we could go and see them fairly soon. I believe that Bertha visits them quite often."

Mentioning her sister made her realise how lucky she was that Oswald had come back home safely. Bertha would never see her husband again. "It was good that Bertha was near to Mama and Papa when she heard that Gustav had died," she said in a quiet voice as if thinking aloud, "it must have been a terrible experience for all of them." She paused before thinking again about her parents.

"Clara calls round regularly too and the last I heard they were all living quietly in Charles Square."

"Have you ever heard anything of your two brothers?"

"Neither Charles nor John have had hardly any contact with the rest of the family. The last Bertha heard was that they were both living with their wives somewhere in South Wales."

Otilia recalled how she felt at the time when she had gone to Brighton to have Rosa and the distress that the family endured from the events that followed. When she had told her mama that she was going to have Oswald's baby, her two brothers had condemned her for what she had done and disagreed with their papa for accepting her back into the family.

"As far as I'm aware, no one knows exactly where they are, or what has happened to them," Otilia said, "so please, Oswald, let's forget about those times."

Otilia now called for the girls to come down, and together they told their papa all about what they had been doing throughout the long years he had been away. No one questioned him as to the life he had been living and he had no desire to tell of it. As they talked, he looked into their faces hardly being able to believe that they were really his daughters. All of them seemed so grown up since he last saw them and now over four years older than when he last kissed them goodnight or sat the younger ones on his knee.

"You haven't asked Edie about her boyfriend," Rosa blurted out, "Nor about mine for that matter."

"Oh! you've got one too?" Oswald said trying to sound surprised. He recalled that she had had quite a number of so called boy friends before he was taken away.

"I don't know about one." Otilia interjected. "More like two or three."

Rosa threw back her head and let out a squeal.

"So what about this young man of yours Edie? Do you love him?" her father asked.

"Love him? She can't stop talking about him and bores us all to tears," Rosa shouted out, in what Oswald took to sound like a jealous outburst. He ignored it.

"From what your Mama said in her letters, I'm looking forward to meeting him. Edie."

Rosa gave an audible sound of disgust and shrugged her shoulders as she picked up the Yorkshire Post and glanced through the pages.

Edith blushed and Otilia said, "Well, I'm sure you will meet him very soon."

When Oswald had eaten the meal that Otilia had prepared for him, she noticed how tired her husband looked. After the girls had gone upstairs to bed, they just sat for a while, holding hands and staring into the fire in their warm and cosy living room. It was so good to be home. Oswald had thought that as soon as he arrived home to Otilia he would have an insatiable desire to make love to her, but he could not help wondering what had happened to all the men he had known in the camps. He knew that sadly many were unable to sit quietly with their wives or sweethearts in the way that he was now doing. Soon his eyelids closed and he fell into a deep and contented sleep. Otilia put a blanket around him, kissed him on his forehead and crept silently upstairs to bed. She lay there alone as she had done for four and a half years, but Oswald was home and there would be plenty of time to reawaken their marital relationship.

Two days later, Oswald put on his suit, which Otilia had kept, neatly pressed for him, and set off to the city to visit his old employer. He had lost some weight since he last wore it and the jacket hung heavily on his narrow shoulders. The trousers were also a little baggy but he felt good to be well dressed again. A corner of white handkerchief peeped out of his top pocket and all that was missing from when he had last worn his suit was his usual flower in the buttonhole.

After turning the corner at the top of the road he surprised Mrs. Hulbert in her greengrocery shop by enquiring whether she had any cornflowers. She looked up when she heard his voice to gave him a broad smile.

"Welcome home, Mr.Siebenhüner. It's like old times seeing you come here and such a long time it seems too."

Oswald took off his dark trilby hat and held it to his face, shielding his mouth from other customers at the stall outside the shop. He knew that because of his accent he would never be able to pretend that he was English, but he whispered to her that he would like to be now known as Mr.Oswald, "Richard Oswald," he said, "and I'm Swiss." He winked cheekily.

"I think you are very wise," she whispered back to him and, as he walked away, she called to him in a loud voice so that her other customers could hear, "Good morning, Mr. Oswald, so nice to see you again. So sorry there are no cornflowers at this time of the year."

He turned, giving her a broad smile and, lifted his hat in a polite gesture, replied. "Good morning to you, Mrs.Hulbert. Nice to see you again too."

"He's a right nice gentleman, that Mr. Oswald," she said, turning to the other people waiting to be served.

"I didn't know him," said one of the women. "Is he from around here?"

"You'll no doubt see a lot of him in future," Mrs.Hulbert told her. "He's been away, but he's back now."

Oswald caught the tram from outside The Friends Meeting House which took him to City Square, then along Boar Lane and into The Headrow. He enjoyed the ride: the sound of the wheels scraping on the rails, the shaking and rattle of the tram as it crossed the points and the ringing of the shining brass handle as the driver turned it first one way and then the other, every one of the friendly noises making him feel once more at home. He handed over his two pence to the conductor and watched as he punched a hole into his little green ticket, the bell on the machine ringing sweetly as he did so. It was a sound that he had hardly noticed previously, the whole journey being a pleasant nostalgic ride. After he had alighted, he walked towards the barber's shop where he had worked before the war.

In his imagination he heard a voice calling to him from behind, but when he turned there was no one there. Was it really over four and a half years since Miritz Heuer, then a complete stranger, had spoken to him near this spot, fearful of being interned and of what might happen to them? He recalled that night when they had all been taken to Lofthouse camp and wondered what might have become of Miritz and the two young boys who had gone with them. Many men had been repatriated to Germany from the camps and he wondered whether the older Miritz might have gone too. He gave them no more thought as he entered the shop. The owner took him to the back of the shop after giving him a fairly cool reception and asked him what he proposed to do now that he was back. "You know of course that I won't be able to re-employ you."

Oswald was aware of the restrictions placed upon all unnaturalized aliens as far as seeking employment was concerned and knew that he was still categorised as an enemy alien. He would only be able to get employment by getting permission in writing from the Director-General of National Service through the Labour Exchange. This he was reluctant to do especially as Otilia had also lost her British Nationality when they got married. He was about to ask where his fellow workmates were when he noticed two photographs on the wall of both young men in army uniform, recognising them immediately. There was a piece of black ribbon tied to each frame.

The barber nodded in their direction." They won't be coming back," he said quietly. Oswald lifted a hand to speak, but then found that he had nothing to say. It had been a horrible war.

Oswald explained that he'd changed his name and then said that he planned to start up on his own. But first he was taking Otilia to London.

"Tilly wants to visit her parents. She hasn't seen them for about nine years since we came to Leeds. I will need to obtain a special permit to travel there, but hope that because of the reason for the journey I should be able to obtain it without difficulty."

His employer still had some respect for his former employee, and wished him luck in what he proposed to do.

Otilia and Oswald arrived in London a few days later and made their way to her parents' house in the Hoxton district. Her mother looked well and was delighted to see them. She made a great fuss of Oswald as well as her eldest daughter, but Otilia was surprised to see how frail her father looked, her mother telling her afterwards that he was not in the best of health.

Amelia explained that they still did a little work for what remained of their friends, "but so many have returned to Germany," she told them, "and others are still reluctant to trust us with the work."

Otilia looked at her mother's hands noticing how frail they too appeared. Amelia saw her and turned them over to look at her palms. "Our fingers aren't quite what they were, so it takes us a lot longer now to complete each job, but Henry refuses to give up, so we keep going. Now tell me all about your family. You must be very happy, Oswald, now that you're home again."

Amelia looked longingly at the studio photographs that Otilia had brought of the children, and they talked for a long time about what had happened to their friends and the other members of the family during the last nine years.

"You've managed to look after the children so well through the difficult times you must have been through. They are a great credit to you, Tilly. Your papa and I are so pleased that you are so happy now."

Otilia's thoughts turned to the time when Rosa was born, and then to her first three children when she had been married to Ernest. She realised that Henry would be twenty-eight now, Marie nearly twenty-six, and little Emily almost twenty-four. It had been over twenty years since she had seen them but there were often in her thoughts. She had a new family now but she would never forget her three little children that Ernest had taken away from her.

Amelia could see her daughter deep in thought and, in view of what she herself had just said, guessed what she was thinking. She reached out to take hold of her daughter's arm.

"Tilly." Amelia said her name quite loudly to bring her out of her dreams.

"Tilly," she said again, "Bertha and Clara are coming this afternoon to see you."

Otilia realised that it would be the first time that she and her two sisters had been together since she had left London and was looking forward to seeing them both again. When they arrived they had an emotional reunion. It had been so long since they were all together. Amelia watched and listened to them recounting their tales of the early years but she would have liked her two sons to have been there also to make her family complete.

Upon returning to his home in Leeds, Oswald settled in his own barber's shop in the converted front room of his house in Winfield Mount, and it seemed to mark the beginning of a new life for both he and Otilia. One of the first customers to enter his shop was a familiar face that he had not seen for over four years. Oswald recognised him at once although the man's hair had gone grey and he had aged prematurely. The two men stood facing each other warming shaking hands and saying nothing at first, then hugged each other in a tearful greeting.

Oswald was the first to speak. "My dear Miritz, it's so good to see you. How are you?"

The two men talked for a long time telling each other about their experiences and Oswald was surprised to learn that Miritz had been repatriated to Germany. However, what Miritz had learned from his brother about Otilia's first husband and her three children he thought it best to keep to himself. He had decided before he came not to tell Oswald what he had found out, although he wondered whether he should have told Otilia. It was only the fact that her eldest son had been killed fighting for Germany that prevented him from doing so. He considered that it was best that she would still think that they were all living happily in their adopted country, but wondered whether he would always be able to keep that secret from her. For some reason that Oswald never understood, Miritz never came to see him again.

The next two years went by quickly but uneventfully for Oswald and Otilia. Oswald was making a fair living from his hairdressing business, having both men and women customers. Bertie was discharged from the Army and became a commercial traveller. In 1921, he married Edith seven days after her 21st birthday as he had promised.

CHAPTER NINETEEN

1921

Amelia was sitting at her husband's bedside recalling every moment of their own lives together. Only a few days earlier she had read out Otilia's letter and they had talked about how they had thought that Tilly had made a complete mess of her life when she had become pregnant with Oswald's child. They had believed at the time that she would regret what she had done, but they were so pleased that everything had turned out for the best. As Amelia sat there in the cold bedroom, she relived in her mind the births of her own children that had given them so much joy. She also remembered with terrible sadness the time when Otilia's first husband, Ernest, had suddenly taken their three grandchildren away to Germany without a word to anyone. It would have been heart-warming to have received news of what had happened to Henry, Marie, and Emily, but they had heard nothing about them since that fateful day. It was probable that they knew nothing of their grandparents. Henry, who was the eldest, would have been in his early twenties at the beginning of the war but she would never know whether he had been interned in Germany as an enemy alien, or perhaps conscripted into the German army. She had seen the sad faces of the Londoners when they received news that their loves ones had been killed during the fighting, and she prayed that her grandson might have survived the bloody trench warfare that had taken place.

She recalled the awful squalor in Artillery Lane and the slum property where her first babies were born and then, thankfully, their much better house in Earl Street, where their six children had given them so much happiness. She remembered the traumatic experiences they had gone through during the early years of the war, and also the kindness of their friends who had helped them to come through those difficult times. Much had happened over the years, and, as the memories came flooding back, her eyelids began to feel heavy and soon she too fell asleep as she sat by her dear husband's bedside.

Henry's eyes opened slowly. A couple of painful minutes passed by before he was aware of his surroundings. He knew that he was lying in bed but he couldn't focus properly. He screwed up his eyes trying to see more clearly then realised that he was not wearing his spectacles. He moved his head slightly to one side and looked with blurred vision at Amelia sitting in the chair by the side of his bed, sleeping. He longed to be able to see her more clearly and called out, "Amelia," but he uttered no sound. His lips moved again, shaping her name, but once more the only word he heard was inside his head. As Amelia made no movement, he lay back staring at the ceiling, the pain unbearable.

He was aware of the clock on the wall ticking loudly, echoing round the stillness of the room. Suddenly all pain left him. He experienced a feeling of weightlessness as if floating. He turned his head again to see now more clearly Amelia asleep in the chair, and noticed the net curtains billowing in a gentle breeze that was coming in through the slightly open window. He looked lovingly at his wife, her face changing to how beautiful she looked on their wedding day. He smiled and wanted to hold her hand but was unable to move his arm. Even if he had been able to, he had no desire to disturb her.

"It's not so bad after all," he said to himself, and took his final breath.

*

Amelia spent the next five lonely years with her daughter, Clara, never properly recovering from the loss of her beloved Henry. She became terminally ill during the summer of 1926, and died in her sleep aged 74.

CONCLUSION

Otilia and Oswald, now happily reunited, continued to live a fairly normal life with three of their unmarried daughters, their son George left the army and got married soon after his sisters Edith and Rosa.

Thirty years later Clare married a widower, but Mabel and Lily remained single, always referring to themselves as two of the 'unclaimed jewels of the 1st World War.' There were many of these 'unclaimed jewels' as a result of the war, when millions of young men were killed in the four years of that bloody conflict, which left comparatively few eligible men available to marry.

As Oswald grew older he closed his shop and became a gentleman's hairdresser, and was well known to many people in Leeds, including the managers of the cinemas and theatres in the City. One of his customers would telephone him to make an appointment then send a chauffeur-driven car to collect him. His routine most mornings, was to shave with a cut-throat razor, keep his moustache well trimmed with his long pointed scissors, then cook his own breakfast on the one gas ring in the corner of the room.

With his shoes highly polished, and dressed immaculately in a well brushed dark suit, he would set off on his calls carrying his brown attaché case containing al the articles required for his trade. He had a neatly folded raincoat over his arm and a black felt trilby hat placed squarely on his head. Often, his first call would be to the corner shop where he would purchase a blue cornflower, when available, for his buttonhole - the German National flower.

He enjoyed life and was always full of fun, telling jokes and relating anecdotes as he chatted to his customers. With his German accent, his stories were much more colourful in the telling. As with the thousands of other German aliens who had experienced internment during the 1st World War, he never ever spoke about what he had endured, neither did Otilia ever tell of the difficult years that she and the family went through while Oswald was away. Little was known about the sort of lives they led before moving to Leeds, and, until it was researched, the family history of both Otilia and Oswald was left undiscovered until after they had died.

In 1939 when Britain declared war on Germany for the second time in

The author is Edith's youngest son

Explanation. In the 1800s, the family nam Walling was changed unofficially to Nelsor but reverted back to Walling in 1939.

25 years, Oswald had to report to Leeds Town Hall to be again considered for internment. However, this time, after only a brief interrogation, he was allowed to go home and was not troubled again. During that Second World War, their son, George, again joined the army and was wounded, this time by shrapnel from a bomb-blast soon after D-Day while serving in the Pioneer Corps. Rosa's only two boys were both killed in action in 1944. Arthur, the eldest, died in a tank during the battle at Imphal in India. Six months later, his younger brother, Donald, died in a ship hit by a mine off the coast of Normandy whilst serving in the Navy.

Otilia suffered a slight stroke in 1953 and died the following year aged 83. Oswald lived on for another six years and died of heart failure, three months before his 87th birthday. All their children lived into their 80s and beyond, Clare being the last to die in September 1999, aged 93.

Edith was the only one to leave Yorkshire with her family to live in the Midlands. She died soon after her 95th birthday.

FAMILY HISTORY

Oswald Richard Siebenhüner was born in Riestedt In the German province of Saxony-Anhalt on 7th November 1872. His godparents were Anna Wagner, Anna Kautz, Bertha Agthe, and Auguste Siebenhüner. He was the 8th child out of twelve children born to Carl Gottlob Friedrich Siebenhüner and Johanne Wilhelmine Auguste, who was a Wagner. They were married on 8th December 1861. Friedrich's Father, Johann Gottlob Christoph Siebenhüner, was a brick maker, and married Johanne Sophie Schobeß, on 30th June 1833. The Schobeß family tree goes back nine generations to 1555. The Siebenhüners' to 1660.

In the Middle Ages, a noble family (the Lords of Morungen) had a farm in the village close to the church. In 1790 the land was sold to the parish of Riestedt and three small houses were built there. It is known that in 1869, Friedrich Siebenhüner was living in one of the houses, number 40 known as the "Old Castle." In spite of its name, there is no record of an actual castle being there but was probably just the name of the original farm.

Oswald's mother's parents were Franz Julius Wagner and Dorothee Theresie, nee Kalbe. There were eight families with the name of Siebenhüner living in Riestedt during the 19th century, and also many with the name of Wagner. Nearly all had large families and Oswald had seventeen cousins either still living, or who had died, by the time he left for England in the 1890s. Although there are still many families with the name of Siebenhüner living in Sangerhausen in 2002, there were none with that name still living in Riestedt.

The author has since discovered the true story of what happened to Augusta Bansmer and her husband Johannes Weinerlein. They did not return to Germany as in the story, but stayed in London.

Johannes died on 31st October 1893. They had five children. Their third born was Anna Louise Maria, who married John Christian Reul, a baker from Hof in Bavaria at St George's German Lutheran Church, Whitechapel, on 28th April 1895. John acquired British citizenship by being seven years in business in London. In 1903 he was called to serve as a juryman in the High Court in London. Anna and John had seven children and emigrated to Johannesburg just before WW1. Following the sinking of the Lusitania, he was interned on 19th June 1915, at the age of 53, in the camp at Pietermaritzburg. This was in spite of being a naturalized Briton and that no civilian over the age of 45 should be interned in the event of a war, as stated in a statute signed at The Hague. Tragically, he was not released until 27th June 1919 and then deported to Bavaria from where he had originated.

During his internment, his wife was committed to an Asylum at Pretoria apparently because of her mental state being affected by having to defend her small children from being assaulted. She was still in the hospital when her husband left and was not allowed to go with him. However, his two eldest boys went with their father and continued their education at Emmasdale School in Heidelberg. One of his daughters died while he was in prison and, although he applied to attend her funeral, there is no evidence that he was allowed to go.

Another of his other daughters married in Johannesburg but later moved to England with her family.